# OUT OF THE ASHES

MARTIN EASTLAND

Copyright © 2024 by Steven Macintosh

All rights reserved.

No portion of this book may be reproduced in any form without written permission from
the publisher or author,
except as permitted by UK copyright law.

Published by Unveiling Nightmares

*Kathleen Kelly,* for saving me when I needed it most! I love you more than you'll ever know!!!

My grandparents – maternal and paternal – for unshakeable love and wonderful childhood memories...I LOVE and MISS you all!!!

My beautiful children

Carlene, Bridget, Roman & Riley for worshipping their old dad.

I LOVE AND CHERISH YOU ALL!!!

John Steven – my boy, forever!

Love ya loads, son – no matter what!!!

(You're my world – my best creations!!!)

My parents and family who were always there, in good times and bad...

I love you!!!

**SPECIAL THANKS TO...**

Sam M. Phillips and Adam Bennett of

Zombie Pirate Publishing (AUS) –

'Thanks eternal' for giving me my break!!

Thank you to Crystal Baynam, for making this happen.

**THANKS TO... (In no particular order)**

Sian Staley, Shelley O'Sullivan, Belinda Brady, Brandi Fox-Young, Rebecca Brown

Dr. Jesu Maria Estrada, Faith Lynn, Tamara Kerr, Cecilia Hopkins

(All of you read my work, gave your time and effort to me when you had your own work to do - you are *all* invaluable to me!!)

# CONTENTS

| | | |
|---|---|---|
| Praise for Martin Eastland | | VII |
| 1. | Suffer the Little Children | 1 |
| 2. | Deadline | 27 |
| 3. | Carry Me Off | 50 |
| 4. | Dark Harvest | 52 |
| 5. | Death Awaits Her | 70 |
| 6. | Home, Sweet Home | 76 |
| 7. | Homecoming Queen | 82 |
| 8. | Evil Is... | 87 |
| 9. | It Smarts, Don't It?! | 92 |
| 10. | Mind Games | 111 |
| 11. | One Night Only | 136 |
| 12. | Out of the Ashes | 146 |
| 13. | Perfect Stranger | 157 |
| 14. | A Ride to Remember | 182 |
| 15. | Screenshot | 190 |
| 16. | Storm of Rage | 211 |

| 17. | The Ivory Smile | 216 |
| 18. | The Maze | 236 |
| 19. | Behind the Stories | 249 |
| 20. | Now for Something Completely Shorter... | 258 |
| 21. | Being a Writer | 266 |
| Also By | | 273 |

# PRAISE FOR MARTIN EASTLAND

*"...HOMECOMING QUEEN by Martin Eastland is a piece of quintessentially American flash fiction, reminiscent of classic pulp horror works..."* – Unknown, discovered on Google search

・・・・●・●・・・・

*"...Twisting through Martin Eastland's dark passageways of prose is a chilling delight...one in which we find the rules can always change..."* - Sian Staley, Author

・・・・●・●・・・・

*"...Martin Eastland gave me thrills, chills and lots of scary, horror. His work is amazing – a must-read. Definitely an up-and-comer in the horror genre and the writing field. Reader be warned – his stuff is intense!..."* - Tessa James, Author Of 'FROM THE ABYSS'

・・・・●・●・・・・

*"...[of PERFECT STRANGER] I can't remember when I last read a story so fast! Says so much for Martin's talent as a writer. Any*

## MARTIN EASTLAND

*author who can make their characters come to life in their stories says tremendous things about them..."* – Faith Lynn, Poet and Author

• • • • • • • • • •

"...Martin Eastland is a very talented writer. From the intricate details in each scene to the realness of his characters, his words make you feel as though you are a part of the story. A truly gifted storyteller..." - Belinda Brady, Author

• • • • • • • • • •

*"...Martin Eastland...what can I say about this author? His stories really hit the mark. They have it all. I turn pages with baited breath. When a story ends, I have to take a deep breath. Well worth reading anything he has written..."* – Becky Brown

• • • • • • • • • •

*"...CARRY ME OFF Stormy Valentine's night filled with supernatural elements. It's an intense, atmospheric setting. The way you depict Jacqui's inner turmoil and her encounter with the mysterious entity is haunting. Beautifully captures the essence of loneliness and the desire for connection."* – Editor, Wicked Shadow Press

# SUFFER THE LITTLE CHILDREN

*'Give us your children and they'll be ours forever.'*
*– old maxim of Roman Catholic Church, alluding to baptism.*

*Drogheda, Northern, Ireland...1995*

Her screams shattered the night as she pushed harder and harder still.

The head was still not visible except for the crown, and it reached the point where the man thought they should have gone with a hospital birth instead. Blood was running down the mother's legs as the midwife took her scalpel from her bag. The man's eyes were wide–with a mixture of fear and anger rising within him.

He snapped.

"What the hell do you need *that* for?" he demanded.

"If I don't allow room for the baby to vacate, *it will die*, Mr. Murphy. It will die and, quite possibly, take your wife with it. Now, please, get out of the way before I lose them both!" Her voice contained no ambiguity–it was a controlled voice, an undeniable order.

He stood back and watched as his beloved Mary, growing paler by the moment, was haemorrhaging blood from her womb. The midwife made an incision to the perineum, and, amidst the fresh flow of blood, the child's head appeared, its heavy head of black hair matted by the blood and amniotic fluid emerging from her mound. It was a miraculous sight. More so than he had been told it would be.

The midwife's stern, accented voice boomed throughout the room.

'PUUSSSHHH!!' she roared with the voice of an Olympian Goddess.

Mary, exhausted and pallid, gave one more violent push, accompanied by a scream that would haunt his heart for eternity. The child was born and a flash of lightning from outside the window lit the entire room.

"It's done," the midwife proclaimed, exhausted herself. "I have a few things to finish before I go, so you may as well put some tea on the stove. You've been through as much as she has, from the look of you. I'll take care of her; don't you worry yourself. I'm giving her a sedative to help her sleep. Go have a cuppa. I'll let you know when I'm done."

He nodded wearily and headed for the door, rubbing his face with both hands. Turning to say something, he thought better of it and left the room.

It had been a good ten minutes before she appeared in the living room, bag in one hand, umbrella in the other.

"I'd be watchin' yourself out there. Pretty wild, getting!' he said, gently. She ignored him.

"Right. I've sorted your wife out with stitches around the perineum area and bandaged her to keep it sterile. We sedated her and she will remain unconscious for a while. Check on her every half hour, but don't talk unless she speaks first. She'll be needing the rest. The baby's fine. She's asleep now, in her crib."

He opened the door, and the wind imploded inwards on them, knocking them both back a little.

"Jaysus, Mary, and Joseph!" she exclaimed. She didn't even bother shaking the hand he proffered, instead opened her umbrella. As she stepped outside and rushed to her waiting car, the gale swallowed her last words - goodbye. He shrugged and closed the door, locking it behind her. *Crusty old cow,* he thought and headed upstairs to see what the Lord had bestowed on him.

He sat on the bed, silent and happy, not wishing to wake her or their daughter. His hand was being held by her fingertips, but he felt a sharp tightening and he turned to see her. She was almost purple, her eyes glinting; wild and feral, as she choked on something unseen. He panicked and jumped to her aid, thumping her back in vain, trying to release whatever the obstruction could be. Her grip tightened, and he watched her eyes roll back into her head; then as she collapsed on her side.

Dead as Dillinger.

He searched for a pulse, anything to indicate remaining life. But there was none.

He cradled her lifeless form in his arms, looking up to the heavens in a heart-wrenching askance. Too tired and empty to say much, he opened his heart, and the pain evacuated him in sobs only the archangels could hear. The baby lay dormant in her crib, two feet away. He looked at his newborn daughter, regarding her, and felt a new, growing sensation.

Hate.

· · · • • • • • • • ·

The storm raged as Mike Murphy locked the cottage door, carrying the baby seat to the waiting car. He fastened it and drove off into the heavy mist, which was growing thicker by the hour.

*The orphanage wasn't too far off,* he thought.

Despite his resentment of the baby, he wasn't about to leave her to the elements. That would be unforgivable too far too many in these parts. Surrendering her to the good sisters was far more merciful. The roads were quieter than usual, and he only just made the foliage-draped entrance to the long, winding side road leading to the child's new lodgings.

*Permanent* lodgings.

He stared at the bend inside the driveway, sensing something dark in there, like he was about to enter a labyrinth from which there was no escape. A feeling so strong, it almost made him relent and turn back. His resolve returned, and he proceeded, taking the bend, then another, to discover a long stretch of dark country road, leading to a formidable wrought-iron gateway, the sign over which stated his destination.

*St. Mary of The Immaculate Conception Orphanage.*

Swallowing hard, he slammed his foot on the gas pedal, barrel-assing up the darkened road toward his imagined freedom.

He reached the orphanage, and the rain was hammering on the windshield. He looked up at the building, his nerves jangled. It was an old gothic structure, its stained-glass windows staring down at him with an unforgiving gaze as if it were saying, *You evil bastard...how can you abandon your own flesh and blood*?

He got out of the car, grabbed the baby out of the seat, and slammed the door shut. The lightning flashed across the sky, lighting up the entire building, as he ran towards the entrance. The building was dark and uninviting, with only one light visible on the top right. He took the heavy knocker and slammed it brutally against the metal holder.

Looking at the baby for a moment, almost hesitating, he kissed her on the cheek, hugging her quickly. He put her in the large alcove, at the rear, sheltered from the storm, looking back almost with regret, before getting in his car and gunning it back along the dirt driveway to the main road. He lit a cigarette as he drove, his hands shaking as he tried to light it. Out of fluid.

*FUCK!* He tossed the lighter over his shoulder. He hit the main road, and he disappeared into the night.

The orphanage door opened, and a tall nun appeared, looking around, and then down at the newborn lying prostrate at her feet, helpless. She smiled sweetly, picking the infant up and taking the car seat inside. The door slammed with the inevitability of finality, which, had he stuck around, would have haunted his mind for eternity.

··········

Mike arrived home, locking the door, his expression one of relief and unspoken guilt. The kid had killed his beloved Mary. He couldn't have faced looking at that kid every day for the rest of his life. He made coffee and stared out the window into the distance. From there, he could barely see the spire of the orphanage (it had been a church back in the day) and an involuntary shiver rushed up his spine.

A large cloud was forming above the structure, with an ominous pulsating light within it. He rose and closed the curtain and, as he turned towards the table, back to his coffee, he gripped his chest. A massive jolt of pain had shot along his arm and hit his heart like a sledgehammer.

It felt like his heart was being crushed, as dark shadows scurried across the walls, all screeching at once, joyous at his agony. Blood began to cascade, slowly at first, from his nostrils, then his eyes, as he fell to the floor.

The pendulum of his parent's grandfather clock stopped dead as it began to chime 3 times, each of them deafening, the countdown of his delivery to the devil.

3 AM.

The witching hour is when evil holds sway against the powers of light. God would not be with him tonight. He gave up the ghost and his eyes rolled back into his head, as his life evacuated him.

He was gone.

In the distance, the clouds above the orphanage had relented and all was peaceful in the darkness.

There was still a light on up there.

·･･●●●●･･･

**Five Years Later...**

The crunching of the gravel filled the air as the car drove up to the orphanage. The driver killed the engine, and the husband and wife got out of the car, taking in the enormity of the place.

"Jesus! Sure, it's big enough?' he laughed.

'It's a church, Dom. Have a little respect, dear.'

He rolled his eyes and took her by the hand, as they walked to the door. He saw the large lead handle hanging from it... There was no doorbell or intercom. The handle would have to do. He lifted it and slammed it against the solid wooden door.

'Great knockers, huh?' he cracked. His wife, Sammi, laughed despite herself. Footsteps could be heard, and they composed themselves. The door opened to reveal a young Catholic Priest, Father Eduardo Martinez. He had a strong Latino accent, but his English was impeccable.

'Good morning, Sir...Madam. What can I do for you?' he asked sweetly.

Dominic Mansfield (his mother *loved* Italian names, although his old man hadn't been so convinced) offered his hand and Martinez took it (Dom would later tell his wife that the little priest shook hands like a fish, with no grip at all).

'Dominic and Samantha Mansfield. We're here to visit Callie Murphy.' The priest nodded and stood aside. They entered; the door slamming shut like a prison cell door behind them.

'If you'll be kind enough to wait here, I'll get someone to attend to you,' he said smiling.

'Thank you,' Sammi offered, returning the smile. They looked at the artwork on the walls, created by the children, no doubt.

A young nun, obviously a novice, entered and took Sammi's hands in hers.

'Good morning, Mrs Mansfield. I understand you are here to visit young Callie?'

'Yes. We came before to adopt a child and we saw Callie. We just fell in love with her after five minutes. She's beautiful!' The nun smiled brightly.

'Yes, she is one of our friendlier children.

Well! I have five minutes free now if you'd like to follow me to my office.' Dominic looked at Sammi, puzzled. Sammi asked her, politely.

'Won't she be in the playground?" The nun looked confused, and then she smiled. 'You must sign papers to spend time with the children. Nothing personal, of course, but we can't just allow anyone in off the street. Right this way, please.' They shrugged and followed her up the staircase and into her office. The door closed.

They had been in there for at least twenty minutes before the nun slid the papers in front of them.

'What are these?' Dominic asked. He had a funny feeling and wasn't one for revealing anything when it hit. He played this like Texas Hold'em – close to the chest and poker-faced.

'Adoption forms. Just fill them in, signing on both sides and you can be on your way.'

Dominic and Sammi looked at each other, fully knowing that this nun didn't have a damn clue what they had been told the last time they had visited. Instinctive to the nerve, they followed her instructions, and the nurse placed it in a file drawer.

'Well, congratulations to you both. Let's go find your beautiful daughter, shall we?' She walked to the door opening it for them, and Dominic returned the favour.

'Thank you,' she said quietly, smiling, as she led them to the foyer.

'Callie's in the library at the moment. We keep her reading because she loves it so much. She doesn't have any belongings. We have some limited items of clothing on offer until you can get her some more. I've taken the liberty of providing her with another child's clothes as that child passed away last week, sadly. Tuberculosis, poor thing. You can have those as they're already hanging up and bagged." She opened the library door and called out for the child.

The doorway was filled with the elfin figure of Callie Murphy – daughter of Michael and Mary. The girl looked up and grinned, realising who they were and ran to them, her arms outstretched. They knelt and embraced her warmly, then returned to full height. Smiling, they took the clothes offered and left the building.

Their car was waiting - and their new life with their daughter. They said a final goodbye and walked to the car, getting Callie inside it. They drove in silence until they passed the hairpin turn at the exit.

The door to the orphanage slammed shut behind them.

··········

*'You did what?'* the Mother Superior screamed, her face a mask of simultaneous hate and terror. She crossed herself, falling to her knees, moaning repeatedly in anguish, as the novice nun looked on in terrified confusion.

*All this for an adoption*, she thought. Something else was going on here – and something she wasn't privy to.

'You must leave the Order at once. You can no longer serve God in the Holy Catholic Church. Go directly to Sister Elisabeth – she has your disavowal papers ready, then be on your way. You have damned us all! The child, your fellow Sisters, the Church, and that young couple,' she hissed. 'They were here a week ago, and they were told *then* – by *me* – that we do not adopt permanently, as a rule. As far as I can tell, they either came back to visit the child and took advantage of your weakness, or they deliberately deceived you by their intention to adopt the child against our wishes. Either way, you have no idea of what you have done. May God have mercy on your soul.' She crossed herself again, her eyes staring up at the large crucifix suspended above her head.

'What is this place, if not an orphanage? Why are all these children here, if not to be adopted? Why wasn't I informed of the truth in either case?' the nun asked. 'If I am to be expelled from the Order, do I not have the right to know the truth?' she continued.

There was silence.

The Mother Superior slapped her hard. Her face was a mask of fury, as her tone descended into contempt.

'You have no *right* to be told anything. One specific order was laid down and followed by everyone. You couldn't even follow *that*. Get your belongings and get out of here. Go now, and never return. You will report tomorrow to St Francis Church in town where you will be formally excommunicated. 10 am. I trust you will not be late,' she said frostily.

With that, she entered a door to her right, and the nun jumped when a piercing scream could be heard on the other side of it. She went to her room to collect her things and returned five minutes later to be escorted out by another stern, ashen-faced Sister. The door of her life, thus far, slammed hard behind her with a finality that made her skin crawl under her jeans.

She began the long trek along the dirt road towards the village below, and her new life, whatever the hell that may be.

••••••••••

The street was silent. The Murphy cottage was dark, the only light emanating from the upstairs bedroom. The house had been vacant for four years before the new tenants, the Mansfields, took possession. They knew nothing of the dark history of the property, being probably the best thing for it.

The Mansfields were agnostic, and extremely sceptical on the subject of aliens, ghosts, and evil spirits – or...*other* things. They neither entertained nor indulged, such foolish notions, mocking anyone who *did* mercilessly.

Their new daughter, Callie Murphy, was sound asleep next door; warm, happy and, best of all, sated. She had never known such luxuries. Compared to the school lunch-type dinners, what her new parents had given her was heaven on Earth.

A full roast chicken dinner dragged through the Sunday roast garden. They had felt sorrow at how fast she wolfed it down, with Dominic jibing, 'Christ! What the fuck did they feed 'em on in there, gruel?' Samantha snorted unexpectedly, covering her face, and laughing.

'I'm sorry,' she said, 'but that made me laugh.'

They had dessert, settling down afterwards to the night's movie, the 1972 animated version of *Charlotte's Web*, and they observed her quietly, revelling in the sheer wonder she was displaying. Dominic shook his head, annoyed, whispering to his wife,

*'Fucking Catholics,'* who smiled in sympathy.

She, too, felt much pity for the girl. What kind of existence do you call it when a bloody cartoon is a major event in a kid's life? Well! She was about to be immersed in the fun-loving Mansfield ashram, a family environment where fun was the mantra, and love was the meditation.

Something this poor kid had never known.

She and her husband had heard about her father, Mike Murphy, a week after they had taken possession of the house. The neighbour, old Mrs Kernaghan, had told them that Murphy's wife had had the baby in bed, and died after childbirth.

That her old man had had a heart attack in the night after returning from a late-night trip...funny, she had said...she never saw the baby again. She could only assume that he couldn't handle the child and had taken it to family members to look after.

But, no, she had no idea where he had taken the child. The old woman's tone had kept Sammi awake the following night. The old dear's recollections...the way she had recalled "the church up the road having an orphanage attached to it." Rumours of that place sent shivers through her over the years.

*Dark...evil...reprehensible things, perpetrated under the eye of God, Himself, held court in that place, that monument to evil - she felt sure of it.*

They got Callie off to sleep quicker than they imagined. It must have been good for the girl to get a nice bed, a decent meal and two lovely people as parents.

The parochial control had been tangible in that orphanage, tinged with the overpowering aura of a stealthy evil permeating every movement within it. And that was in *daylight*!

Sammi dreaded to imagine being there at night, as a young child; the imperious hierarchical atmosphere embedded in every statue; the brutal discipline meted out to the children for the slightest infraction; but the worst, she had thought, the worst was the images of rampant child abuse which had plagued the Catholic Church, which continued to this day.

The thought fleeted across her mind; had little Callie fallen victim to the unwanted attention of a chastity-sworn collared devil posing as a servant of light? Had they gotten her out just in time?

They lay in bed together, in complete silence.

Dominic had crashed out for the night, but Sammi was awake as awake could hope to be. She got out of bed and went downstairs to the kitchen. Switching on the coffee pot, she happened to look outside the window. The sight that met her made her pale under her tan.

The damn place loomed over the town like an evil talisman, a *boyar* of sorts, overseeing the activities of his peasants, intermittently lit by the whip-like cracks of forked lightning which flashed over the roof. Chills lurched up Sammi's spine, catching her breath. It almost seemed to have a face, she thought.

Maniacal, tortured, abundant malevolence as she had never known…grinning at her, *challenging her* to confront the sheer evil contained within those stained-glass windows, each featuring one of the ten stations of Christ. She hastily closed the blinds, and poured her coffee into a waiting Beatles mug, before walking to the large round wooden dining table. She sat there for hours, her hands trembling, thinking about deals with the Dark One.

·········

Sammi jumped at the sound of banging filtered through to her subconscious state.

The kitchen clock claimed five afternoons. Dominic would be out getting the last of his errands done, unlikely to return for yet another hour or so. She ran up the stairs, taking two at a time, and stood outside Callie's room. She knocked lightly and, receiving no response, entered. She had gone with Dominic, by the looks of it.

*At least the goddamned knocking had stopped*, she thought. She walked towards the upper hallway and the knocking started again. Cursing under her breath, she stormed down the stairwell, to answer the door. It was a young woman in her mid-twenties.

'Sister, what a lovely surprise!' Sammi said with as much enthusiasm as she could field from within. She didn't like the look of it. Was she here to take Callie back to that shithole? Would they be indicted for fraudulent adoption, or something worse? Those questions and more flooded her mind as she opened the door, beckoning the young nun to enter out of the rain. Sammi closed the door.

'What brings you out on a day like this?'

Sister Mary Theresa went on to explain how she had been cast out of the Church, and how she felt the nuns – mainly the Mother Superior and the elder staff – seemed to be petrified of the place.

'So, what're ye tryin' t'say, it's possessed or somethin'?' Sammi burst out laughing, covering her mouth with her hand, and looking apologetically at their visitor. Sammi was silenced by the matter-of-fact tone in her voice.

'Yes.'

They sat in silence for a moment as the Sister detailed what she had discovered since leaving the Order.

'I gave my life to the Lord, but the moment I entered that accursed place, I felt...*something*. To that day, I put it out of my mind. When I saw the look on the Sister's face, I knew I was right all along. It was sheer terror, like being reminded of something that had scared her so *badly* that she blocked it out completely. I did some digging and found out from a friend in the Vatican archives that a young Priest - Father Eammon McDonagh of Drogheda - had been possessed by a powerful demon and had died due to the injuries he sustained from it. He fell over the stairwell bannister and broke his neck. The unclean spirit was believed to have been banished but this had not been so. It clung to the walls and windows of that place, refusing to be cast out from the building. It was de-sanctified as a cathedral soon after, with intentions to sell the place to the Board of Education. Once the rumours got out on the exorcism, they pulled out of the deal. To make it work, they had the building re-sanctified, and it became an orphanage. From what I can gather, some local kids had been sneaking in at night before the re-opening, y'know – sex and boozing, that type of t'ing – but the janitor found little pieces of scrap paper with letters on it. The Parish Priest, at the time, said something about them most likely using a make-shift spirit board. According to spiritualist sources, that could easily open a portal for a demon to infiltrate the place once again. To be honest, I'm inclined to steer the wheel that way, mesel'. I think those kids up there have been taken by the unclean spirit of that same demon. I've stayed overnight on several occasions, and I've heard distant screaming...tortured, and painful ...echoing through the corridors at night. All that got me through it was saying the rosary over again until it stopped. Those kids in there are only allowed to be adopted for a month at most, and only to parents suffering stillborn births or miscarriages, where it can ease suffering. Your daughter was one of those children, Mrs. Mansfield. I made a mistake and gave you that child officially, so there's little they can do to reclaim her. But—'

She took a deep breath in, and Sammi's eyes opened wider.

'But *what?*' Sammi asked, cagey as hell. She didn't like this shit.

'This house, Mrs Mansfield...is the house Callie Murphy was born in. Your *bedroom* is where she came forth, killing her mother in childbirth.'

Sammi covered her mouth in shock.

'From what I can gather, there had been a terrible storm that night. The midwife's car was found half a mile away, buried in a tree, her face non-existent, destroyed by the impact of the car's windscreen as she passed through it. I've been collating the events of that night from the scant information I could find from neighbours and newspaper articles of the week following her birth. Her husband, Michael – Callie's biological father – appears to have, in resentment of her, driven to the orphanage to abandon her there, driving back home. The report stated he was found dead two days later by a family friend. Heart attack. Seems reasonable you might say. My belief is somewhat more disturbing,' she started, pausing.

Sammi encouraged her on. 'Which is...?'

'Based on knowledge of spirituality and...other things,' she said, allowing herself an awkward smile. She knew how all of this must have sounded to Sammi, the ravings of a religious crank.

She continued, '...I think he's come home, unknowingly bringing the spirit of the demon into this house, where it has been allowed to roam without let or hindrance ever since. The moment Callie re-entered this threshold, I think it acted as a catalyst for the fragmented evil lying dormant within her, still. The unquiet spirit must be laid to rest before her possession takes effect. She has a short time left – as I said, it appears to return in the children after that time, hence the reason any adoptions are strictly temporary. They must be returned to the Orphanage before the occupants of that house are possessed themselves. It's like a virus, a contagion of sorts. You see—'

She stopped in mid-sentence, her eyes turning to see the front door opening and a happy, contented Callie entering with Dominic.

Callie saw the former nun, her eyes narrowing, her heart racing.

*Would she have to go back...there?* she thought. Her heart began beating like a jackrabbit as she progressed slowly towards the smiling nun, she had been fairly friendly to for so long. Callie sensed the fear in her. Fear of the child she had comforted in times of colic pain, of frustration caused by toothache and from occasional church reprimand for minor infractions.

'Hi, Callie. Do you remember me?'

Callie nodded, her eyes boring through her, her stare intense and probing, as if she were trying to read the woman's thoughts. Mary

Theresa was, at once, both captivated and reviled by the intensity of the child's glare, fully realising, now, that the child thought she was to return her to that terrible place.

'I just came to see how you were, sweetie. I don't go there anymore. *This* is your home, now, okay? You're safe here.' When Callie's expression turned to what she could only deem to be a resettlement of sorts, she heaved a sigh of relief. The poor little tyke had been through enough. *Had* she still been with the Order, with instructions to return the girl to that 'hell-on-the-hill,' she seriously doubted her conviction or resolve would be intact enough to execute that task. Callie went to her room to play, and the adults sat outside at the picnic table.

'Sorry, Sister. I've forgotten your name already,' Dominic started,

She laughed lightly. 'That's fine don't worry. My name in the Order was Sister Mary Theresa. We are all rechristened before taking our final vows. My real name's Kathleen Monaghan.'

'You said *was*. Past tense. You...don't work there anymore?' he asked, gently.

'No. I was expelled from the Order the day after you took Callie home. Glad to be out of it, to be honest. I still love our Lord, even more so now, but I couldn't stay there even if I wanted. I can serve Him in other ways without the regimented approach. Narky old bags were getting on my nerves, anyway.' They laughed out of sheer surprise.

'I'd better go. It's getting on a bit. I imagine your wife will fill you in on everyt'ing I'll call in next week, if that's okay?' she asked.

'You'll always be welcome here,' Sammi said.

'Anytime you're passin,' pop in for a cuppa tea and a gab,' she continued.

'I'll hold you to that,' Kathleen said, smiling.

Kathleen stood and walked towards the foyer. Something made her eyes travel upwards, her eyes locked to the stairwell... Callie was standing there, hands on the wooden railing, looking down at her. Her face morphed, momentarily, into a monstrous entity, with a knowing, malevolent smile, only changing back to the young girl she had taken care of.

Kathleen's heart jolted, although she betrayed nothing to the child. A dark shadow lingered behind her on the ceiling. She waved again, turning towards the open door. The child was not *quite* as free as she had first hoped. There was only one proper way to deal with it.

And one proper time.

···•••••···

Dominic had never experienced fear like this before. The overwhelming sense of dread lurking in his soul infested there and spreading through his coiled body like a brush fire was staggering. He tried the side door to the building, expecting it to be locked.

It creaked open a few inches and stopped. He turned to look at Kathleen, who swallowed hard. They both entered, and he closed the door again. Dominic switched on the torch he had brought along, surveying the room, a storage room with an annexing door up a small flight of steps in the far corner. He turned to Kathleen, indicating the steps.

'You ready?' he asked her.

'No. But sure, I'll have to be, eh?' she quipped nervously. He guided her to the door, and helped her up the steps, grabbing the handle. It opened like the previous one.

'Am I the only one here who t'inks that this is a wee bit too easy?' she asked.

Dom replied, 'It *would* appear that way, I s'pose. Let's be gettin' on with it. We haven't much further to go, now.'

They entered the main cathedral section. It was impressive, to say the least. One thing he did notice was that instead of looking up to the heavens, exalting God, all the statues of the angels were high on pedestals, holding their spears downwards...as if trying to keep 'something' in submission. Looking around, they noticed that the large cross suspended above them was anchored more rigidly than he had ever known, its supporting beam having been reinforced to bear tremendous weight, in itself drawing only one possible, if unlikely, conclusion.

'Holy Mother of God! Pure gold!'

Kathleen stared hard at it.

'How can you tell from here?' she enquired.

'The reinforced beam holding it. That's not what's bothering me, though,' he stated, his voice hazy.

'What then?' she asked.

They're usually made of gold plating. Most catholic trinkets are gold-plated. It would cost far too much to waste pure gold on such things. Especially for a bloody orphanage chapel, never mind a church. You ought to know this shit since you worked here. What can you tell me about this place I wouldn't know?'

'Novice nuns aren't told much of anything. It's like we're on a need-to-know basis.

We're helping hands at the beginning, to be honest,' she replied. Dominic looked around and saw another door to the far left of the altar. He nudged an increasingly edgy Kathleen, pointing to it.

They walked quickly to it and entered.

··········

Sammi lays on the couch, watching a movie with Callie, herself lying on her front not too far from the TV set. Sammi's eyelids started to roll down, and she tried to stay awake. But she was unable to fight the urge, slipping into the lost world of REM sleep, a temporary resident of dreamland.

It was about ten minutes later that Sammi was dragged violently awake to the screams coming from a writhing Callie, her face scratched and bleeding, having torn it to shreds, her eyes black as opals, staring hypnotically at Sammi like she was sucking her soul through her eyes.

Sammi backed up, petrified, as Callie stood up, limp and lifeless as if she had been picked up by her collar.

She looked directly at her new momma with hatred and disgust before gliding towards her, her bloodied arms outstretched, reaching for Sammi, her hands livid. The guttural sound emanating from the child's mouth hurt the woman to her soul, deep and full of darkness she had never imagined. She stood, looking around her. And she saw the only thing she could conceive that might help her - her mother's bible. She picked it up and held it against Callie's head, eliciting an unholy scream from the child, and blinded by the blue flash that spewed from her upon contact.

The smell of charred flesh was overbearing, but she held the bible firm, calling out loudly to the God she had rejected for so long. She had cried inside, begging forgiveness for her years of scoffing and ridiculing others. The soft voice coming from her breast made her heart implode and she withdrew the smoking bible to see a badly burned Callie, free of the evil which had temporarily taken her soul. Exhausted, they both knelt in each other's arms and wept openly.

·· · · · · · · ·

The room was dead, completely devoid of any signs of life. A simple, chess-board floor with statues of the Blessed Virgin in each corner. They walked across the floor and Dominic stopped dead in his tracks. Kathleen's hand gripped his arm so fiercely that he winced in pain.

'What is it?!' she asked, hoarsely.

'We're being watched. Can't you feel it?' he asked, his doubts beginning to question themselves as he progressed slowly, step by step. She *could* feel it. Intense malevolence washed over her body like a lover's hands. Something caught her eye, and her head spun around to gauge what it was.

Was she going crazy? she thought or was that statue turning its head towards them? She nudged Dominic hard in the ribs, and he turned just in time. She had not imagined it, after all. They both looked on in horror as the statue slid to the right and forwards towards them as if it were executing a chess move; its alabaster head having come to life, its eyes red as hellfire itself, lapped in a storm of rage, its forked tongue slithering from its once solid mouth, taunting them as it worked its way towards them. They looked around and the other statues were converging on their position.

Kathleen held up her cross, eliciting a cry in Latin as light flooded over the gold-plated trinket, surging up her arm. The scream of rejection which came from the statues reverberated through their souls as Kathleen, her authority resolute, pressed on, commanding them to depart.

They did so, reluctantly, and the room returned to its original state as if nothing had transpired. They looked at each other and continued through the door ahead, concealed by a heavy, long red velvet curtain.

The room they entered was shrouded in darkness and the musty, mothball smell assaulting them almost overwhelmed them, but they switched on their flashlights, revealing a large storeroom, containing many large, olive green filing cabinets.

'Bingo receipts?' chided Dominic as Kathleen stifled a laugh.

'Maybe it's the lost episodes of *I Love Lucy*,' she countered, eliciting a snigger from him in return. She opened the cabinet easily.

'If it's unlocked, I doubt you're going to find the Grimoire of Astoroth in there.'

'This place isn't exactly a tourist attraction, Dominic.

There's little point locking doors in a neglected building, you might say. We may find out the truth about this place in these files,' she whispered, rifling through the file tabs. Leaving her to search, he walked off, scouring the floor with the flashlight before each section he looked at.

'Oh, dear Christ! Dom. It's here. It's *here!*'. He hurried back to her, peering over her left shoulder.

'What've you got, there?'

'I hate it when I'm right. Did your wife mention the Priest whose possessed spirit couldn't leave this place, even after the extensive exorcism performed for him?'

'She said something about a young priest, but I think she was finding it hard to take in,' he said. 'Why? What's it says?'

'This place *has* been subject to unholy acts, as I suspected. Right from a few weeks into the time of it being completed, till about five years ago. There's sworn testimony from sisters past and present, attributing all manner of Satanic idolatry, and child abuse – the exposure for which they were thrown out of the order and slapped with a confidentiality order upon pain of excommunication. It's all *here!*'

Dominic stood dumbfounded.

'So...what do we do?'

'We must destroy this place. Burn it to the ground.'

Dominic was incredulous.

'Are you fuckin' *insane*?! There is no WAY I'm about to burn a building full of sleeping kids!'

Kathleen put her hand on his shoulder, firmly.

'The kids have been taken to Lourdes on a trip, and there's only a handful of older staff upstairs sleeping. And it's the ones who know most about it. They're the most complicit.'

'But for fuck's sake, Kat'leen! Come on, now! You're still talking about burning nuns to death, here,' he cried.

'Fire purifies, you know that, right?'

'So, I've heard.'

'Right! When those kids get back, they'll be cleansed of their demons because the presiding evil has been purified.'

'Still no excuse for murder, love,' he stated, uncertain.

'It's me that has to take the shit for it, so don't you be worryin' yerself about it.'

The door was wrenched open, startling them. The Mother Superior stood there, her face a mask of fury.

'I might have known it would be you. So...you've discovered our little problem.

Good! It's just too bad neither one of you will live to tell anyone about us.'

Dominic laughed, faking a shocked gasp of disbelief, his hands mockingly lunging for his cheeks.

'The Catholic Church involved in a scandal?!

Say it isn't so! The shit your lot have been up to the last fifty years *alone* will have the whole fuckin' world drooling at the mouth with this shit, and you know it.'

The Mother Superior walked to the left, tilting her candle to the area at her feet.

'You see these paintings? These artworks were created one thousand years ago by an Aramaic-fluent artist who, it is said, turned from God in anger, and pledged his soul to Lucifer. His entire line of succession was betrothed to the service of evil, and each male born of his line had, subsequently, been possessed and used to further his purpose.'

Kathleen probed. 'And?'

The old nun sighed, continuing.

'The purpose was to create a coven of children, all of whom were to be pure and intelligent, who would help to, themselves, possess and corrupt the children of this nation. It's but a small cog in the wheel of demonic supremacy. We are here to do his bidding, to prepare for his arrival. These children will be arch demons, his guiding light to the throne he is destined to occupy.'

'Hold on just a second here? You're telling me that from the start, this place was built to usher in the *antichrist?* You can't be serious?'

Dominic sighed. 'No, I think she's deadly serious.'

Without warning, the old nun pulled a baseball bat from the pile of wood behind her and, screaming, swung it at Kathleen's head, barely missing it. Shocked, Kathleen shoved her and the old woman hurtled backwards, impaling herself on a long wooden spear (a gift from the African missions several years back), the large, thin arrowhead emerging from her spine. With a muffled scream, her head flopped to the side, her body bereft... Kathleen recited the last rites and crossed herself.

She looked around the room, finding some large containers of gasoline. She unscrewed the cap, flooding the room with it as Dominic got out of her way.

Leading a trail out of the door, all the way back to the main altar area, she lit a match.

'*Carpe diem!*'

She dropped the match, and the floor came alive in a powerful torrent of flame, consuming everything combustible within reach.

They hung about outside until half the entire building was a raging inferno. Satisfied, they walked off towards their car. A window crashed, making them jump and turn. A large jelly-like 'mist rose sharply into the air above the orphanage, and they watched in horror as it elicited a scream of shame-filled rejection so piercing that it shattered every window for miles, before being sucked back into the raging inferno.

The sky went back to darkness again as if it hadn't happened, the only light coming from the flames which were annihilating the remaining structure of the cathedral wing.

The spirit of Father McDonagh was returned to God, purified by the fire of light.

The car drove off as Dominic leaned back, looking out of the rear window at the carnage they had inflicted.

'Looks like we might have a bit of rain!' he stated, cheerfully.

Kathleen stared hard at him, horrified at the idea, then her face softened, and they both laughed, as they drove into the center of Drogheda.

···········

She watched the fire from the house, glad to see the terrible place burn.

She had hated it, but it was all she had ever known. The fire had burned the entire structure to a state beyond repair. It would have to be rebuilt. Not that *she* cared, though. All they had done for her had not been in her best interests. She turned out the light and went to bed. A low whisper of filtered voices whispered in her ear.

*'CAAALLLIIIIEE'*

Her scream was ear-shattering.

# DEADLINE

Ron Kramer sat hunched over his desk, taut, irritable and exhausted as his screen flickered above his head. The evening edition had stopped its run and he had promised Sam Daniels his story would be ready by six AM. The phone rang, startling him. He punched the speakerphone button.

'Yeah?'

'Ron Kramer?' the voice demanded.

'What did I win?

'Oh, my God...it's really *you*!'

The tone sent his radar into orbit. This was not anyone he recognized.

'Who are ya, and what can I do for ya?'

'You can die.'

The line went dead, leaving Kramer staring at the phone. He picked up the receiver and replaced it, standing up, ruffling his thick hair with both hands. He scoured his mind but could find no-one's face in it to attach to that voice.

*Terrific. Fucking* great*!*

He walked to the coffee pot and poured some into an available mug. He tried to think of whose toes he had stepped on.

*That's gotta be one hell of a long list.*

He *was* an undercover investigative journalist, after all. All the slime he had exposed over the years? Hell, it could be any one of them, or someone they'd hired, maybe.

It wasn't as far-fetched as it sounded.

Powerful people don't like being exposed for the shit they get up to. He had gone undercover in the White House as a janitor to discover that the most powerful man in the world was giving a little more than dictation after hours.

He had uncovered a CIA plot to finance arms to a small Bolivian militia to act as insurgents against a smaller, but more aggressive, regime whose leader was threatening their illicit cocaine racket in that area. These were just two of his most notorious exposes, cementing his standing in the paper but, while being their best writer, he could be an intolerable pain in the tits. A womanising, feminist-hating asshole who never let up on the more aggressive females among us.

He had even enraged old man Randolph's wife with his scathing article on the current gynocentric push in the States, and the third wave feminism which had subjected the national birth rate to an all-time low, endangering the American family unit. It had been researched with due diligence, and he had handed it in. It had been the *truth*, ascertained from statistical analysis and personal testimony from countless interviews held over three months. He had never gone to such an extent over a human interest sidebar before, but he felt this had been worth the extra effort.

The results had been awe-inspiring. The phone grid lit up the entire day of its printing, half the calls hailing "the bravery of the writer," the other half demanding his printed retraction or resignation, if not both.  He had thanked God for his old boss at the time, Mike Avery, who had refuted any suggestion of losing Kramer as being "the most instinctive goddamn writer this ledger's ever known!"  ("Probably why we put up with his shit," he had added later during a board-room meeting break).

Kramer turned off the screen, grabbing his coat and briefcase, and headed for his car.  He emerged from the elevator and walked to the entrance.  Henry, the old Irish concierge, wasn't there.  Probably off patrolling someplace, Kramer thought, wondering what Henry was gonna do if this nut got past him and went upstairs.  A beautiful old man by all means, but not exactly terrifying to anyone.  He pushed his code into the keypad (a new one was re-issued each day by morning email, eliminating the opportunity for early morning infiltration) and pulled the handle.

The rain was bouncing off the sidewalk.  The car had been parked across street before he came in to polish his recent article on non-compliant auto union bosses in Detroit.

'Shit. Goddamn rain never stops,' he said as he pulled his coat over his head before unlocking the car from where he stood.  He quickly ran down the wide steps of the Chicago Herald-Tribune awning and ran towards the warmth of the battered, old Lincoln which awaited him.  He only hoped the piece of shit would start first time.  Narrowly missing a few angry drivers, he got his keys out ready to open the door.  He stopped dead.

The voice of that lunatic filled his ears again.

*Die.*  He checked under the car, just in case.

*FUCK!* There it was, staring him in the eye. A small package, fixed to the underbelly. No doubt wired, he surmised, to both the door handle *and* the ignition. Most only bothered with one wire. Two would be more befitting a person determined against failure to kill his or her target. In technical terms, the guy – if it *was* - was covering his ass. Standing up, he pulled out his cellphone and dialled 911, as he negotiated his way across the road, and back to the office.

··········

The apartment was pitch black when he opened the door, exhausted. Ron locked up and headed straight for the refrigerator, scanning its contents; the remnants of the previous night's Chinese take-out; four bottles of Budweiser; half a loaf of granary; and a quart of milk. He grabbed a beer, and swung the door shut. Collapsing onto the couch, he picked up his newspaper, turning to the features section. His story sprang from the pages he could barely see and he allowed himself a small, half-hearted smile before tanking the beer in two long mouthfuls. He lay down on the couch, staring at the ceiling fan rotating, as he slowly fell asleep, death on his mind.

His *own*.

He awoke with a start. Something was amiss, here, he thought. He could feel eyes on him; malevolence itself, personified. He got up off the couch and walked through the apartment, checking cupboards and under beds. He forced a nervous laughter. He hadn't done that since he was a kid. Satisfied that he was alone, he re-entered the living room, walking to the window overlooking the park across the street.

*Fucking* rain *again*. The condensation crept down the window beside his face, forming a small pool on the window ledge. The street was silent, and for that he was grateful. Peace and quiet appealed to his baser instincts and always had.  Being heavily introverted in high school and, later, at NYU, he had shunned the popular set, preferring the solitude of the library carrels to eternal stresses of gaining popularity.  Not that he would have been accepted, but he wasn't overly concerned with their opinions of him.

He worked for the high school editorial, focusing on publicising the extracurriculars and covering the varsity pep rallies when they came up.  He had made quite an impression on the NYU in-house magazine, writing a brutally incisive column on various current topical issues affecting the studentry.  He liked that word better than 'student body,' having read it from the late, great William Strunk, Jr.  It held a certain resonance and relevance, as opposed to any implication of the students walking around like the walking dead – much like they do today, as he had observed.  Entitled, smug, their lives controlled completely by their social media status.

*Shee-it! The goddamn fuse blows in Facebook HQ, and it's like a fucking zombie apocalypse! They can't function, and lose the power of rational compensatory thought.  But that's what social media was created for.  It was a highly-addictive platform to condition its end user into dopamine-dependent quagmire, where if someone doesn't answer them within five minutes, friendships are off-limits.  The price of being 'in' was a heavy price, indeed!*

His train of thought was shattered by the loud ring of the cordless phone, causing him to jolt out of his internal social commentary.  Cursing under his breath, he walked to the phone.

'Yeah?'.

'Sorry if I'm disturbing your general malaise, there, Ronnie.  I just wanted to see how you were see how you were coping.'

'I'm up to my neck in shit, here. Either tell me what you're after, or get off the line. I've got no time, and even less patience. So, speaketh thee, or fucketh off!'

'You're not being very polite, Ron. I'm your friend,' the voice crooned.

'I'm sorry. Let's start over. Would you please tell me why you're calling?,' he asked with *faux* fawning.

The caller responded in kind.

'Certainly, Ronald. I just wanted you to know that your so-perfect existence is drawing to a close.'

'Okay, so I'm a dead man walking. Mind telling me why I'm being so singularly honored? It would be nice to know who my benefactor is before I get to take my eternal vacation in the Lake of Fire.'

'Just think of me as...uh...someone who doesn't like you very much.'

'That's gotta be one helluva long fucking list! Can you volunteer a few cryptic clues before I'm manacled off this mortal coil? Since you're planning my demise, I'd say you owe me that much at least.'

'Not yet. Maybe later. I *will* leave you with this final thought, though. Ever play charades? One word, two syllables...Boardwalk.'

With that, he hung up. Slowly, Kramer replaced the handset, his face registering the memories that flooded through his mind. He shrugged, and walked to his bedroom, closing the door after him.

· · · • • • • • · · ·

The office was jammed with reporters...unusual for the time of day, Kramer thought. He sauntered casually to his desk, hanging his sport jacket over the chair, and walked to Sam Daniels' office, rapping twice on the door.

'Come,' a voice replied and Kramer opened the door.

Sam Daniels, the editor-in-chief, lounged backwards in his leather recliner, talking on the phone, signalling Kramer to take a seat. Instead, Kramer walked to the window, staring out of it, his troubled reflection betraying his true feelings in the moment as he waited patiently for Daniels to lose the caller.

'Look,' Daniels said in his imperious tone, 'just get a more solid source next time. I can't run that story with the half-assed shit you're givin' me now. Come back to me when you got somethin' more concrete than wild conjecture and horse-shit. Talk to ya later, kid.' He hung the phone up.

'Jesus Christ on a popsicle stick! They write a few local accident reports for their high school rag and they think they're Woodward and Bernstein! What can I do for ya, Ron?' he asked, smiling. Kramer was a pain in his ass, but he respected the hell out of him. The best, most naturalistic writer he'd known in years. This fucking guy buried the Surgeon-General four years before, and he did it with a photograph – a fucking *photograph!*

'I was working on the Vargas piece last night when I got a phone call. Funny thing is...I recognise the voice but not the person on the end of it. It was pretty weird.'

'Well? What did he want?' Daniels probed gently.

'Not much at first. But when I asked him what I could do for him, he said "Die" as plainly as you'd say hello.'

'You think it's someone fucking around?' Daniels asked, more intrigued than before.

'I don't know *what* it is. Just freaked me out a little, to be honest about it. Not something I hear on a paper phone every day. Could be someone I exposed, an angry ex-husband from my extra-curricular days, or it could be Karon The Ferryman – the list is staggering. What should I do? Forget about it or take it seriously? He called me at home last night, around at about 2am.'

Daniels stiffened in his chair. This upped the ante. This wasn't any disgruntled reader.

'He called you at home, you better start takin' it seriously. Have you called the FBI, yet?'

'Not yet. I wanted your take on it, first.'

'I'll call it in for ya. Guy called Fred Dorfler. He's a Forensic Psychiatrist and Profiler when he ain't out at his lakeside cabin spearin' trout. If he's in, I'm sure he'll take this.' He dialled the number, waiting a few moments and then spoke in the customary brash, commanding tone so often reserved for staff meetings.

'Hi. Yes. Fred Dorfler, please. Thank you.' He winked at Kramer and hit the speakerphone button, as a male voice came over the phone.

'Dorfler, here,' he said.

'Freddie! Sam Daniels. How's it goin'?' he asked his old friend jovially.

'Fuck me – Sammy! It's been a while. How are you?'

'Pretty good at my end. What about you? How you been?'

'Ah, the ulcer's giving me shit again. What can I do you for?' he asked.

'I'm not sure what it is yet, but one-a my boys got a stalker on his ass. Called him at the office, and at home later last night. Was wondering if you'd be kind enough to check it out if I send him over to you,' he asked.

'I'm full, but I can have lunch with your man today, and he can tell me all about it. If that's agreeable,' Dorfler suggested. Kramer nodded.

'When and where?' Daniels asked.

'Salerno's. Corner of Vine and Haven. 12.30. Table will be booked, so he can tell the Maitre'D to seat him ahead of me if he gets there earlier. It's on me,' Dorfler said.

'Very kind of you, Freddie. My treat next time,' Daniels replied.

'It's about time you paid for one, you old fraud,' Dorfler joked. Daniels chuckled.

'Take it easy, Freddie. I owe you one.'

'Anytime,' the voice said before clicking off.

'Dorfler's a salty sonofabitch, but he's one of the best profilers the Feds have ever had. He'll tell you the best course of action to take. Go get some petty cash from the fourth floor. I can't have the Feds sayin' we're cheap-skates. I'll cover you for two hundred. Salerno's is a little too pricey for me, but Christ in Heaven, the food's the best this city has to offer. I'll call up and authorise it. Get outta here, ya dumb schlep,' Daniels said, grinning at Kramer. Kramer stood, and walked to the door.

'Ronnie...'

'Yeah?'

'I...uh...you know I'm not one for kissing ass or holding anyone's hand in this place. You're the best I've got. I guess you suspected that by now, anyway. Don't let this prick kill you, alright?'

'Yes, Sir,' Kramer said, smiling, gratified to hear it. High praise, indeed.

He walked out of the office, leaving Daniels staring out of the window, and notably more perturbed.

··········

"So, you're telling me there's nothing you can do about it? Is that it?' Kramer asked the man sitting in front of him, tucking into a large steak dinner. Fred Dorfler was a heavy-set (but muscular) man with slicked-back, jet black hair, sporting a thin moustache.

He was a man who liked to dress well. Although not being able to afford thousand dollar Brioni suits, he was extremely stylish in his choice of apparel, and *how* he wore it. *A la page,* as they called it, where the socks matched the shoes, the shirt the suit and, overall, the suit the man.

Kramer himself was a slob in terms of dress code – happier in jeans and t-shirts, electing for a simple chocolate brown suit and shoes, and khaki shirt with, more often than not, a plain black tie, usually loosened a little. Slightly under-dressed for a ritzy place like Salerno's.

'I don't know what else I can tell you, Mr. Kramer. I haven't exactly got a lot to go on, here, except a possibly veiled death threat and a voice on the telephone. A voice, I hasten to add, you don't even recognise yourself! From what you've told me, he hasn't made any *specific* threat; more suggesting your killing yourself. All we can do is to put a trace on your phone to track where he's calling from, I guess, but even that's not guaranteed to work. He's hardly going to call from home, is he? I doubt he's dumb enough for that. He'll be calling from a pay...'. He thought of something.

'Are there any pay-phones around your property?' Dorfler asked.

'Yeah. There's one down the street, and one in the park across from my apartment. You think that's where he's calling from?' Kramer asked, a little more hopeful.

'It's a strong possibility. We can bug those easily, and without a warrant. Just in case.'

'Why bother? Can't you just run a wiretap out of mine?'

'You really want us listening in to your private conversations, Mr. Kramer? What happens if you wanted to call out for some 'company' shall we say?'

'You really think I'm that desperate?' Kramer laughed.

'Not at all. In your line of work, I'd imagine your sources are important to you,' Dorfler said, warmly. There was an awkward pause hanging in the air.

'Look, here's what I'll do. We'll hook up your phone for a week. You get your sources to call your cellphone instead, that way they're not compromised, and we'll try to nail this freak. Sound good?' Kramer stood, placing a fifty-dollar bill on the table, shaking Dorfler's hand.

'The tip's on Sammy,' Kramer said, grinning. 'Thanks again, Sir,' Kramer said before turning away.

'Oh, Mr. Kramer...'

'Yeah?' Kramer said, turning to face him.

'Remember the golden rule of wiretapping...always keep 'em talking.'

Kramer nodded, smiling thinly, and exited the restaurant, as Dorfler continued his meal as if the meeting had never taken place.

••••••••••

He ate the last of his TV dinner, washing it down with the last of the Budweiser sitting next to it. He had finished the polish on his expose, and would email it to the Copy desk later. He had nothing to do for the rest of the evening. Walking to the cupboard beside the tv, he opened the door, revealing a mountain of DVDs. He had them all compartmentalised by genre and 'star' – it was easier to find the good shit that way. He flicked his finger across the spines, reading them aloud as we went, finally fingering a few of them for the evening's movie fest – *Cool Hand Luke*, *All The President's Men* and *Casablanca*. Oughta be good enough to take his mind off this shit, he thought. Call out for pizza and chill out for the first time in months. Sounded like a plan.

He called Fat Tony's, ordering two large Double Pepperoni with sausage and jalapeños, and Hawaiian (although, he thought, why in Satan's butthole *anyone* would think of putting pineapple on a pizza was way over his head. But this was *America*, dammit! You could get French fries and *Oreos* on a pizza, as long as you fuckin' paidfor it!). He thanked the girl on the phone and hung up, rubbing his hands together. It was going to be at least 45 minutes to an hour before it got here. He lay down on the couch, his left arm behind his head, watching as Renaud's men rounded up the usual suspects.

Within minutes, he was lost in dreamland.

··········

The banging on the door made Kramer leap out of the comfort of the couch, angry at being woken like that. He had fallen asleep after the pizzas and beer had evaporated, and was full up and cranky. He reached into the box in the hall cupboard, pulling out his Cubs baseball bat, a gift from an old college friend, and stood behind the door.

'Who is it?'

'I've got a package for a Mister Ron Kramer,' the voice said flatly.

'It's two a.m., for Chrissakes! Who the hell delivers at this time?' Kramer snapped.

'Leave it at door and get out of here!'

'I can't leave it. I've been ordered to hand it to you,' he replied through the door.

'Take it the fuck outta here. I don't want it,' Kramer yelled. Then he chewed on his bottom lip.

'Who sent it?' he tested.

'Somebody called Fred Dorfor...Dorflan...or something like that. Can't make out the last name on it.'

Kramer, hearing close to Dorfler's name, lifted the chain latch and opened the door, revealing a dopey-looking Fed-Ex courier, barely out of puberty, complete with crumpled uniform, scratching his mop of ginger curls as he looked over his rocket scientist spectacles at the clipboard.

'You wanna sign this so I can leave, please?' he asked Kramer, his voice strained and over-tired. Kramer didn't like it but he signed, taking the parcel, and closed the door, locking it again.

He walked into the lounge, putting it to his ear. It wasn't too big a package – but just large enough to lift without difficulty. It had a little weight to it. He started to unwrap it and he heard static from inside. Whatever was in that box was interfering with the cable signal. He walked to the rear window in the bedroom, opening it, and launching the parcel out of it, towards the perimeter wall adjoining an alleyway.

The explosion was loud – and blinding, blowing out every window within immediate proximity, including his. Kramer, having dived to the carpet, looked up at his shattered window frame, at the flaming lace curtains billowing inwards, and shook his head to clear the light from his eyes. He stood up and walked to the small refrigerator he kept in a cupboard under his well-stocked bookcase. Shaking, he managed barely to fill a small glass with whiskey, gulping it down in one shot, exhaling sharply. His laptop sounded. He walked to the desk, lifting the lid, and touched the mouse pad. One word appeared in an email before him.

*Boardwalk.*

Kramer closed his eyes. This was more serious than he had imagined. He closed the laptop lid, and poured another whiskey.

He was going to need it.

··········

"So, you got no idea who this person is? Not even anything he's said to you that could give you a clue? I'm sorry to press you on this, Mister Kramer, but these types usually *want* their targets to know who's doing it to them.'

'I'm a reporter. I write investigative pieces and, sometimes, they implicate important people. It could be one of them, someone they hired to take my ass out...an angry husband from my youth. I couldn't say. He only said 'board walk' on the phone, as he did the lap top. The only board walk in my life is the one in Asbury Park, New Jersey, when I was at NYU. Jersey was much cheaper to rent in. I met a girl there, and we spent a lovely day together.'

'Maybe it's someone connected to her,' the Detective posed.

'Since she's been dead these last ten years, I very much doubt it,' he said, bluntly.

Detective Harry Winston looked at Kramer, disliking him but, almost as strongly, loving his sarcasm. It was a gift which deserves constant practise. He smiled to himself at Kramer's poker-faced response - so quick, so...economical in its inherent brevity. He sighed and, flipped shut his notebook.

'Okay, then. I think we're done here. The lab boys are outside checking the building for prints and fibres. We've got the IP address for the email they sent you. I'll get it checked out through our Cyber Crime unit and get back to you if we find anything.'

Kramer extended his hand. 'Thanks!'

Winston smiled thinly, a bare crease of the corners of the left side of his thick lips. He walked out, followed by the other uniformed cops, leaving Kramer to assess and clean up the mess.

'On your own again, kid,' he told himself, as he attended to the scattered glass shards.

He decided – not being far wrong - that this was some fucked up shit.

··········

He had the apartment back to the way it was, except for the window frame, but that was going to take a little more than a vacuum and dust. His property insurance would take care of that, being fully paid at each renewal call. He sat back, crashing his head against the cold, cracked leather, wondering what this crazy bastard was going to throw at him next. His car, his apartment...would it be his life? Who knew with this guy? He stared blankly at the tv and realised he couldn't be bothered even turning it on. He was too burned out to watch anything. He found some wood to secure the exposed window and grabbed his coat, pissed off, and left the house. He needed a drink.

Kramer walked the near-deserted street, populated only crack whores and johns on alternate corners, as he ambled aimlessly along looking for a bar. He found one a mile further down – McDavitt's – and opened the door. He was relieved to find it relatively empty, and walked the counter, ignoring the few young women in the corner, tossing him cool, appraising looks. He slapped a twenty on the bar.

'Bourbon and a glass. Leave the bottle, will ya?' he drawled in an uncharacteristic languid tone. Jay, the barkeep, raised a questioning eyebrow but relented. A twenty *was* a twenty, and he wasn't exactly rolling in patrons these days. He put the bottle on the counter, sitting the glass beside it, and walked off to start the dishwasher under the pumps.

He was lost in his own universe when a voice shattered his haze. His periphery told him it was one of the 'corner hoggers.' He didn't even acknowledge her. Why the hell should he? he thought. The last thing he needed now was some skank trying to hustle him for her next drink.

She waved her hand in front of his face.

'Hello? You in there somewhere?'

'Look, Miss…I'd really, *really* like to be alone right now, y'know. I ain't got any money left, and I've got shit on my mind, okay? So if you wouldn't mind, try someone else.' Irritated, she stormed off, cursing him.

'Fuckin' queer!'

He laughed inwardly, 'Yeah. Queer. Right!' He poured himself another triple, and stared at his own eyeballs in the bar mirror as he downed it in one shot, savoring the taste.

The car pulled up across the street, its occupant eagerly watching the bar.

'You sure he's in there?' the man asked.

The woman sitting beside him, also looking over at the building, replied, her voice distant and mysterious.

'For sure. Helena called me and told me. He doesn't drink much, and when he does, it's usually the first bar from where he is at the time.'

'He with anybody?' he asked.

'Nah. He's a loner. What do you expect from a reporter!' she said, enjoying the ensuing laughter from the man beside her.

'Hand me the cellphone, Natalie,' he asked. The woman handed it to him and he began punching the number in.

'Watch this, my dear,' he said, a wry grin creasing his heavy aquiline features. There was something behind that grin, she had felt. And it made her uneasy, almost regretful, about her part in the whole mess. But she had to do her part.

The dialling tone was heard and Jay's voice came over the other end.

'Yeah?' the voice crackled.

'The gentleman sitting at your counter. Kick him out. Now. I don't care how. Just *do* it.' He hung up.

Jay stared at the phone, replacing the handset to the wall holder. He looked over at Kramer, and truly felt for the poor bastard. The guy on the phone had been a pivotal influence in his bar being closed for over four months with a single call to the cops, citing suspected narcotics trafficking as the cause for a search and seizure warrant. Of course he knew the old man had both supplied and arranged to have two full kilograms of pure junk planted in the back room of the bar. The closure had damn near broke Jay who, the old man knew, could ill afford to close for a week much less four whole months. Jay was a tall, tough, stocky guy who was well abled enough to be a doorman in any rough bar in the city.

He would do *exactly* what he was told if he wanted to stay in business.

Jay walked to the back room, and dialled the bar from his cellphone, setting it on the table as he emerged, towel over his shoulder as he answered it cheerfully.

'Yell-o,' he said, pausing a few moments as if listening. Kramer looked up at the change in the man's pitch, squinting.

'Look, Marie, calm down... listen to me carefully...where are you?' he asked, his voice obviously panicked.

'Alright, stay right there. I mean it, Marie. Don't you fuckin' move. I'm lockin' up, now,' he said, almost reaching fever pitch. 'I'm comin,' now. Just stay right there!' He hung the phone up and ran his hand through his thick dark hair, before going back to the room to retrieve his cellphone. It had worked. He grabbed his jacket for added effect, putting it on as he emerged from the rear.

'Alright, everybody. Closing time. I've gotta go. Drink up and I'll see you tomorrow. You don't have to go home, but ya can't stay here. C'mon, c'mon...let's hustle.'

Disgruntled, the few people in the bar finished their drinks and left the bar. Jay locked the door behind him, and an overwhelming guilt washed over him. He didn't know what the guy at the bar had done, but whatever it was it was fucked up. He took his coat off, poured a double from the bourbon bottle, and knocked it back sharply.

When Kramer walked into the cold, moonlit night, the skanks had gone.

*Thank Christ for small mercies*! he thought, as he raised his coat collar. Looking around, he saw little of much to hang around town for, and started the long walk home.

Or, at least, what was left of it.

· · · • • • • · · ·

Kramer entered his building around an hour later, cold and dejected. He had work in three hours, and he felt the worse for wear as the barrage of bourbon worked on him. He tried to get his key in the door, dropping them on the doormat.

*Shit!*

Fumbling around in the dark, he found them and tried again, this time with more luck. He put his hand against the door and it swung open. Someone had broken in, by the looks of it, and he sobered up quickly as he reached for the tire iron he kept behind the hallway bookshelf.

Nothing. Now he *was* in deep shit, he thought. He closed the door quietly, and slid off his shoes, proceeding carefully through the house, praying the floorboards wouldn't betray him. Was it the crazy sonofabitch who had bombed his car...who had destroyed his apartment? Or was it...someone *else?*

As he approached the living room, Kramer saw a faint light emanating from the bottom of it. He swallowed hard, pushing the door open to find it was exactly as he had left it.

*What in Christ's name was going* on *here?* he mused. As if in answer, a voice boomed through the room as the leather recliner chair swing around, taking him by surprise.

The man sitting there had a smug grin plastered over his face, triumphant and vindicated.

'It's been a long time, Mr Kramer,' he said, examining his fingernails.

Then it dawned on Kramer. That *voice.*

It was the same voice who had called him in the office earlier the previous evening.

'Who are you?' he demanded.

'Now, don't tell me you don't remember me, Kramer. You put me in the can for thirty years. Ring any bells?'

Strangely enough, it did. Kramer had been part of a grand jury that had locked him up and threw away the key. As Kramer recalled the verdict being read out by the Lead Juror, he could recall the ashen grey face of the man sitting before him, now.

'This can't...this can't be. I heard you died in Atlanta!' Kramer exclaimed, not believing what he was seeing. He took another look through his bleary eyes and noticed a faint outline around the man and it became apparent that this...thing, whatever it was had come from somewhere. Kramer composed himself enough to speak.

'You killed that girl in cold blood. I saw the evidence, myself. We *all* did! You deserved what you got, Mister.'

'Actually, Mr Kramer, you forget your history. Six days into my incarceration to the service of the State, the very same thing happened to another girl in Vermont. They caught the killer. He had exact same M.O. as I had so they ran DNA comparison tests on her, and it came out that it was the same person who had brutally raped and murdered young Miss Carswell on the Asbury Park boardwalk. I was the scapegoat for an embarrassed system. But before they could release me – and they tried – I was shivved through my mattress two days before they came to release me. A most unjust set of circumstances, I would say. Wouldn't you?'

Kramer couldn't believe what he had just heard. Maybe it *was* true. There *had* been some minor mitigating factors in the prosecution's case but it had all pointed to him. There had been no other suspects. Unless...

The full horror of the reality occurred to Kramer in that instant. It *had* been purely circumstantial, and they had been too deep in to stop it from going ahead. The publicity had been on such a level that they had had to cover their asses to placate an angry public. They had found a man who had been seen on the boardwalk around same time, and that was all they cared about. Politics had demanded that someone take the fall for that whole mess, and to prevent a class action lawsuit against the system, they had manufactured enough compromising evidence to place an innocent man at the scene. With no other leads, and no-one else seen in the vicinity, they had their closure on the whole sorry affair. Kramer felt a wave of nausea rise in him. He swallowed harder, and braced himself.

'So...I acted on the evidence they presented at the trial. It's unfortunate at best; a disgrace at worst. Question is, here...why come after *me*? I was only doing what I had to, erroneous or otherwise. What the hell were you doing at the boardwalk at that time of night...cruisin' for hookers?'

'Yes. I had been divorced that day and was feeling lonely. I was hoping to find someone of, shall we say, (he made air quotes with his fingers) 'horizontal persuasion' to indulge me. Next thing I know, I'm surrounded by cops and slammed against the hood of a squad car being read my rights. Not a very auspicious start to my new life,' the thing said.

Kramer knew truth when he heard it.

'So what do you want from me?' Kramer asked a little too tersely. He wanted to get to the end of it.

'I want you to die, Kramer. I don't believe you have the slightest remorse for my...predicament. It's time you left,' he finished.

'You really expect to cross over with an attitude like that?!' Kramer asked, tut-tutting. He took a breath, continuing.

'You're dead. You've got no use for money, and I'm not ready to leave yet. What'll it take to help you across? I can't go back in time to change anything, can I?', Kramer asked, his tone risen and indignant.

The woman who had been in the car with him emerged from the foyer behind him, a .9mm aimed at Kramer. He turned to face her.

She was tangible, and of flesh and blood. His mind raced as his body froze. He stood there, immobile, the adrenaline pumping through him.

'What are you gonna do with *that*?' he asked her. He knew it was pointless wasting breath on her, but he had to berate her, a petty attempt at getting in that final word before he ended up on the wrong end of that slug.

'Oh, I'm sure, being a reporter, you can figure *that* out for yourself, Mr Kramer. I'm just the trigger. Nothing personal, of course,' she said, smiling coldly.

'Of course. You're gonna waste me to get me wherever he is. Then I'll be as empty as him. Right? He can't do any damage *here*. He can't touch the living, right? You gotta kill me so he can take me apart in the next life? That it? That's pretty vacant, lady.'

'Enough of this shit. Shoot him. Shoot him now!' the thing commanded her. She cocked back the sliding barrel, aimed, and –

*CLICK! Misfire.*

Kramer snatched the pistol from her as she studied the gun, angry, trying to figure out why it hadn't gone off. He looked it over, aiming it at her.

'You forgot to take the safety off,' he said. He pulled the trigger, decorating the wall with an arterial spray and whatever brain she had been harboring underneath that maze of blonde bangs. She froze, the disbelief showing in her face as she dropped to the floor. The 'thing' in the chair screamed and flew against the wall, passing through it. Kramer stood, looking down at the dead blonde leaking cerebral fluid and blood over his laminate floor, wondering what this was going to do to him. Murder one – or self defense? How would the DA and a jury play it, he contemplated. Probably not a good idea to tell them a ghost had a blonde try to kill his ass.

Maybe there *was* a life after prison, after all, he thought as he lifted the phone and dialled 911.

As he waited, he asked himself if there were any catamarans in Jersey.

# CARRY ME OFF

The chimes rang twelve as a loud peal of thunder roared through the small cottage on the east side of Colwyn Bay. The storm had reached fever pitch at 120mph gusts and, miraculously enough, the reinforced roof had remained intact. Jacqui was all alone for the first time in seven years. She and her ex-partner, Miles, had spent many 'happy' times in this place but neither had ever come alone. Now, as she looked out of the window, she wished she hadn't been so impetuous on that last argument. It had been a petty disagreement which had ballooned to a shouting match – during her 'bad time' of all moments.

She had kicked him to the kerb, and was only now beginning to regret it. She was a frisky, ambivalent young woman with a little fire between her legs and, it being Valentines Day, she was feeling the 'burn.' A flash of lightning, too close for comfort, lit the entire window frame, making her jump, lurching away from the glass pane, having been lightly scorched from the impact. The lights flickered off and on and Jacqui swallowed hard.

'*Okay,*' she said to herself. '*This is* not *good!*'

The door slammed open, the brutalising gust gaining its previously-denied entry to the lounge. The room became a maelstrom from hell. Framed paintings flew across the room, smashing into the wall with terrifying force; glass ornaments were sent to the hardened oak floor, obliterating themselves; magazines and newspapers became possessed as they flew across the room, held in place to the kitchen hatch by the sheer, undeniable intensity of the icy blast penetrating the sanctuary of her solitude. Jacqui was cowering in the corner, when it came in, it's eyes dark crimson, glowing, as it glided across to where she sat crouched in terror. In seconds flat, she knew she was no longer alone in this pithy little cottage.

She looked up and saw the tall, dark, brooding figure hovering over her, her petrified eyes wide as saucers as she felt her soul being drawn inexorably from her body. She felt unable – and, strangely so, un*willing* – to resist the power radiating from those bottomless red pits. It was commanding her to come to him, to be his – and his alone. It was deal day with the devil. But his sheer force of will had taken leave of any resistance she imposed on it. She felt herself being levitated, his dark clad arms embracing her waist and legs as it carried her - *willingly* – to the door to hell.

# DARK HARVEST

"Thou shalt not suffer a witch to live!"
The Bible, Exodus 18: 22
*Salem, Massachusetts...1692*

The tall man arrived without fanfare, quietly taking possession of his room in the small village property he had acquired through the local realtor. He had heard of the puritanical influence in the area, and hadn't been overly impressed at the treatment of the native Indians who had been condemned to the outskirts. He was here for one thing, and one thing only. To barter his goods among the village women, and then get out of this god forsaken hell-hole for good. He spent the evening at the local tavern, made some potential sales connections, and adjourned to bed. The journey had been arduous, and had taken a lot out of him. He would start afresh in the morning. He turned out the light, plunging the room into darkness, and fell asleep quickly, so deeply that he did not hear the screams of the young girl being tortured by invisible forces.

So it had begun...the darkest chapter in the history of the Massachusetts Bay area, forever after to be immortalised in history as the 'Salem Witch Trials.'

He could have had no concept of just how close he was to be involved in it. But, for now, he slept like the dead.

··········

The village was teeming as Jonathan Lerner emerged from his lodgings the following morning. Women were standing around gossiping as they went about their barter; men, also, loitered in the passageways discussing the business of the day, mostly the recent arrival of their new church leader, the Reverend Samuel Parris, reputed to be a failed businessman, himself only recently ordained as a minister. He had had some contractual problems with his salary, and there was much fighting within the community over land, money and religion. Parris' own daughters had been diagnosed with 'witchcraft' when they had mysteriously been stricken by invisible bites and scratches. The doctors', unable to diagnose conventional ailments for a person's malady would usually be inclined to determine one was afflicted by devils – heaven forbid, they could ever bring themselves to forfeit the 'god-like' status conferred in them by their patients.

The village had been condemned by God, Parris had preached, the young girls having been seduced by darkness and converted to the infernal magic of the dark one. He had condemned his own daughters and niece to the hanging gallows, sparing them the mental anguish they would surely suffer by way of the demonic machinations inflicted by the left hand path. He could not possibly, therefore, allow such evil to prevail without let nor hindrance in his own parish. His own precarious position was at stake, and he would ensure his daughters were not vilified alone. It had not escaped his fervent eye that a stranger had infiltrated their once peaceful village, a salesman of sorts it was claimed. Perhaps he was the cause of it all – and perhaps not. He would be carefully watched, his movements scrutinised to make certain he was as he presented himself to be.

The devil was, after all, more than capable of transforming himself into human form. Perhaps this Lerner fellow was evil incarnate, made flesh to supervise and protect his followers. Who could truly say? Such things were not impossible. Would that it were that a person can be infested by demons, why not then can't their Master avail himself of the power to be seen in the form of another? Parris hadn't ruled out the possibility, and had sworn to hunt the man should he once be caught fraternising with the young women of the village. In the meantime, however, the good Reverend had bigger fish to fry. He had caught a young village girl in a barn the night before last, convulsing violently, and she had been taken to the local physician who, unable to diagnose her condition, had declared her to be possessed by unnatural forces. She had been detained in a converted barn, her family's wealth used to keep her *in situ* for the duration leading to her trial and assured conviction, as it had been following the village coffers being gradually reduced when the outbreak had first began. The town couldn't afford scandal, therefore it had been agreed, unanimously, that the evil must be destroyed at any cost.

Lerner walked the dirt roads, taking the air, surveying the landscape and its social architecture, both separate and in whole. He was entranced by the village and its intricate web of underlying secrecy. He noted that, while the gossip flowed freely, those engaging in it clammed up when asked a direct question. There was darkness in this village. A darkness which dared not speak its name, lest the speaker be shunned by their peers or, worse, banished completely.

He had learned from hearsay that they had been obliged to finance their own (albeit, unjust) incarceration. Their personal finances were billed until such times as their funds were drained. He had scarcely believed that such injustice could be common-place in modern day 1692. It was beyond the pale, to say the least.

He took lunch at a small inn on the outskirts of the village. He had found it very pleasant and the serving girls were stunningly beautiful – obviously the best the village had to offer. They were off-limits to outsiders. The merest word spoken to them out of turn, and overheard, could result in their being repudiated and, should you be caught alone with one, there was the reasonable likelihood that she would be pilloried as a practitioner of the dark arts, and hung in the village square by the puritannical hierarchy administering the area. This Parris fellow had been forced by his own beliefs to condemn his own blood when they were overawed by a mysterious malady spreading rife throughout Salem, and he wasn't about to let another walk free in light of that. They were made swift examples of, without let or hindrance.

Lerner stood at his stall in the village centre until shortly after noon. Business had proven less than admirable but he was always prepared. He still had a small amount of money in his purse, but the value of the Colonial Pound varied from state to state. He gathered up his wares and walked to the Inn, where he was bidden to table near the window seat, overlooking the village square. His lunch – a simple affair - soup and bread – was pleasant enough, he thought. His eye caught movement outside and he was riveted to the sight he beheld.

A small group of puritanical leaders emerged from two buildings, followed by a hog line of four women and one man (likely in his late 20's, Lerner thought) were shepherded to a large multiple wooden hanging range and led up the short flight of steps to the platform. As the masked executioner placed black hoods over their heads, the town crier began pealing his bell, alerting the village to this morning's little redemptive soirée.

'Oyez, oyez! In this day of our Lord, October 30, 1692, *Anno Domini*, we bear solemn witness to the purification of these unfortunate creatures, whom have fallen foul of God Almighty by renouncing His word, falling into the graceless state of eternal damnation. To save the eternal souls of our dearly beloved, they must be purified. Only then can they pass from this world to the next. These people have been found guilty of the practice of witchcraft, as deemed most appropriate by leaders of good standing, present of this village of Salem in this year of our Lord, 1692. Let the dark ones be warned. By this act we consecrate our beloved village in the lifeblood of Jesus Christ, and drive out the evil within their corrupted shells.'

Lerner was rapt with attention, amazed at what he was saying. He had heard tell of the Puritans and their religious fervour – but witnessing it was something else altogether! He supped at his meal, unable to detach his eyes from the monstrosity outside. The rest of the inn was watching with a mixed reaction of pity and equal fervour matching that of the leaders...

(*...Ha! Leaders? Damned barbarians and religious maniacs so convinced of their own piety it made you want to puke!*)

...outside. He continued to watch, despite his every urge to turn his head from it. It commanded his attention with a powerful draw.

Without warning, there was a simultaneous loud crack as the trap doors opened – then another as their necks were snapped. Lerner screwed his eyes shut, attempting to dispel the image from his mind, but was unable. He reopened his eyes, slowly returning them to the scene barely fifty feet away. The bodies were being cut down and checked by the local physician to make certain the task had been acquitted. The old medic nodded, his expression cold and grim, as he executed the crisp, quick hand gesture across his throat Such was not a moment for gloating or revelling.

These people were their *friends*, and should be mourned as such. They had been touched by demons and, as such, had those demons

# OUT OF THE ASHES

vanquished in the most humane (it was humane in *their* view; bloody insane to his) manner according to the word of God. What was it the bible said? He couldn't remember it chapter and verse, not being in the remotest way religious, but he recalled it as being *"Thou shalt not suffer a witch to live,"* or words to that effect. He left the inn, and walked through the crowd, making his way to his rented room. All he wanted was to sleep.

For a week.

··········

The lamp lights in the village were out when he woke up in absolute darkness. He reached around for the gaslight and his matchbook. Tearing one off and lighting it, he lifted the small amber-glow kerosene lamp and walked to the window. He had overheard someone commenting on the street, something about the lamps being doused early to save the Village coffers from being depleted any more than necessary. He heard screams in the distance...tortured screams of a young woman terrified out of her wits, and a chill ran up his spine as he tried to imagine what she could be enduring enough to elicit a scream as bad as that. He walked back to bed, thoughts of witches walking the dark corners of night running through his mind before sleep finally took him.

··········

She was, in her own quiet way, remarkably beautiful. Pale skin, the colour of fresh milk, set against eyes of emerald green, made his heart jump every time she caught his gaze. Her resulting smile made him want her even more. Try as he might, he fought the urge to let her catch his eyes taking in her ample bosom and curvature. A comely wench, indeed, he thought. Was it just his imagination or was he being afforded preferential attention? He noticed that, although he wasn't the only man viewing her attributes, he *was* the only one being smiled at with an open mouth. Every other man was given a closed-mouthed, pursed-lipped smile, polite and socially acceptable. But when her eyes met his, those emerald eyes assumed a glint of undeniable attraction, almost as if she bore desire for him alone. She wasn't of the village it was whispered, instead hailing from neighbouring Salem Town.

Not that it would make any difference. If she transgressed against God, she would be tried, convicted and dangled from the same blackened rope as quickly as any other. He could not even approach her lest they be seen conversing where, he knew all too well, she would be held accountable as a 'harlot,' and her life made unbearable until she left the area of her own accord. She returned to the counter to fetch another order and he caught her name for the first time.

Rachel. No surname was forthcoming, at least not yet. Just *Rachel*. He had no idea of the importance she would bring to bear on his future, for at this moment she was to be regarded as unattainable. A position in which he felt unduly aggrieved. He returned his gaze to the snow-covered fields outside his window, dreamy thoughts of Rachel inescapable from his mind.

The Reverand Samuel Parris stood at the lectern, his heavy imperious frame as righteous as his manner. He surveyed his flock with a cool, appraising, pious glare, wondering not for the first time what his Lord and Saviour would have made of them had he stood here in his stead. He decided that the prognosis wasn't a particularly good one. There were sinners in this village – just as there had been in the first flock he had tended.

'Here there be sinners, ladies and gentlemen. Among all of *you*. It matters not of what sin you commit, but the mere fact that you have shamed God is sin enough. He knows all. All of your fornicating. All of your licentious cavorting in the corners of your mouth, courting the regard of men. There be an unholy aura in this town. As you will doubtless be aware, my own child and the child of my brother have been the beneficiaries of this darkness. They were good girls with a strong moral compass. They did not hold free verbal congress in the pathways of this village. Nor did they dress provocatively to enslave a married man for financial accoutrements. They were *stricken*,' he said, enunciating the last word with a crash of his closed fist on the lectern, making everyone jump, 'stricken by Satan Himself. As a man of God, I was forced to expel these unfortunate children to the gallows, an act I was proud to instigate to preserve the sanctity of their eternal souls. Let no servant of the serpent sit here, in this house of mercy, masquerading as god-fearing human beings when they be cursed of the stars. Let their glorious redemption in God be a shining example of the efforts of Salem Village to renounce Be'elzebub and all his works, lest he be loosed upon the world once more. We cannot dismiss the fact that the curse of witchcraft is with us, my friends, and we – all of us, not one – are susceptible to the charms of the infernal spell of the devil's handmaidens. Let us pray!'

His voice held a contemptuous yet commanding tone, demanding yet caring, as the congregation bowed heads in silence – and in their collective unspoken shame. They repeated each line like the Catholic Catechism they had rebuked so many years ago.

'Our Father, who art in Heaven...hallowed be thy name...'

A dark grey, billowing *stratocumulus* gathered over the church as the skies turned hostile, a distant rumbling gaining on the village as his voice boomed through the church-house, projecting through the drywall panels, through the clapboard, ringing through the stiff, whistling breeze which was picking up fast.

・・・・・・・・・・

Cotton Mather had always been a great conversationalist. Indeed, he was regarded as the World Champion of Great Conversation. He could sweet-talk the hardest class most pessimistic banker into financing any venture he chose to broach, when everyone else was rejected. Cotton Mather had the *gift*! The gift was most evident on the day he met Rachel. He had taken a great interest in her, much to her annoyance – and the consternation of Lerner, who had watched the prowess of Mather in seduction mode. Rachel, however, had rebuffed him time after time. She knew - all too well – how the village viewed lewd behaviour in its female contingent, and the consequences should a village girl be found to have engaged in any out-of-wedlock trysts. It was marriage, or public shaming in the stocks.

Lerner had taken his evening walk when he heard screaming. Following his ears, he traced the sound to a isolated barn on the road to Salem Town. A young man, dressed in black, was accosting a young woman. Lerner grabbed a nearby axe from a log stump, walking to the barn doors. He heard the woman's voice. There was real panic in there, he thought. It was now or never. This was not his usual thing, normally electing not to get involved. But this was different.

*He* knew *that voice.*

He had his suspicions and prayed he was wrong as he grabbed the handle on the door, yanking it open, surprising the young man. He was about a head shorter than Lerner, but more imposing in height and menacing in manner. Lerner had suspected Mather as being the one to be facing off, but the man was not familiar. He looked down at the woman who, ashamed to have been caught in such a position, regardless that nothing had happened – yet.

'Be you okay, my dear?' he asked her.

She looked up, her eyes tearful, her face distressed.  It was Rachel.

His heart turned black with rage, desiring nothing more than to kill this defiler, this spoiler of young women.

He stormed towards the young man, axe at the ready, who ran out of the barn, pursued by an enraged Lerner.  He watched the degenerate running for his life and returned to Rachel.  He sat down on the straw besides her, his legs hunched to his chest.

'I think we ought to get you home, Miss,' he said softly.

'I...I didn't...do anything,' she said, visibly shaken.

'Let's get you home,' he said standing to his feet, extending his hand to pull her to hers.  As she stood, the barn doors were burst open from outside, splintering in the impact.   Rachel's eyes opened wide as a small group of men holding gasoline-wrapped torches and pitchforks walked in their arrogant, righteous swagger as Rachel backed off in terror, knowing exactly what was to become of her.

'You're making a serious mistake, gentlemen,' Lerner accused them, his face stern.

From behind them, Reverend Parris entered the barn, his voice making the posse turn and part to afford him access.

'On the contrary, Sir.  In your position, I should say it is *you* who has made the mistake.  Miss?  Come here.'  She looked at him, her eyes bulging as her pallid, fish-white skin lost the last remaining tint of colour.  She was petrified beyond belief.

'You, young lady...are in very grave trouble.  We have our ways, and our ways have always been known since our arrival, here.   It is our belief that you be possessed by the devil...a witch.  You will accompany us to Salem Village where, on the morrow, you will face trial on a charge of witchcraft and licentious disorder in public when, if found to be guilty, you will be hanged by the neck until you be dead. Thankful be you that we do not consign you to the flame. Take her!'

As two of the largest men walked towards the screaming Rachel, Lerner's fist crashed into the face of the tallest of them, knocking him out cold. As he landed in the haystack, he elicited an excruciating scream as a hidden pitchfork ripped through his chest, his shirt becoming a blossom of claret as the blood poured from his wounds. His head rolled to the side, his eyes wide in shock as they gave up the ghost and life left him.

Parris was apoplectic with rage.

'You, Sir, are guilty of murder! The crime has been witnessed and confirmed by the presence of the people here. I am confident you will join the girl on the gallows, and I, for one, will relish the prospect of hearing thine neck crack,' he said, his face smug and sneering. 'Bring them! Our work, this night, is done.'

Lerner's eye caught sight of the butt of a matchlock pistol near his feet, partially concealed by hay. He quickly bent and picked it up, and fired it into the air. The village men began to back off. He was right about them, he thought. And he wasn't in the least surprised.

*Damned cowards. It's so very easy to hunt weak women who are less likely to resist you, but try it with someone stronger...*

Lerner pulled Rachel toward the barn doors, keeping the pistol aimed at them.

'You will be hunted across this state...this land, entire. Have no fear of this. You will be found and punished for your crimes. You have one chance to redeem yourself before God Himself decrees you face the hangman's rope. Come with us while you still can. I beseech thee,' Parris said, but his voice contained no sign of genuine concern for them.

Lerner, detecting it, his face stern, backed out of the barn, loading Rachel into the horse-drawn caleche, firing a shot at a gasoline vat near to the barn doors. The posse of villagers cowered from the inferno as the sound of the whip crack horses sent them galloping out of there. They would pay dearly for this night, and Lerner knew he had signed his own death warrant. The death of the *de-facto* posse member had been unintentional – Lerner had no way to know there was anything submerged within the hay. How *could* he have? At most he could be charged with aggravated assault. He had tried to save one of their own from being violated *by* one of their own! The irony stultified him into submission. He would hide out in the snow-capped wilds of rural Maine until he decided what to do.

And what was the alternative, exactly? he reasoned. It didn't bear thinking about. He knew it was wrong to run. They were both victims of a terrible confluence of circumstances. Her almost being raped; his crime being having, albeit accidentally, the unwitting manslaughter of a villager. The injustice would be swift and unrelenting. They would care not for the girl; care not that she was about to be brutally spoiled by an upstanding member of their own parish; and, further, care not about bringing the proper parties to account. Their minds were made up, and he knew it. There would be no reprieve for either of them this night, or any other.

The caleche was beginning to slow as the winter snowstorm began to thicken to an alarming degree, becoming more savage in its voracious assault on their near frozen, reddening skin. They had passed by Salem Town by going cross-country, and were close to the Maine State line. But that would take another two days of constant wheel-rattling, he estimated. They would have to locate a barn where he could tend to the horses and then their own comfort, all out of sight of any passers-by, who might hear of the evenings events. The people of the day were more vindictive and bloodthirsty, it seemed. He had recently heard tell of one woman who had been accused, tried and convicted of witchcraft, all because she had disagreed vehemently with her husband. She had been hung according to their laws, and other such cases were not exempt from being tried through the grapevine. A vine that had been, and was still being, well-squeezed these last few months. Was there no end to the madness? Time would tell, he thought. Right now, however, he had to take care of her. He turned to her, seeing that she was asleep.

*Asleep? Or dead? Too hard to tell, looking like that*, he mused. He couldn't stop now or they'd both be popsicles. He shielded his eyes, scouring the land, and his dejected heart skipped a beat. A large estate loomed in the near distance. A ten-minute ride to safety, he estimated. The horses did their duty, and they arrived at the gates, one of which hung haphazardly on one hinge. He reined in the horses and climbed down, opening them enough to fit the conveyance through and resumed his seat, corralling the horses into the last journey up the long, deserted, snow-blanketed road, praying to good God Almighty that it was hospitable or – better yet - as deserted as this godforsaken road.

Thoughts of love were the farthest thing from his mind, as replacing that he heard the repeated sound of his neck cracking like a stuck record. It grated him – more deeply than he could have imagined.

Casting it off, he drew the caleche into the opened barn doors, themselves a god-send. He closed the doors, struggling to close them from the freezing -2 Celsius gale which threatened to rip the doors from his red, raw hands.

Time to resuscitate Rachel as best he could.

*If*, the thought entered him, *she wasn't frozen stiff*.

The meeting took place quickly, there being little time to lose.  Parris knew his tenure would be at risk even further, beyond a simple salary dispute.  He had to find them, and find them fast, he would.  His position – and the stability of it - was of paramount importance.  He addressed the men before him.

'Gentlemen, the hour has come and the fate of the village be at a desperate juncture.  A stranger hath come to our village.  Not only hath he caused the death of one of our own, he has taken the innocence of a young woman of Salem Town, working in this village, entrusted to our care.  He hath cast a spell on her with his evil, and that evil *must* be vanquished at *any* cost!  To this end, until they are found, we shall currycomb the countryside.  They shall both face the rope to prevent our beliefs and our way of life from being dishonoured.  Let us ride!'

They stood in unison, racing after Parris as he stormed out of the church.  They mounted their horses, galloping after him as he took flight into the night.

..........

They would not be there anytime soon, Lerner thought.  He would remain in this shed with Rachel until the last, until the blizzard re-commenced, when he knew that their hunters would have to take rest from the snow-storm.   They were weak, and their manner haughty just enough to reveal their presence, leaving  enough time to beat their retreat.  They would tear the place apart looking for them, but no matter. They would be long gone by that time.  Indeed, the idea of them doing so filled him with amusement, wishing he were a fly on the roof to witness their frustrated rage.

'W-who's there?' he heard her ask, her voice frightened. He walked to her, sitting beside her. She looked at him in kindness, remembering him from the previous barn as the one who had saved her from being violated. She smiled that smile he had come to love even wider and his heart leapt inside his chest. She saw his pleasure and made a mental note in her mind to smile more often.

'Are you well?' he asked her.

'I be fine, sir. Thanks be to thee,' she replied.

'We should get out of here, and soon. They are cowards but they will return – and in greater number. We should be far from here when they arrive. Thanks be to God I know of a place these charlatans dare not enter. You have a choice, of course, save that it be not much of a choice. But it be yours to make, all the same. Come you with me to this place?' he asked. She smiled as her eyes softened. She was starting to *really* trust and like this stranger who had so readily fought and killed to save her honour from being taken by that Neanderthal. Her voice was as gentle as he had ever heard as she smiled even wider, and replied, taking his hand in hers.

'I choose to be with you. Always and forever.'

He was stunned into submission. Had she just proposed giving herself to him, or had he imagined it? He was sure she had, but could not be certain.

'Always?' he asked, ascertaining what he thought she had said.

'You know not what you have done, Sir. You delivered me from certain dishonour. Tradition demands that I take thee as thy husband. Do you accept?'

Lerner was speechless for a man not easily lost for words.

'I accept you. We shall be wed at the first opportunity. But for now, we should leave before the only consummation should be at the end of a hangman's noose. Come, help me saddle the horses. The hour draws near.'

He helped her to her feet and made a move towards the horses. She pulled him lightly and he turned to face her. Her eyes were soft, her bosom heaving as she leaned into him, kissing him gently, but passionately, on the lips. Her peachy scent was one of such delight that his legs quivered at the thought of them together, her bountiful form entwined around him, taking him with all the love she had inside her. She seemed to detect the thought as when he snapped out of his reverie, she was looking at him where the horses stood waiting.

There it was. That *smile*, the smile that killed a thousand hearts. He slipped a sheepish grin and walked towards the horses, saddling them. He opened the door to the caleche.

'No. I will ride with you...my husband,' she said, pleasantly defiant. A gentle soul, with a fiery side.

'As you wish,' he said, helping her up to the seat he would occupy. He opened the door a fraction, looking around the area.

There was nothing in sight.

'Quickly. We are short of time. We must make haste before our enemies bear down on us. Lest you forget, we pass through the Wampanoag nations. Fortunately, I have good standing with the Indians. I've made peace with them over time, before they were aggrieved by our friends back there. They be driven out, but they be a strong people and staged a brutal revenge where the Puritan folks were savaged most horrifically by the tribe. A fair exchange, considering the hell on Earth to which they had been subjected. They will hurt us not, have trust in me,' he explained. She her arms around his waist, as the whip cracked lightly over the horses, sending them galloping into the fresh blanket of snow. As before, the heavy snowfall would cover their tracks, covering their escape. They *must* escape, he thought. To face what alternative? A hangman's rope, and hellfire and brimstone?

The choice was no choice at all as they disappeared into the wilds, towards the Maine State line.

And the freedom in which they would prosper together.

·· · • • ·• • · ··

The house looked to be deserted, Parris ventured, as they approached, making more noise than Lerner had first anticipated.

'*BE SILENT!!*' Parris commanded. His command was observed, his mob jolted into obeyance by his imperious timbre.

'*God cursed peasants,*' Parris muttered under his breath. He signalled for half the men to repair to the rear, and they rode silently to cover the rear, while led the rest of them in equal silence to the property.

He dismounted, followed by the villagers.

'Search the entire building!' he barked.

They stormed towards the house, ramming the door, with a huge log lying nearby. It caved in the third hit and the doors splintered open. The men, all afraid yet more fearful of their zealous minister, searched the rooms thoroughly. No signs of their quarry were to be found. Dejected, they and the rest at the rear returned to their master.

'Burn it. Burn it *all!*' Parris commanded, his own weariness betraying him in voice.

Hence, the immolation of the old Gardner estate was instigated. Burnt to the ground, Salem's inferno raging like the fires of hell themselves, as they stood in silence, watching it collapse.

# OUT OF THE ASHES

· · · · · ● ● · · · ·

The tent was not without its comforts, Lerner thought as they lay together, nestled in each other's arms. The elderly Wampanoag Chief had conducted the union, albeit in his own traditional manner. They cared not, for the Union was a religiously-binding one. To make it legal, in official terms, they would have to register it officially at a government office in Bangor, the closest main town where they would be living until finances permitted him to take her out west with him, to their rightful home waiting for them in Oregon.

The lovemaking had been at first painful, then sweet as her body acclimatised to his, her nerve receptors alternating to receive pleasure than pain. She had lost her innocence, but in a respectful manner, and not in the way she might have had her new husband not interceded at the right time. Had that attack taken place, she would have been compelled to take her own life, due to the scandal it would surely provoke – not to mention, more than likely, facing a charge of witchcraft by her assailant to prevent a damaging indictment against him.

She hadn't known it then, but the day she had first laid eyes upon him, she would never have guessed that he would be her husband.

In the cozy confines of the tent they lay, contemplating their life together.

*In September 1692, having lasted around six months in totality, the Salem Witch Trials (so-named thereafter) were decried by the good people of the Massachusetts Bay Colony, and the practice of hanging those deemed to be reborn to darkness, came to a final resolution.*

*In 1696, after his salary contract was honoured by an Ipswich Court but, due to societal complications arising from the case, he found his position to be untenable and he resigned. He died on February 27, 1720, in the town of Sudbury.*

# DEATH AWAITS HER

'I'm not a woman who takes a great deal of chances," she said.

The man in the brown moulded-plastic bleacher was too intent on admiring the Porsche that had pulled up outside the auto shop across the street - and the hot chick that got out of it, even more so. Tall, brunette, mid-thirties; no need to figure out her measurements - he could nail them on sight. Just his type. He brought himself back to the interview, just in time to have caught the rest of her statement enough to be able to surmise its entirety from experience.

'...but I can tell that you have the pre-requisite skills that my client has asked for. I am in the position of offering you the post. Do you accept?' she asked.

Expertly, he smiled his most winning smile. Without betraying her inner desires, she kept her composure.

Oh, *shit*!

That smile sent a tingle up Kelly Leyton's entire body. She wanted to clamber over her large overly- officious mahogany desk and tear his ass apart but, afraid he would notice it, she dismissed the idea. As she was before that smile, she extended her manicured hand and said, her eyes sparkling, 'Welcome to Leyton Security, Mr Kenner.'

· · · · · • • · · ·

The memory of their first meeting flicked through his mind in a flash. He would never have expected to be guarding his own boss. But she had powerful enemies. He looked at the array of weapons sitting on the table and wondered, not for the first (or final, he hoped) time, how the hell he had ended up doing this for a living. Thoughts of his childhood dream of going into space made him smile to himself.

Innocent enough. But, twenty-five years later, he had become a gun for hire. A freelance close protection agent, with skills in weapons, surveillance, martial arts and spoke basics in several languages. He looked down at the .9mm on the pillow. Begging him...pleading with him...to load and cock it.

*Not just yet*, he said in their own quaint telepathy.

He glanced over at her, sleeping soundly on the king-sized vibrating bed and caressed her with his regret-filled deep blue eyes. A mix of emotions crossed his mind.

*If only I was...*

He shook the image from his mind, moving his gaze to his circumvented security device, one half of which lay behind the curtains, the other clipped to his shoulder holster. A baby monitor with split-screen worked wonders, he thought. No peeking at corner of a frayed old set of curtains, and taking a risk being detected. The view outside was covered by two cameras and he could view the parking lot outside from where he stood. They would be here for her, soon, he thought. It was only a matter of time. They were gonna poke their heads into the rabbit hole and when they did, all fucking hell was gonna break out in that pissant little hick town they were hiding in.

But for now, at least, they were safe. She woke slowly, looking over at him as he cleaned the spare .45s he carried in a large case. She bit her lip lightly before walking to the en-suite bathroom, and closed the door. He heaved a huge sigh of relief. She was a temptress and he could see it clearly enough to tell that she would demolish him given an ounce of encouragement.

It was against his code of ethics to get *involved* with a client, much less fuck one. He had resisted all advances from her, assuring her that it was inappropriate but, still, she persisted with her harangue. He was beginning to weaken with each day they were together. He knew it was wrong. Knew it all too well. He had tried to explain that it wasn't professional to breach the code of conduct, *his* code. He thought back to his father, who had been on his mind for days, now. The day trips to the beach and walking along the sand together. He smiled at the thought, and began cleaning his weapons. So intent was he that he failed to notice her exiting the bathroom and walking toward him, revealing herself to him. She felt sure he would not resist her now. She *wanted* him. *Had* wanted him from the moment he set foot in her office at Leyton.

Tapping him on the shoulder, he turned and before he could protest, her mouth was on his, gently caressing his lips. She was beginning to turn him on, and he couldn't have that. He prised her lips from his.

'No, Kelly,' he said as gently as he could.

She wasn't about to take that seriously. She could *feel* his desire for her.

*Root no denial!*

She persisted by rubbing him slowly, ever so gently until he lost all resistance. She wanted it, she was gonna get it. He wasn't dumb – there was a third camera facing the window, where she couldn't see it, taking in the entire room. He knew how conniving a horny woman could get and his career meant too much to him to leave anything to chance.

It wasn't put there solely to catch her, but it had definitely proven useful, he thought. Nothing wrong with being self-protective. You *had* to look out for yourself these days.

He lifted her up, her legs wrapping themselves around his abdomen, as she released his jeans belt, slipping her hand down his pants. She didn't have to put in much effort – he always went 'commando' as it was called. She massaged him, guiding him to her, and he carried her to the bed. He couldn't believe he was doing this. But if she wanted it, by Christ, he thought, she was gonna get what she came for. With alternate feet, he removed his jeans, and reached up under her luxuriously thin satin nightgown, pulling off her matching panties.

Within moments, he was lost in her, and she him. She quickly climaxed, completely fulfilled, a rarity these days. It had been reported by the sex set that orgasm was rarely achieved by penetration itself, but rather through direct stimulation of the clitoral gland, or a combination of the two. She moaned as he kept going, his thrusts arching her back until he broke, and she felt his seed flood her completely.

Exhausted, they lay together for a few moments. Disgusted by his weakness, he got off the bed, entering the bathroom, slamming the door behind him. She lay there, sated – and smiling between her pants of breath.

···········

It was starting to get dark, now. Four hours after their ill-advised moment of weakness, they still hadn't made an appearance. He would give it one more day, then he would have to move into the next State, maybe Ohio or Pennsylvania, he wasn't sure. He just wanted it to be over. She had compromised his ethics and he, like a fool, had allowed it.

*Well*, he thought, *at least it's on tape. She starts anything, I'm covered.*

She had fallen asleep soon after it, and still lay in the bed, out of it. It *had* been amazing, though, he said to himself. She had been involved as a juror in a murder case, but the defendant wasn't your average run-of-the-mill murder suspect. He had been the son of a prominent higher-level politician, who was up for election in the coming primaries.

A murder trial with his son as the only suspect would severely destroy his credibility. The boy had been found guilty, thanks to the unanimous jury verdict, and his father's campaign wiped out.

He had used 'political connections' to use corrupt FBI agents, using them to locate the jurors places of work, and had had them followed by reliable 'people' who had taken them out one by one, a week apart. One was run off the road; another, their house burned to the ground while she slept with her family; others falling victim to various convenient accidents, resulting in their deaths. The cops investigated it for a while, but were ordered off the case to take care of their backlog of unresolved cases. The old man had lost the election, having to deal with the public aftermath of his son's murder case.

The light in the motel room was off, and he sat in his chair, his two .50 Eagles waiting on the table beside him, within easy reach. Two headlights filled the car lot, as a car pulled in, the blinding beams filling the window. He cocked both pistols, readying himself.

*SHIT!* He looked over at her. She was still sleeping. If they opened fire, she was fucked. He sniped across the carpet to the other side, roughly pulling her off the bed, startling her. It had been perfect timing. The windows imploded with a long hail of gunfire - machine pistols by sounds of it – and he waited till it had ceased. She had screamed a few times, and he allowed her to. It would convince them she was dead. He had clamped his hand over her mouth, to give the illusion that the occupants of the room were dead. He put his finger to his lips, silencing her, indicating to her the bathroom.

The room was still dark enough to pass it off. They wouldn't see her. She crawled in, half in shock, and curled up against the wall, cringing in terror. He waited for them to come in. They would have had orders to ensure they were dead for sure before they left. If they found their faked dead bodies, no doubt they would waste the corpses a little further to be 100% on it, or it would be *their* ass when she poked her head back into the limelight. He heard a car engine start, and braced himself. Sirens could be heard five blocks away, and the car screeched out of the lot, driving out of there.

He quickly got their stuff together and, checking the lot was free of anyone in a suit, they got into their miraculously-untouched car, and tore out of there, slowing down after two blocks.

Seconds later, the cops turned into the street where the motel sat. Close call at second!

Curled at the bottom of the seat, cowering in fear, she said little, unable to find her voice.

He smiled at her, as he pulled onto the on-ramp – a straight run to the 'Bama State Line.

It was over.

# Home, Sweet Home

Samantha Harding stared out of her bay window at the blizzard outside, and thought of Ray out there someplace, near frozen and alone, and unable to get home. He had gone out to his friend's house for a couple of hours, but that was at five after ten. The light was almost gone and there was still no sign of her boy, and her nerves were beginning to fray with worry. She had called Danny's house to tell him to get a cab home, but was informed by his mother that Ray had already left hours before. That held a less than desired comfort for Samantha, and she felt the fear wash over her like an invisible cloak of darkness. Her son had only just turned ten, and had bad circulation all his life, exposing him to the elements far more than others his age.

He was susceptible enough to viral infections as it was, she thought, without the flu coming into the mix. His immune system had taken a nose dive these past four years, landing him in hospital more times than either of them cared to remember. Now, here he was...stuck in the snow drift someplace, trying to find his way back home to his Christmas Eve dinner (now cold and deserted, and almost snaffled by Terry, the family beagle if he hadn't been distracted by his chew toy in time). The house, in contrast, was warm, and festooned in Christmas finery, the huge tree, taking pride of place in the corner, fully loaded and extravagantly lit. Samantha looked at her watch, growing more irritable as the seconds ticked by.

*I can't even go out and look for him! What kind of mother am I?*

A very good one, as fortune would have it. It was two under zero out there, and she looked over her younger two children playing on the rug, completely unaware of their mother's panic. She couldn't take them out in *that*. Her husband, Mark, had died at work a year earlier, and she had been on her own, since. She trusted no-one with her children, so leaving them with a neighbor wasn't even part of the equation. It simply wasn't an option. Maybe in the past, she thought, that might have been a possibility, even a likelihood. But the way it was these days? *Fuhgeddaboutit*! She had called the cops an hour earlier and she had heard nothing back yet. "Maybe he had holed up somewheres," they had told her, trying to offer comforting alternatives,"kids ain't as dumb as we think, ya know! It's *possible*."

She appreciated the effort, but wasn't buying it. Every ounce of her instinct told her that he might be lying out there under a mound of snow, possibly hurt or, worse, unconscious. She knew that she was preparing herself for the worst by expecting worst case scenario, but what other option does a parent have in such cases? It's always the worst thing imaginable we think of, first.

No, she would stay put and pray to Jesus that the cops would find him hiding in a barn someplace, lying awake on a bed of straw, perhaps even sleeping, as he rode out the storm outside. It was all she had left to hope for. She used that image to sustain her only hope of his safe return. Of course, thoughts of lesser pleasant things had infiltrated her as the inaudible tick-tock of the hallway grandfather clock reverberated like a death watch beetle through her soul, a demon of torment planting ideas of his abduction across state lines by some homicidal maniac – or worse, a predator chancing upon him in passing. That would be worse than dying, she thought.

You live *through* that shit. If you *were* lucky enough to walk out of that, you'd be scarred for life. From that perspective, she recalled that line from Stephen King...'Sometimes, dead is better.' But she had chosen to cast aside such notions in favour of a more pleasant one. The 'stranded in a barn' theory was working out nicely for her.

She jumped out of her skin as the phone rang. Running across the room, she grabbed the receiver, breathless, and prayed it was good news. Her eyes began to well up as she listened, her hand at her face.

'Mrs Harding, this is Officer Samuels. We've found the body of what appears to be a young boy. I don't want you to worry just yet. We've had a few missing kids in the last months, and it's a good possibility it's one of them. I've alerted all the other parents and advised them to do the same. The body is frozen stiff, and the County Coroner can't do any tests until they thaw 'em out. I'll keep in touch and let you know when you can come and identify the body. At the very least, you may have the closure of seeing it ain't your son, but we're duty bound to alert you of what we find in these cases. Has your son made any contact yet?' Samuels asked, his voice vaguely hopeful.

'No,' she answered, her voice cracking with super-charged emotion. Her heart was beating like a freight train. She prayed silently it wasn't Ray.

*Oh, PLEASE, GOD, don't let it be my boy!*

Samuels continued.

'Alright, then. Just sit tight and keep thinking positively. There *are* other kids we're looking out for. There's every possibility it's one of them. Are there any special places your son might go to to seek comfort? To hide out if the weather's as bad as this?' he asked.

'Can't think of any, off-hand. He always loved playing in the woods when we went on nature walks. There was a deserted cabin there. Safe, but it's been empty for years. The old couple who owned it used to rent it out to summer folks from New York and Boston. They died four years ago. I guess he could have shacked up in there when the storm started getting too heavy,' she managed.

'Okay, great. We'll get a unit out there and see what's what. Better to check these things out while we can. You try your best to focus on your other kids, now. There's little point worrying until you hear from us,' he said, his voice warm and caring. He was doing his best, all things considered, and she appreciated it more than she could tell him.

'We'll be in touch soon,' Samuels said, and the line clicked off at the other end. Samantha replaced the handset, her nerves shattered, and turned to face her other two children – two and four – only to find them sleeping peacefully. For that, she felt relieved. At least she could panic freely without them being aware of it. Kids aren't as stupid as we might believe. They are more than able to sense these things, like their mother going out of her mind with worry.

She grabbed a blanket from the drying rack, and threw it over them, kissing their cheeks, careful not to wake them. They were still young enough to take a four-hour nap. At least, she told herself, she would have time to herself until the doorbell rang. The thought brought a temporary elation, an adrenaline shot to her soul, as she sat smiling with tears cascading down those reddened cheeks, thinking of how she would run to the door, wrench it open to find her half-frozen, snow-covered and shivering son standing there.

She dried her eyes and stood, walked to the kitchen, with a lethargy she had never known. She poured a coffee and returned to the living room. A gust of wind blew the rear porch door wide open, rattling the door's window blinds as it hit the counter. She put the cup down, staring at the door in shock.

*I know I locked this after I got back from town*, she thought. She locked it, putting the key on the key rack next to the knife block, and picked up her coffee. As she set foot across the threshold of the living room, a loud creak of the floorboards resonated from upstairs. She jumped, terror coursing through her veins as she dropped her coffee, backing up against the wall, staring in dread at the ceiling. Again, the creak came, less pronounced this time, but definitive.

*There was somebody up there. Somebody's in here with us!*

She grabbed a Red Sox baseball bat from the umbrella stand, walking quietly to the staircase, her eyes darting from her sleeping babies on the rug to the upper landing, bracing herself. She was impotent with fear.

It took a great deal of effort but she forced herself to take the first step up the seemingly-endless staircase to meet who – or what – was waiting there for her. She moved slowly to avoid detection, but the tension was too great to handle, propelling her up the steps. She barged into rooms, hitting the lights – and finding nothing. One room left to check – the most painful of them all.

Ray's room.

Biting her lip, she reached for the handle, closing her eyes, halfway to irrational hope, and swung it wide open, her hand returning to the bat, in full readiness for what may come.

Her hand reached for the light, and pressed the switch.

As the room was bathed in light, her breath clogged in her throat.

Lying on the bed, sprawled across the sheets, was Ray, his comic books strewn across the bed at his feet. Her heart jumped and her hand flew to her mouth, covering it, and she slid down the wall, a mess of emotions, the most predominant of which being relief. Ray lay there, completely unaware of the drama his unannounced return home had instigated. She would have to alert the cops, she thought, but that could wait for now. She just wanted to look at him, caress him with her tear-stained eyes.

Her baby boy – home safe.

Where he belonged.

# Homecoming Queen

The rain hammered on the roof of the farmhouse as Christina – or Tina, to her friends and family – sat down, finally, after a particularly hard day at the office. She had endured 4 years in UMASS for a degree in I.T., and a second in Business Admin, only to discover that she had wasted her time. Jobs had been a nightmare to find, having eventually settled for a sideline in interior decorating, to tide her over in the interim.

The farmhouse had been bequeathed to her by her parents, both dead within five years of each other – dad first, mom soon followed (Tina liked to believe it had been a broken heart – it was the romantic in her that had survived against the odds).

She emerged from the kitchen, holding a tray filled with snacks and a bottle of white wine. Date night with the DVD player – again!

*"Well, if there were any guys actually worth investing time and effort in, maybe I'd entertain them,"* she had told her friends, all of them chasing the "bad boy" types, most not ever knowing what having a good man was like. These were the women who sat at home every weeknight, stuffing their faces with pizza and Ben and Jerry's, while they waited on the phone like an order at Wendy's. They always moaned about "where all the good guys went?" and Christina, raised

by a caring father, kept silent. A thousand times she wanted to scream in their ears,

*You chased them all away, ya dumb ass bitches! You wanted the assholes and you got 'em. What the fuck are you complainin' about?*

She knew the value of a good man, and she had kept her distance from that whole "he hasn't called in a week!" set.

Tina knew her man would surface like a K9 Widowmaker soon enough. Why rush it? Her view? Simple. She would wait for *him* to do the romancing from now on. That way it would eliminate the chaff from the wheat; the pedigrees from the strays – or however that ol' melody ran.

She sat on the black leather, throw-encased couch, the remote control in her hands, preparing to watch a few old movies (*Casablanca* being her favourite) when the phone rang, making her jump.

Cursing under her breath, she paused the movie just after pressing play on the screen menu.

'Hello?' she said, politely, but itching inside to tell whoever it was to '*get lost*'.

It was her Aunt Cindy (Cynthia, proper). The irreverent pit bull pissing on the Miller family tree.

'Hi, Aunt Cindy...no, I was just about to go hit the hay. Been rushed off my feet all week. Gonna catch up on some sleep, y'know? Ok, you too. Bye, now!'

Tina replaced the handset on the cradle (one of those novelty retro phones) and exhaled her lack of patience into the air. She started the movie again, and looked fondly, smiling, over at Scratch, her little beagle, sleeping soundly in his basket. She stifled a laugh as a sneaky fart escaped the basket. She had it all, right here. A beautifully-appointed, tastefully decorated refuge to come home to; a full roster of consultations to last a month; a fully-restocked freezer; and Scratch, the farting beagle – what more could a girl possibly want?

· · · • • • • • · · ·

She woke up with a jolt, looking around her. Scratch had vanished, nowhere to be seen. She stood up, walking to the bathroom, fixing a sink of hot water as she left for a moment to attend to the fridge. The steam began to form, clouding the bathroom in a shroud of rose-scented mist, fogging up the mirror. Tina re-entered the bathroom with fresh towels and a new bottle of mouthwash. She turned off the hot faucet, and looked up at the mirror. Her heart skipped a beat, her eyes bulging, as she saw what was written in the steam.

From places unknown, a deep, low growling voice repeated the phrase:

*'DIE, BITCH!'*

Backing out of the bathroom in terror, screaming, Tina fell against the toiletry shelf which collapsed to the tile floor from the impact. Bleeding from the shoulder, she ran to the front door to get out.

*Fuck! Where are the goddamn KEYS?!*

She tried the kitchen door, which led to the rear patio decking. That door was locked.

*Shit!*

Only one way left, now, and she knew it. She would have to go through the fruit cellar. The *same* fruit cellar that her eldest aunt had killed her self in by hanging from the centre beam.

That cellar had been off-limits since that day. No member of the family was allowed *near* it, much less to enter. Tina had laughed at the decade-long insistence after she reached her eighteenth.

She grabbed the fire-axe from her dad's rusted old toolbox, smashing the lock with everything she could muster. It broke apart like a cantaloupe, almost completely off its hinges, and she ran for the bulkhead door, the axe at the ready, only to find that door had been left unlocked. She wrenched it open and flew out of there, running to the crumbling, decayed perimeter wall that bound the property.

Her eyes were closed, as her head hung low over the edge. She opened her eyes as her nostrils flared out in reaction to a peculiar odour, putrid and copper-like. She screamed...a ear-shattering scream of terror and grief, obliterating the silence hovering over the farmland.

There, beneath her gaze, lay Salem, her Appaloosa stallion – dead. The sight of it repulsed her and violated every sense she had been inspired to embrace.

The horse had been decapitated, it's eyes mottled and haemorrhaged, as it lay there motionless, the drenched sinews bathing in the enormous blood loss which painted the field.

Holding her hand over her mouth, backing away for what seemed to be an eternity, she finally turned to confront the evil that had pursued her.

In a blink of her gorgeous green eyes, it engulfed her in darkness.

··········

She awoke in the field near where she had found Salem brutalised and, with bleary eyes, she looked at the farmhouse, burnt to its foundations. Her new life shot to shit – and for *what*?

Entranced by the ruins of her beautiful refuge from the world, tears cascaded down her face as she walked weakly towards it, her legs almost dead, she was released from her reverie by a welcome sound in the near distance. There was no breeze in the air, but the wheat stalks were moving in one section of the harvest. Like a lion, a small, bulky form sprang from the camouflage of gold straight into her arms, tail wagging like a rattler, licking her face to a pulp. She held Scratch tightly and, in regretful resignation, she walked the short journey into the nearest town.

# EVIL IS...

The door had barely hit home when Alison was on the phone to her boyfriend. The baby was asleep now, and she wanted some company until the Gage's returned from their dinner date. It was their tenth wedding anniversary, and they had gone straight from City Hall to the restaurant, handing Alison the keys to the house. She had worked for the Gages' before and knew them well. Retaking their vows had been a promise they had made each other should their marriage remain strong after that time.

"Let's face it," Ross had said, plaintively, "if you can last *five* years these days, it's a minor miracle! Nice way to thank each other for their perseverance in such a serious commitment," he had continued, adding with a mischievous glint,

"...considering all the ways marriage can fuck you up." Alison had been chatting for about twenty minutes and stopped dead in her tracks. Her boyfriend – Danny – noticed her silence, asking, 'What's up, Ali? You there?' She had her ear cocked to one side, convinced she had heard something moving upstairs.

'Gimme a sec, babe...I gotta go check the baby. Hold on, ok?' She put the receiver on the coffee table, walking to the staircase, ascending it, tentatively, her hand gripping the handrail. She reached the top and looked down the hallway towards the nursery. It was ajar, barely. She walked slowly towards the room, her throat clogging up as she crept towards it. As she entered, the room was cold as hell, the window open quarter way, the lace curtain blowing inward, wild and blustery. She walked to the window, amidst the flashes of lightning filling the room. She closed the window and turned back to the crib in the corner. The baby – Thomas, five months old – lay screaming from the top of his lungs. Something had disturbed him, but what could have gotten him so bad? She picked him up, walking him up and down the room, comforting him. One big crash of lightning filled the room, making her jump, almost tripping over the life-sized clown in the corner. Cursing, she regained her feet and put the baby back in his crib, asleep once more. She left the room, quietly, leaving the door open, this time, and returned to her call.

··········

The clock chimed 'seven' as she woke up on the couch, rubbing the sleep out of her eyes. She sat bolt upright, running to the stairs, taking them two at a time, as the baby's cries pierced the silence in the house. She rushed through the door and looked in the crib. The baby was awake, thrashing around, and she picked him up, looking around the room. The window remained closed, but that goddamned clown! was it her or were its legs slightly more skewed than before? She finally got Thomas back to sleep, returning to the kitchen, switching on the kettle. A cup of green tea was just the ticket, she thought. God knew, she needed one!

··········

The baby awoke, staring silently at the musical mobile above him, smiling at the cloth animals swaying in the breeze of the air-conditioning vent. He closed his eyes, giggling. As he re-opened them, his eyes opened wide.

*THERE IT WAS!!*

Grinning maniacally at him...that white face, those red, feral eyes burning like the lake of fire, those razor-sharp yellowed teeth...this *monster* staring down on his tiny form, about to render some horrific acts on him. He found his voice and began to scream louder than before. Too young to understand the terror, he felt it throughout his entire body. Numb, frozen in place, waiting to see what those teeth were for. The thumping of the stairs as Alison stormed towards them did not help at all. He opened his eyes. The thing had gone...as if it had never existed. She barged into the room, picking him up, and taking him downstairs with her, his cries of fear reverberating in her soul. The phone rang, causing her to jump in an involuntary start. She picked up. She was relieved to hear Ross's voice on the other end.

'Hi, just thought i'd check in – make sure you're alright. We were gonna bring some pizza back. Would you like some?' he asked. He detected something untoward. 'What's wrong, Ali?' he asked, the fear rising in his voice. 'Is Thomas, okay?'

She tried to keep her tone in check, but he could sense something was wrong.

'Yeah, he just woke up screaming. I've got him downstairs with me, now. He's been like that, on and off, the past hour. I damn near broke my neck on that stupid clown on the rocking chair, though,' she said.

There was no way Alison could see it, but Ross Gage's face had gone pale, all colour drained from him. He recovered quickly, swallowing hard.

'*WHAT* fucking *CLOWN?!* He hasn't got a clown – doesn't like them!' Alison's heart stopped. The reality dawning, she slowly looked up at the upstairs landing. It was walking along, its fingernails scraping the handrail, the sound screeching in her ears. The thing's face held such malevolent fury that it was entirely possible that she would never see evil so singularly personified than what she saw walking casually towards her, a large steak knife caressed in its white gloves, that *face* smirking...cajoling her almost. Ross screamed down the line.

'*ALI...GET THE BABY OUT OF THERE!! NOW!! DON'T LOOK BACK!! I'm calling the Sheriff right now! Stay on the line!*'

She heard him telling Mrs Gage – April – to take the phone, and she talked to her as she found the keys. Opening the door, she ran out into the storm, running down the street, the rain lashing against them, as she ran for their lives...hoping, *praying* for a black and white to turn the corner.

· · · · • • • · · ·

Bob Latham s**at** in his squad car as the call came in. He had almost choked on his pastrami when he heard about a joker dressed as a clown chasing a young girl down Faulkner Drive with a baby in her arms. He dumped his sandwich on the seat next to him, and slammed his foot on the gas pedal, no siren so the nut wouldn't hear it and skip the scene. He was three streets away, now.

*Oughta be in sight, soon* he mused, as he screeched the car into the south entrance of Faulkner Drive. He could see her in the distance, but there was nothing following her. No sign of anything untoward – except a young girl running barefoot in the rain, holding onto a baby for all she was worth. He cranked his foot down harder, sounding the siren, pulling up ten feet in front of her. He opened the back door.

*'Get your ass in the car – NOW!!'* he yelled. She got in, gratefully, and the car took off around the corner towards town.

He got on the radio.

*'Jarvis, come in!'*

Nate Jarvis, his deputy, was heard over the radio.

'You catch the circus yet, Bob?' he laughed.

Latham was not amused.

'Cut that shit out, Nate. This shit is serious, boy! I want every car we got out here, armed to the tits. Right now!'

Nate had never heard his boss sound so pissed.

'You got it! Coming now. Hold on.'

The thing stood in the awning of the only unoccupied house on the street, watching the car screech around the corner out of sight. Ruefully, it turned and walked into the burning hedge and vanished into the inferno before the hedge returned to normal, as if it had never happened.

# IT SMARTS, DON'T IT?!

It *had*, happened whether she liked it or not. *She* had been the instigator, and not he, as people had thought. It was the oldest story in history, and he had the oldest motivation in evolution as a crutch should he be discovered in years to come. Of course she would deny it were she directly challenged on it – precisely the reason he came to the decision he did. It was a stroke of genius and a milestone in the annals of sexual revenge psychology. Nathan 'Nate' Woods stood at the upstairs bay window watching as his beautiful wife, Natalia, unpacked the groceries from the SUV, closing the trunk and carrying them in. Her hair was dishevelled, and he could tell, instantly, that the foul weather outside hadn't been solely responsible for it.

*No matter*, he thought. *It won't be long, now.*

He got into character and walked downstairs to help the conniving whore store the groceries and watch her preen herself on how ignorant he was.

He was *far* from ignorant, in point of fact.

He was just getting started.

· · · • • • • • · · ·

## OUT OF THE ASHES

It had just happened,' as things in life tended to occur. It happened, also, to be the first thing to spill out of a cheater's throat-hole when he got busted for playing 'Hide The Salami' with some little tramp from two streets down. Natalia Carrick had been a cheerleader in High School, one of the popular set who shat on the science club nerds and the glee club prisses with equal enthusiasm. It was the 'done thing.' Instilled in grade school, refined by Junior High (if you had been lucky enough to actually make it that far), and perfected by freshman high school, the worst years of high school were the first years. You soon realised your caste in that first year. It *defined* your chances of survival. Dependent on whether you were the 'giver' or the 'taker,' it would make your time in high school either moderately enjoyable or, for many if not most, hell on earth. Natalia was a stunner by anyone's standards.

She hadn't started out that way. It had taken a few years to break out of her 'ugly duckling syndrome' and it hadn't been easy. She was a chubster as a kid, constantly enduring the grade school taunts of *"Hey, fatty boom, boom!"* and the occasional call for the "lardass" to budge over during class A/V sessions. Such cruelty was the norm in school life. You either survived it, or it drove you fucking nuts. Little 'Natty' (she *hated* that name with a vengeance!) had broken her ass trying to get thin. Diet after diet, none of which worked, came and went and she decided to take up swimming as a last resort. It worked. The excess weight fell from her like autumn leaves, and she soon raised eyebrows - and a few temperatures – with her svelte, new figure.

By the time she strutted into Wellman Consolidated Junior High School – at fourteen, she had transformed herself into a thing of staggering beauty, so much so that some of her old grade school friends failed to recognise her without having to look twice. The change wasn't only cosmetic, but also mind-altering. She exuded such confidence that she was soon courted by the populist clique, and even sooner accepted into their cold, callous arms, where her training in the art of 'revile the odd and uncool' would promise a BI (Bachelor of Ignorance) upon graduation. She had – goes without saying, really – been Prom Queen in her Senior Year, and had her 'night in the moon,' as it were. Then school was over, and she was forced to face the real world, where no-one gave a flying fuck if you *were* 'Miss Dairy Queen' from some shitty high school in the asshole of the world.

Natalia Woods, as she was now, was so self-assured in her own attraction and status that, after years of playing with the hearts of men, she had it down cold. But the day she met her future husband, her entire manner changed.

Everybody noticed it, and she had admitted in private that she realised the horrendous treatment she had inflicted on lesser mortals during her tenure at Wellman. Nate Woods was not of the popular set, but he had gained enough admiration to be able to float in and out of both social circles with relative ease. He possessed a natural flair for flirtation and charm that had gotten him through his High School years. Although he had dated science club geeks and cheerleaders with equal ease, he had never dated anyone as beautiful as Natalie Carrick. He had found her intoxicating after a few moments of meeting her at the law firm Christmas party, although he had gone home with one of her colleagues.

Shortly after, in March, he and the colleague, Janelle, had parted ways and Natalia had set her sights on Nate. He was tall compared to her, but he had a light sensitivity about him she enjoyed more than she wanted to admit. She was used to high school jocks, and bad boys. The idea of a smart, intelligent, *mature* man hadn't filtered through to her yet, and she found his teaching her things like chess and day-trading to be strangely attractive. But the thing she loved most was to watch him move in the courtroom.  His encyclopaedic knowledge of the law ensured that he was never at loss for words, and his manner alternated between adversarial and soothing when he felt the need for them.  A kind of barometer went off in his head telling him when to play 'good lawyer-bad lawyer.'  He had an unerring instinct for the jugular, the killer instinct that fed her alpha male fantasies.

And in the sack?  Jesus *Christ*!

The man was a marvel of modern science!  Knew all the switches to flick at just the right time.  There was no *way* she was letting this one go.  They married the following year.  He had insisted it be then due to a heavy court docket (unbeknownst to her, his trust was less than full and he wanted the time to allow her to expose potential toxic qualities which would nullify the engagement in time before the line was signed – his only real insurance policy.  He knew the risks sadly inherent in the 'modern marriage,' and wasn't taking any chances.  He even had a vasectomy two years before to prevent kids as he was too career-minded.  It was his right *not* to have them, so who had the right to make judgement on it?  It *was* his ass on the line, after all.  Kids deserved better than being weaponised in a toxic relationship or divorce, as was known to be a highly-frequent practice in recent times.

*Not happenin,' baby!  Not to* me*!.*

Nate opened the fridge and slid out another beer from the rack, swinging door shut as he headed back to the couch, wondering where the fuck his life was headed.  The prognosis?

Not good.  His head craned towards the window, the stone driveway crunching under the tyres of his wife's Lexus.

·· ·· ·· ·· ··

It had happened over a series of months, as these things usually do. Very rarely anyone meets someone in the street and decides to risk losing it all over a 'piece of patch.' It had started the the way they all did – a random friend request, a few flirtatious jokes leading to the obligatory bonding phase. A pussy pic led to a dick pic, in turn leading to words of unbridled lust as things escalated beyond the compliment assignations. Then came the plans to meet one day. Usually, these were pointless, as the vast majority of Facebook friends lived overseas and unlikely to pose the remotest possibility of their 'passion' being fully consummated – to some, this was an unspoken godsend, as their misguided love was caused by mere confusion related to issues in their relationships, usually their significant other withholding sex or emotional affection. Why the hell else would anyone in a relationship go on a monkey-branch race? Wishful thinking, for the most part.

The danger presented itself when the subject of one's affections lived in the same general area, or at least within a train ride or two's distance. The hotel would be booked in advance; the first awkward meeting at the railway station; the silent taxi ride to the hotel or, if you were the cautious type, two separate cabs; finally, the sneaking into the agreed room where the wine would be opened and the clothes annihilated from each other, as the pre-ordained lust promised over the past few months was finally enacted for real. That temptation was all too real for some preferring, instead, to have the safety of improbability as their saving grace, knowing there was no way in God's earth they could get to the States, or wherever the hell their digital lover was waiting patiently for their oft-declared, imaginary ravishing.

Natalia had been growing more and more enamoured of Chris Markes as time passed over the months. His witty repartee and picture-perfect manner had enamoured her to the point where she was getting leakage in her basement at the mere ping of her Messenger app, hoping it was Chris looking to deepen their growing bond. He was one of the few rare ones who she had been flirting with who lived within the Maine State line. She with her husband in Orono; he, alone, in a two-bed apartment in downtown Bangor. Natalia had sat, precariously perched, on the edge of her seat on the Trailways bus, the desire tingling in her.

This was the last time they would meet at his place. Too many people had seen her come and go, and the fact her friends and family were frequent visitors to Bangor, was of paramount concern to her. She loved Nate, yes, but he was working too much and what they once had between them had suffered in the interim. She had gotten the itch, and he was far too pre-occupied with work to focus on her as he always had. She had grown tired of waiting and began to spend her time on social media. Had she known then what was about to happen, she would have steered clear.

Nate was a hard-working man, raised by his grandparents for most of his childhood, until his parents, one-by-one, lost their jobs at the paper mill in Hartford, Connecticut. They had had little choice but return to their rural safe haven in Hermon to lick their wounds, and reclaim their son from her parents who, they had both agreed, had done a remarkable job. From a rugged, non-conformist child into a quiet, introspective teen with a gift for the written word, the boy had made them the happiest parents in the world. As Nate grew older, he put aside the writing to get 'a real job' in his father's auto-repair and station. His scholarship to UMASS was a major source of pride for Fred and Kate Woods, with Law being his major. It wasn't long before he met, and became inseparable to, a young lady friend, introduced to them by letter and photograph, as Natalia Carrick, reading Humanities at the time. He aced his bar exam, and found a home at Conn, Kavanaugh, Rosenthal, Peisch and Ford, one of Boston's most prestigious law firms, proving himself to be an asset there in a relatively short period.

They had moved to Boston, and life was good. They married in the Fall of '86, and their son, Daniel Frederick was born a year later, after several failed attempts throughout those heady nights at UMASS. During the leave he took in the third trimester of her pregnancy, the urge to write returned with a vengeance. It was as if his childhood gift had never left him. He wrote short stories with a furious intensity, producing some very controversial work. When he was first published in The Boston Review, paying the unheard of sum of $50 per word, she had been taken aback, his having never mentioned his childhood much.

He had splashed out on a discount model of his favourite car, a fire-engine red 1976 Chevy Nova. The fact that that car was later to be own son's casket would be soul-destroying had he known, then. Danny had been late for dinner and an asshole drunk-driver on his cell-phone had smashed into him head-on, the sheer impact breaking Danny's neck in the whiplash.. The funeral had been numbing for them both, and it was his insistence that no other child be sired by him that prompted him to secretly undergo a vasectomy on a trip to Boston later that year.

He had kept it a secret from her.

Although regretting his deception, he couldn't bring himself to face the pain of facing another child each day, although many friends claimed it would be therapeutic if they *did* have another. Natalia, after a few months and under the illusion that nothing had changed, threw herself into the habit of sex three times daily to facilitate a second child, hoping that the new arrival would sway him. She felt the same as he about their tragedy, but her approach was to carry on as before, celebrating rather than mourning their 17-year old boy.

The shit had hit the fan when Natalia had finally discovered the truth about the vasectomy. Nothing had ever been the same after that 'little revelation.' They had gotten past it for the most, but her underlying, festering resentment of him was still bitter and raw, and led to several incidents of it resurfacing in obligatory arguments when she felt he was working "too fucking much." By that time had withdrawn into himself, choosing the office over constant argument. It was then that Facebook made its inaugural appearance on the cybernetic scene. Like most people, she soon became addicted to it's dopamine-laden charm, collecting 'friends' like baseball cards, never suspecting the many illicit temptations it would present.

For Natalia Woods, the temptation would prove *too* great. In more ways than she ever imagined, her final granted friend request would prove to be a fatal one.

··········

Natala Woods lay exhausted on her double-wide, sweat-drenched bed as her young paramour disengaged from her, soiled and nonchalant as he strutted to the shower, contented yet again. This had been the first time she had been unfaithful in this bed, usually meeting the young stud in hotel rooms across Boston, or driving to out of state roach-ridden motels among I-95. At least, that was, until the penny dropped after being recognised by an old friend from UMASS, asking her how she was and if she were still with Nate. She had confirmed her status, telling her all, and then excused herself as Nate would be "back in a while." She had returned to the room, her cheatin' heart thumping like a marching band in her chest.

She had peered out of the Rain Cloud Motel window, watching her old friend drive off, and got them both dressed and out of there before she got back, just grateful that Chris hadn't been seen. The drive back to Boston had been silent, as her mind raced with thoughts of Nate finding out. Regardless of his little *faux-pas*, there was still a lot of love there, and hurting him was not an option. She knew that the divorce would end in her favour, as the recent slew of cases had tended to go the woman's way in such cases. Women got everything. Half of all marital assets, a percentage of his future gross income, with palimony on top of *that*. Financially speaking, she wouldn't be hurting after it, despite sole responsibility being laid at her own feet.

The courts usually hammered the man in divorce cases these days, regardless if he had Johnny Cochrane in his corner or Johnny Chimpo.. It made little difference to the penal system – it was all rock 'n' roll to them.' It was the last thing she wanted, anyway. Chris might be younger and a far better lay than Nate was these days, but losing Nate was never gonna happen. She turned her attention back to lover-boy who, getting dressed in the doorway, was making quick work of it. His leather jacket was on in seconds, good to go. She had to get him out of there before the Hannigan kids next door got back from Spring Break in Daytona Beach. She saw him to the door and he kissed her goodbye, walking down the pathway to the street.

All lights were out in the surrounding houses, and for that Natalia was glad. This was taking a real risk and she knew it – but *shit! What a rush!* She closed the door after he turned the corner. What Chris didn't suspect was the two malevolent eyes burning into his back as he sauntered down the sidewalk towards his car. As Chris gunned the engine of his 1966 Chevy Impala, taking off down the silent, tree-lined street, the lights of another car followed closely enough behind, keeping just enough room between them to avoid detection.

· · · · • • • • · ·

O'Reilly's Irish Bar was, in a town known as a 'fine place for a Mick to lose himself,' was no different from the plethora of other such bars in 'that foine oul' place.'  Chris sat at the bar, feeling pleased with himself. He had pumped the Woods woman with all the gusto he could reach within himself and had been more than pleased with her response, her loud moans reverberating in his ears, still. He laughed to himself and drowned down a Michelob, banging the counter Gaby, the barmaid, to bring another.

'Alright, are we?' Nate asked, standing at the bar next to him, pulling out a twenty. He ordered a double bourbon and coke, downing it in one, then ordered another to take his time on.

'Not bad, friend,' Parkes answered, his eye on a small, large-breasted blonde singing *It's Raining Men* by The Weathergirls.  Nate held his peace but thought, *You little fucker! If you actually gave two shits about my wife, at least enough to ignore other chicks, I probably woulda respected you more...*

'You gonna serenade us, then?' Nate asked, his tongue in his cheek.

'Don't rightly know yet.  Maybe if I get good and loaded enough, I might,' replied Chris.

Nate laughed and walked away, stopped by his elbow grabbed by Chris.

'Why'n't you hang about a bit? I never get anyone in here worth talkin' to, y'know,' Chris said.

'Sure, why not.  I can't stay too long, though.  Got work in the morning, so it's an early night,' he lied.  He smiled, not showing his teeth, secretly ecstatic as the plan to get his revenge was starting out nicely. It was just a matter of time. And he had all the time he needed to make it work the way he wanted it.

He ordered another two drinks.  He wasn't too concerned about the bar tab anymore.

Not when he was gonna take it out of the kid's ass later.

· · · · • • • · · ·

Natalia stood at the front door, smoking a cigarette, staring out at the heavy rain, hoping to see the headlights of her husband's car pulling into the driveway. She hoped he hadn't gotten into an accident. The rain was so thick that she could barely see the houses across the street, and imagined that his view of the road ahead wasn't any better. Finally, she gave up, stomping the butt of her third consecutive Pall Mall on the concrete below, turning to the foyer.

The headlights blinded her, making her jump as the car bounced the driveway, screeching to a halt. The lights went out as Nate killed the engine, getting out, his head under a folded newspaper as he ran for the door. He set his car alarm on the key fob, and ushered her into the house, out of the rain.

They lay in bed together – but, for the first time in their twenty years as lovers, they were oceans apart.

Not a single word was spoken as they fell into a deep, dreamless sleep.

· · · · • • • · · ·

The river was still, barely rippling as they waited for a trout to take the bait. Chris called out to him.

'Think fast!' Nate turned to catch the bottle which was tossed gently, but quickly, in his direction. He opened it and took a long swallow.

He hated this little prick with every fibre of his being but he had to maintain the charade until he was certain of gaining his trust. Then

– and only then – would he see his plans come to their brutalistic conclusion. But for now, it was playtime. He was gonna have to get close – real close – to fool him. The kid was still on edge, touchy as hell at times. It would take a little time yet, but he was gonna win this stupid little asshole's trust if it killed him. He had given Chris another name - Tom Lanford – in case Chris mentioned his new 'friend' to Natalia. No photographs of the two were permitted for that same reason, and she had hid all photos of Nate, anyway (kinda weird, really as, by *not* doing that, she could have indirectly warned Chris).

The boy would find out in his own good time.

But for the moment, 'Tom' it was going to be.

The day was a good one. They caught and cooked four freshwater trout between them, having to throw two small ones back into the river. But all in all, they enjoyed each other's company and were beginning to bond a little more, as Chris began to lower his guard and, for the first time in his miserable existence, trust another human being. Nate drove Chris home, and then made his way to his little whore back home.

Things were about to heat up in the Woods house. In ways she could never conceive.

∙∙∙●∙●∙∙∙∙

*Two Weeks Later...*

Natalia had been out shopping for the past three hours and she was concerned. Usually, Chris would message her frequently as she made her way around the stores, her eyes glued more to the screen, peering up now and then to see where she was going. There had been nothing all day.

*Maybe he's bored with it all...with you? Perhaps he's found another little slutty wife to poke?* her mind asked. She had to admit it was a good possibility. This new friend – whoever he was (if it even *was* a 'he') was pre-occupying most of their usual time together. He had only told her he had met a guy at the bar and had hit it off after that night at her place. And his name...what had it been, again? 'Tom', something? She knew very little beyond that except that the guy was apparently a little older than he, that this 'guy' had been teaching him about the worldly things he never learned in school, and that he made Chris laugh a lot due to his antics in the bar. She caught herself wondering what this new friend was like between the sheets and stopped herself.

As she pulled into the driveway, she noticed Chris's car parked across the street. There could be no mistaking it – especially since only two days before she had been familiarising herself with the rear seat layout, her legs resting on the head rests as he serviced her and, soon after, she him, in a rare break from his all-consuming new friendship. The break had served them both well and the separation renewed her vigour as she took him for all she were worth, resulting in a cataclysmic orgasm neither had felt together till then.

She locked the car, and headed to the kitchen, unpacking her groceries. Her head whipped around.

Was that *glass* breaking or was she hearing things? She stopped the unpacking and headed towards the foyer, her ears focussing in, waiting for a re-occurrence.

There it was again. Her head spun like a whippet to face the closed cellar door. She walked towards it with tentative steps, the fear rising in her, pulsing in her veins. Her hand reached out slowly, turning it, her nerves jangled as she pulled the door open. Looking down the wooden, uncarpeted stairwell at the pitch black void beneath, she swallowed hard.

*Something was down there. Something bad.*

She took the first step, not processing what she was doing. Was it an intruder? Was she going to be violated? Or was it that goddamned cat from next door sniffing around again? She picked a large knife from the ledge of the stairwell as he walked down to the darkness, disappearing into it. Reaching the bottom, finding her feet on the cellar floor, she felt around for the light, and switched it on, filling the room with dimmed light.

Her hands flew to her mouth as she screamed through her fingers. A bloodied and battered Chris sat naked, bound to a wooden chair with thin, suffocatingly-tight rope, his hair matted with dried blood, his face red, with the streaks of the rivulets of dried tear stains still marking his cheeks. He wasn't moving much.

*Damned ropes ripping against his skin* she thought as she walked over to him, kneeling at his feet, tilting his battered face to face hers.

'Whar the fuck are you doing here? Jesus Christ! I thought I told you never to come here unless it was all clear?' Natalia ripped the tape from his mouth, as he elicited a pained, exhausted groan in response. A voice came from behind, a funny voice she has never heard before. She pivoted on her heels, rising to full height, looking around. The light was slightly more dimmed than before she noted, only just realising it.

'I invited him,'

'Come out you sick *fuck!*'

'As you wish,' the accented voice said.

The familiar figure of her husband stepped out of the darkness, and she understood. All of it, finally. She had been busted – good and proper. The party was over. Why else would Chris be here if not for him knowing her indiscretion? She felt a rising nausea surge through her, stomach to head. Natalia hung her head. There was little point in denying it. By the looks of Chris, he had endured a lot thus far, and didn't need more. She turned to look around the cellar for potential weapons. The look on her husband's face was truly frightening, made all the more ominous with him acting so affably, like a sociopath interrogator extracting fear from a subject.

'How long did you think it would take before I got wise to it, Natalia?'

'When did you find out?' she asked in that resigned tone one has when they are discovered doing something they shouldn't.

'The day I was in Boston. The case ended suddenly with the Krieger kid switching his plea. We got an adjournment but he waived the right for a pre-sentence hearing. He knew he was licked but my guess was he got bored with the charade. I came down the street and parked across the street. Thought I'd drop in and out - get some money out of the safe. I was walking towards the drive and the door opened. So I ducked into the undergrowth behind the tree, and I watched as this little bastard sauntered out of *my front door*, *my house*, zipping his fly shut with a stupid grin plastered over his face. So I watched a little *more*. And what did I see? My own *wife* wrapping her arms around him, obviously having given him the one thing she hadn't given me in months. All that time insisting that she wanted to get...' He made air quotes with his fingers. '...closer to God. Well, sweetheart...angel...sugar... God isn't here, today,'.

He turned to Chris, the latter looking on with increased dread as Nate picked up the blowtorch, pretending to inspect it like an art appraiser searching for significance. He extracted a lighter, and lit it. The burst of the blue flame filled the room, as Natalia stared at him in disbelief. She couldn't believe her husband was capable of this. It was beyond her reasoning that he would inflict this kind of pain on anyone. But here he was, with a welding torch in his hand, about to melt a young man's balls into macaroni. This was a scare tactic, it *had* to be.

'You have to understand, Christopher. There is a particular emotion one has when he finds out his wife has been…how do they say it in these heah pahts?…'foolin' around?' It's a curious mix of anger, resentment - shame, even, where no shame should exist. Karma is an age-old Indian concept, echoing the accepted Judeo-Christian ethic of 'Reap what you sow,' and all that jazz. Me? I prefer the other one, myself. You might have heard of it. 'Do what thou wilt.' It possesses certain 'darker' connotations, and most of all for the person in question.' He walked towards Chris, gagging him with tape once again, looking back at Chris whose young eyes bulged with the anticipated agony that torch would bring. He regretted it all.

All the stupid shit he pulled as kid, all the crap he had put his parents through in his adolescent years and, most of all, he regretted ever even *approaching* Natalia Woods on Facebook, much less fucking her. But that was his problem – always had been. Too stupid to know when to quit. Too goddamned dumb to see he was bound to get caught. Now, here he was, strapped to a chair in her cellar with her husband about to inflict upon his young body, the most unimaginable pain his mind could ever conceive. As Nate approached him, he struggled vehemently, his petrified, muffled screams of anticipation drowning in Natalia's screaming pleas.

'*Please,* Nathan! Don't do this. It wasn't his fault. It was me! All me!'

'That's as maybe, dear. Makes no difference to me. You no longer exist. This little bastard's gonna feel what I feel, if it kills me.' Natalia lost it, desperate, now; reaching for something – *anything* – she could find to stop him. She knew from her heart that she would be killed, too. Nate wasn't stupid *without* the extra stimuli, and this weak shit only added to his demented fervour. He wouldn't think twice of killing her, although, she suspected her fate would be far more painless than her soon-to-be-cremated lover's. As Nate grew closer, Natalia saw no option.

He was gonna do it. He was *actually gonna fuckin' do it!* His eyes were filled with shame and rage as he lowered the torch towards Chris. She attacked Nate but received a vicious back-handed slap, which sent her careening hard against the tool rack, knocking her out cold.

'Don't you be worryin,' Chris. I've got other plans for *her*, I promise you. She'll get her end, alright!'

Chris's eyes bulged as he watched helplessly as the sheer heat of the blowtorch seared into his naked glans, reducing it to a gruesome pulp, moving along the shaft as the terrific heat both melted and cauterised his wounds.

'It smarts, don't it, you little motherfucker! That's the last time you accidentally stick your prick in my wife!' Nate yelled, as he tore off the tape, re-applying the blazing torch to Chris's tongue.

Chris's ear-shattering screams were such that Natalia had been snapped out of her own unconscious state, watching the objects of her satisfaction being eviscerated, the thoughts of what would be headed her way afterwards. Her entire body felt weak with dread as she looked on the young lothario.

'*THIS* IS WHAT YOU BETRAYED ME FOR?!' Nate screamed at her, his own internalised agony being made all too apparent to her. He turned off the blowtorch, and threw it to the other side of the room, out of her immediate reach. He reached up to the small shelf on the wall, taking down a small box, placing it on the table. He reached in, the tears flowing down his already stained cheeks, and extracted a .50 Desert Eagle pistol, a gun so powerful that one shot would scatter Parkes's chest to the prevailing winds. He inserted a full clip and cocked it quickly. At least, Natalia thought, the boy's pain would be no more.

'He's had enough, Nate. If you're gonna finish him, do it, and do it now,' she pleaded.

'Oh, this isn't for *him*. It's for me,' Nate said, again calm and collected.

'W-what are you go—' she started to ask.

'What am I going to do with you? Is that what you wanna know? Well, there's a number of things I could do, but I guess I'm just gonna let you go. You're punishment is simple. I want a divorce, with no contest to a file for 'irreconcilable differences.' I'd say that's about the least you can do, wouldn't you say?'

'That's *it?*'

'That's it. Now, get outta here. I've got things to be getting' on with, if you don't mind,' Nate said, off-handedly.

Natalia was amazed – and furious at Nate for putting her through this shit. She backed up away from him, towards the staircase. A groan from Chris made her look over as his head rolled to the side, then slumped forward. He had given up the ghost, finally. As she turned, dejected and never more scared, she failed to notice Nate's hand reaching for the tool rack. Hearing something whistling through the air, she turned to face her fate. The steel of a razor-sharp wood hatchet slammed against her vulva, nailing her body to the wooden stair frame. She screamed in agony, her head thrown back as the pain consumed her. He raised the .50 cal pistol and squeezed the trigger. The shot was synonymous with her brains splattering against the wall.

He took the pistol, carrying it to the staircase, passing her on the way.

'Fuckin' *whore*,' he muttered as he climbed the steps toward the house. Reaching the summit, he took one last furtive glance at her, before closing the door on her memory forever.

The sirens were getting closer as Nate stood at the door with a cigarette. There was no point running from this. Right or wrong, he had fucked himself. But he wouldn't have too long to think on it. The racket of conjoined sirens was about two blocks away, and would be there in moments. He cocked the Eagle and held it near his leg as he watched the squad cars charge around the corner, screeching to a halt outside the house. Officers raced out of their cars, guns at the ready.

'DROP THE WEAPON, AND PLACE YOUR HANDS BEHIND YOUR HEAD!! DO IT, NOW!!' one of them yelled.

Nate issued a wry grin as he pulled out the Eagle fast. The lead cop who yelled fired six shots, one of them a head shot, realising in horror that the Eagle had been dropped upon command. It must have hit the ground before the suspect took the first shot in the chest. He was in it up to his balls this time. His shift commander was gonna have his ass. But it had been a righteous kill – there had been no question of anything else. Several other officers had witnessed the gun in the suspect's hand. The young cop walked up to the corpse lying on the ground as the others entered the house.

'*JES-US CHRIST!*' a voice yelled from the bowels of the cellar.

The side cellar skylight, near the privet hedges was stained red with blood as the cops looked around in there, horrified by what they found.

It was gonna be one of those fuckin' nights!

# MIND GAMES

*Calumet City, Illinois, 2015*

The divorce hadn't gone quite the way he had expected. David and Marlena Kent had not exactly set the world on fire with their marriage. It wasn't toxic in any way, just more than slightly imbalanced. Marlena knew from the on-set of their relationship that marrying a writer one day would, in no way, be a key to spectacular riches or fame. Very few were fortunate enough to be able to reach that level of success, and even fewer had wives that were in it for the long haul. She knew this going in, so she couldn't blame him in the event of its end if she didn't get much in the divorce settlement. She had decided to forgo any claims upon him, leaving him free and clear. They had their daughter to consider and she refused to do anything to destroy her own child's opinion of her. He was a great father, after all was said and done. She would never take that away from him. A great 'daddy' and a great writer, almost to the point where one might say the choice of his words and how he manipulated them possessed an alchemic quality, that peculiar, unexplainable 'star' charisma, entwined within his 2,000 words-per-day target.

*Really!* He was *that* good!

Marlena was a great writer's wife, if no other kind. She would test him frequently at the weekends, giving him timed 'exercises' to complete at night or, as was more usually the case, during off-time with a coffee beside him. The stuff he put out was breathtaking and hard-hitting, with careful and strategic downtime scenes to bring the reader down again – just before he threw something into the mix to send their minds racing, turning the pages like their lives depended on it!

*Yep*, she had always said, *David Kent was a good writer who, with luck and hard work , could be one of the greats!*

David sat hunched over his electric typewriter (he always wrote his first draft on a typewriter, a tradition which reminded him of how he had started out as a kid), his hands clasped, thinking of the good old days when he had courted Marlena; how she always sat listening to his work as he read chapters to her over a coffee; how she would walk up behind his chair, wrapping her arms around his neck, nuzzling it softly when she wanted him where he should have been; and the day that she told him she was pregnant. His eyes began to tear up at this thought, and he laughed it off, draining his near-empty rum and coke.

Melissa would be sound asleep by now, he thought. She had fallen asleep watching Peppa Pig, and he had carried her upstairs to her bedroom, settling her into bed. She was an amazing kid, and always had been, he thought, smiling at her tiny head poking out from the Peppa-themed duvet. He stood at her opened door for five minutes until he was satisfied she was out of it, then blew her a kiss, whispering 'I love you, Missy', and closed the door, plunging her into near darkness (he always dimmed the lights on the upper landing for her).

With that, he had gone to his writing studio in the attic, to finish off the last chapter of his latest thriller. He hoped Scribner would like this one after the two they had rejected in the years before, citing 'conflicting scheduling interests,' which, more often than not, simply meant they had a similar enough tale on their books already.

*Well*, he thought wryly, resentfully even, *I can dream, dammit!*

He felt his eyes beginning to close against every effort he employed to delay them, but eventually he conceded; *enough was enough!*

He finished the paragraph in question, and turned off the typewriter, standing upright, stretching his arms out, exhausted. Walking to the door, he turned off the light.

'Another day shot to shit,' he said as he closed and locked the door.

· · · · • · • · · ·

Something moved next to him, and he jolted uptight, half-asleep, his eyes struggling to adjust to the pitch darkness of the room. The babyish, also half-asleep, voice of his daughter droned in his ear, and he began to relax. It was normal for Missy to wake in the night and seek refuge in their bed – now *his* (she had left him the house and bought another with her end of the insurance money from the car accident the year before they got hitched. She had put it in T-Bills and other safe investments to make it work for her). Missy stayed over at his place on weekends, and he *loved* having her there. She was his light through the remarkably easy, yet still painful, divorce, and she always had a huge toothless smile stretched across her face, her eyes sparkling from the moment she got dropped off till the moment Marlena came to pick her up.

She snuggled into him, and they both fell into a deep, dreamless sleep.

· · · · • · • · · ·

The rain hammered, relentless and cold, against the house, almost as if it were pre-ordained that this house should be particularly aggrieved by the elements.

David woke suddenly, his senses telling him something was amiss, although not *quite* sure as to what it could be. Yawning, he looked over at where Missy had been lying. Nothing.

The only sign of his five-year old daughter was lying underneath the duvet, crumpled on the dented mattress beside him. His daughter knew early on how to undo the popper buttons on them, so it wasn't such a big thing. She was probably watching tv in the den downstairs. He shrugged, resignedly, and got up, slipping on his pants and sneakers. He lit a fresh Camel – the first of many – and grabbed a t-shirt from the drying rack, entering the bathroom, farting as he went.

'Oops! More tea, Vicar?' he joked in a pseudo English accent, as he closed the door.

First, he would have a shower; then he would get his daughter dressed; then it was off to the park for the picnic he had been promising her all week.

He emerged from the bathroom, unsoiled and well-groomed, and walked down the stairwell to the foyer. He stopped dead as a chill darted up his spine like a bitter wind. He listened hard, praying his thoughts were just his own foolishness.

The house was silent, with no sound of a television filtering out of the den. His panic was setting in now, as he ran through the house, checking every room, matching pace with pulse. No sign of anything out of place, no intrusion from without.

*But no Melissa*!

He checked the windows and doors throughout, and even the basement, but they were all locked as he had left them after Missy had gone to bed.

The adrenaline was coursing through him like a burst of life had invaded him, lifting him, but he could do nothing more than what he must - submit to the inevitable, and call the cops. He had no choice in it, but he made the one decision he knew he had to...

He *had* to call Marlena, first.

He pulled out his cellphone, and dialled the number to the most difficult call he had ever imagined placing.

∙ ∙ ∙ ∙ ● ● ● ● ∙ ∙ ∙

The cops had left an hour ago, and David sat at the large bay window in Missy's bedroom, staring out at the dark clouds punctuated by the light drizzle cascading down the glass separating them. Marlena had thought he was 'losing it,' and suggested he get some sleep. Her repeated assertions of "we don't *have* a daughter!" caused him to question her state of mind. He had been there during the birth, had held her in his arms, he had gazed lovingly into her eyes, and every day since. How the hell could she ever deny having a kid when she was the one who had carried and nourished her since her conception? It made no sense, whatsoever.

He looked at the photo of the three of them sitting on the chest of drawers, and the solitary photo of her, resting on the bedside table, smiling, her cute little toothless grin, wide and bright. It had been taken at her second birthday party. Smiling at the memory of that day, tears flowed down his reddened cheeks as he screwed his eyes closed to staunch them. It was useless. If he *didn't* have a daughter, then whose pyjamas had been lying crumpled beside him? The cops had actually questioned his whereabouts the previous night, but he had stated an empathic "being home writing," resorting to offering them access to his laptop file where the date and time of the last writing session would prove, undeniably, that he had, indeed, been home last night. The detective's face had paled upon seeing the document files of the stories he had been working through. They had no probable cause to detain him or even to question him further based on this fact, resulting in him suggesting that David was "over-worked" and he "oughta think on getting some rest." They had said their goodbyes, leaving him to wonder what the fuck was going on.

······

All he could do was sleep to get the thought out of his mind as to whether he was going crazy or not. Marlena was *still* denying the existence of their only child, and he knew she wasn't the 'seein' illusions' type, but how the fuck she could deny such a thing, after going through the hell of the pregnancy that she did, flew way over his head. He got out of bed, and walked downstairs to the kitchen, opening the refrigerator. He looked with disdain at the contents, and wished he wasn't turning into a human waste disposal system. Going to the gym wasn't his bag, as he detested those types; the whole dating scene that come to dominate that atmosphere; and his generalised consensus that they were fake, vain, overly-pretentious assholes, holding their mineral water and 'reporting in' to their social media accounts, letting everyone know (whether they wanted to or not) how much they bench-pressed in that hour, and plastering their wall with dumb-ass selfies no one in real life, observing all this, would give two shits about. Nah! They could stick their tank tops, sneakers and heart monitors straight up their tight, self-obsessed asses for all of him, he thought, laughing at the image of it in his mind.

He scoured the fridge and finally found a pastrami sandwich he had one day left on. He grabbed a canned Starbucks and closed the door with his leg. He walked into his lounge, and sat, picking up the tattered paperback copy of LeFanu's *Carmilla*, and started to read where he had left off. He raised the sandwich to his mouth, and was in the process of taking a bite, when the doorbell rang.

'Christ! Every fucking *time*,' he muttered, replacing it on the coffee table. He got up and walked to the door. A woman stood behind the screen door, her back to him as she looked around the street. He opened the door, sticking his head out.

'Can I help you, Miss?' he asked, trying his best not to betray his irritation.

'Hi. I'm sorry to bother you. Are you David Kent?' she asked, smiling awkwardly.

'Yes. I'm kinda busy at the moment, so if you'd mind telling me what you're after, we can get on with it, maybe?' His tone made it apparent – it was a thinly-veiled order, not a question. He was extremely tired and trying to be as patient with her as it was possible to be for something you had no patience for. He wished she would just get the fuck out of here so he could rejoin the dream he had about walking on the beach with his daughter; there, at least, he could deceive himself into believing she was still alive. She smiled, her awkward eyes darting around, not sure how to put across to him the reason she had tracked him down.

'My name's Kari Hanley. We went to Kennington Consolidated together. I was in a few of your classes back then. You may remember?' she asked, her strong Queens English accent unmistakeable even to this day.

He studied her hopeful features. It was peculiar seeing her face again. The name had struck him as familiar, even if only vaguely.

One of those people you knew well in the past as the class 'freak' or 'geek,' completely out of place in most extra-curricular groups the kids formed from the student body, most of them being an integral part of one clique or another.

*Kari Hanley...Kari Hanley...who the fuck was she, again?* Then it came to him.

He remembered her.

············

They had been talking solidly for around four hours, and he had enjoyed her company more than he imagined. He had tried and failed several times in High School to date her, but it had never got beyond trying. He had been one of the 'art farts,' 'the miscreates,' as they had been not-so-jokingly referred to by the popular kids. She was the typical student geek, but became popular enough to 'play the game' of the American High School hierarchy, and survive it. It could so easily have gone the other way. American high schools were not unlike that of the British class system, constructed in the well-defined sociological strata where every student 'hangs' in their own groups. Deviating from this highly-maintained pecking order could result in abject humiliation, being ostracised by one's original peers, and the relentless practical jokes that you were subjected to – all for trying to abandon one's station in the youth hierarchy.

Kari was different. Having relocated to Chicago when she was a tender 16 (her father, Roy, was a British representative for Ford and had gained a promotion, granting him immediate residency in the parent nation of the company), she had tried and failed to fit in as easily as she had hoped. Jealousy and jibes had engulfed her from her first day, the girls taking an immediate dislike to her, mostly due to their prospects of landing a hot jock being dashed on account of Kari's stunning looks. She tried to improve her situation by ingratiating herself into their various clubs and extra-curricular groups, but was roundly admonished for daring to abandon her post. Giving up, she accepted her fate, hanging out with a few of the lesser mortals occupying the halls, although most of the geeks had given her the silent treatment in return for her defection to 'the enemy.' She was a lost soul without a hall pass in the hell of high school.

They had chatted for what felt like an hour but was actually three.

'I'm gonna have to go. Sorry. I've got to pick a few things up at the hardware store. Maybe we'll have coffee some time?' she asked.

'That'd be nice, yeah,' he replied. He was expertly analysing her tone, listening for signs of fake interest in what she had said, but found none. It was a woman's easy way out, trying to avoid any bad feelings by keeping it light.

*Well, it's much nicer than a savage rejection, ain't it?* he told himself. He saw her off, and closed the door.

He lay on the couch, ignoring the sandwich, and stared hard at the ceiling fan rotors as their gentle motion soothed him to sleep once more.

・・・・●●●●・・・

David stood at the foot of the staircase, his gaze riveted on the landing above as an unnerving surge of dread washed over him.

Fearfully, he set one foot on the bottom step and, swallowing hard, began his ascent to the summit – and whatever beckoned. His hand edged along the pine handrail, gripping it, his knuckles turning white from the sheer pressure he exerted. His heart was pumping hard, his chest hairs vibrating with the hits, as his mind began to crack a little at a time.

*Am I nuts, or is it getting* colder *in here?*

He continued his ascent, resting his foot on the landing, by which time it had grown so cold his breath was tangible, billowing out as he shivered. He turned to face Melissa's bedroom, his body wracked with a fear he had never known, as he crept towards the door. His hand volunteered it's reach toward the knob. He paused briefly, turning his head slightly to exorcise any fear he reserved, and he summoned every ounce of faith buried deep within him.

*One...two...THREE!!*

On three, he twisted the doorknob, shoving the door open.

*Nothing. Not one thing out of joint.*

Stunned and unsure, he began to laugh hysterically, running his hands through his wild, dark brown wavy hair, and down his tired, craggy face. Surveying the preserved bedroom, he sat at the small art table he had bought her for her fifth birthday, picking up the A4 drawing she had left unfinished. So lost was he that he failed to hear the door closing behind him, revealing the solid-yet-spectral figure gliding his way.

Whatever was there caught his periphery, and his entire body was livid, afraid to move. He could take it no longer, spinning his head quickly, only to be confronted by his daughter, her small, elfin, pasty off-white ghostly face staring at him, her eyes black as opals, hypnotic, as she regarded her daddy with a malevolent grimace, her chin dripping with saliva. He felt a peculiar, yet not unpleasant sensation, a release of some kind, draining him of strength as if it were feeding from his life-force...his mortal soul, even!

*Speak to her, asshole! If she's alive at all, she'll answer you.*

David began to speak, but he mumbled a mess of gibberish. His voice, cracked and weak, found its strength.

'Baby...are you in there? Honey, answer Daddy, now!' he called out. 'Come *on*, honeybunny! Talk to Daddy...I love you!!'

His heart was in his mouth when her terrified, distorted voice from...from *some*where...filled the small, yet cavernous bedroom, its piercing pitch ricocheting off everything in sight.

*DAAAD-EEE! Come get me, Daddy – I'm afwaaaaiid!'*

The scream that spewed from the pits of her soul sent his eardrums into swathes of crucifying pain, as he clamped his hands over his head to quell it. He collapsed in that moment, his will to live hereonin barely existent, as the despair of not being able to bring her to safety crushed him.

He was done – the darkness had fought him - and it had won.

··········

The banging on the front door startled him. That had been one doozy of a dream. Shaking himself back to normal, he answered the door. It was Marlena. Cursing under his breath, he slid the chain over and opened the door.

'Come to gloat? Speak your piece and get outta here, I'm too tired to argue with you, Marlena,' he growled.

'I didn't come here to gloat, *David*. I'm here to help, if you'll let me,' she said, looking around her.

'Nice place. How much?' she asked with genuine interest.

'Eight a month. You wanna tell me why you came over? It sure as hell wasn't to see how I was. You gave that up when you played hide the salami with the Monopoly guy from Pigsknuckle, Arkansas. Our daughter is missing, and I really think you should start giving a shit, don't you?' he snapped.

'David, honey...booby...we *had* no children. I think I should know if ever my legs were up in stirrups, with my modesty on display for a bunch of med school interns. I think you should seek help, I really do.'

She walked around the foyer room, picking up ornaments, admiring them. He watched her as she picked up Melissa's photograph.

'Your soon-to-be stepdaughter?' she asked, showing him the frame. David sighed in resignation.

'I thought you'd at least recognise your own child, Marlena. You only went through hell getting her here!'

Marlena changed in a blink of an eye.

'WE DIDN'T *HAVE* KIDS, DAMMIT!!' she yelled. She composed herself, speaking softer. 'We tried for three years. I was infertile, remember? It's just the way it is. I would have loved to have had kids with you. It wasn't to be. Get over it. There's a good shrink with an office over on Wallace and Third. He deals with trauma and PTSD, or whatever. You should see him about this fixation of yours,' she said.

'What *fixation*, for Chrissakes?! My daughter crawled into bed around midnight. I wake up in the morning to find her pyjamas lying there in a pile on the mattress. No sign of her anywhere! Damn straight, it's a fixation! Our daughter is missing, and all you wanna do is alert the men in white! Fuck is *wrong* with you, Marlena?!' he roared.

'There is *no* point talkin' to you, cause all you are is a child grown older! The number's on the sideboard. I've got other things to take care of. Let me know how you get on, okay?' she said, her tone indicative of someone trying to be patient with whom they have no patience for. She still loved him, and it was obvious, but she was growing tired of this crazy delusion of his.

She walked to the door, opening it to reveal a stunning Kari, surprised at Marlena's presence. Marlena's face betrayed her envy. As hard as she tried to conceal it, she failed. Marlena was, in her early forties, still ravishing. But Kari's natural beauty took even her breath away. Dressed from head to toe in a stunning red dress, not too low-cut or trampy – 'elegant' was a far better synonym to use. Marlena offered her hand, accepted warmly by the beneficiary of her apparent misfortune.

'Hello,' she said. The tone was icy, masquerading as pleasant. Kari flashed her most natural winning smile and Marlena was undone in that very moment. If she harboured any submerged hopes of getting David back, they evaporated in the time it took for that smile to evolve.

'Hello. I'm sorry to disturb you. I'm here to see David?' she stated, unsure of the reason behind Marlena's presence.

'I'm Marlena Kelsey – formerly Kent. Nice to meet you. I was just leaving. David's in the kitchen. Go right in. Nice meeting you, Miss-' she said.

'Kari. Kari Hanley. The pleasure's mine,' Kari replied. Marlena smiled as genuinely as she felt she could.

*Christ, there's a lot of cutesy-cutsey in this little bitch!* she thought. Marlena walked off down the path with nary a look back, and got into her Lexus, gunning the engine as she screeched off. She walked into the house, knocking the door to alert him. David's voice called out from the kitchen.

'Whatever it is, we don't want it!'

'That include me?' she called back. David's head stuck out from behind the wall, a sheepish grin strewn across his symmetrical features.

He walked over to her, dumbstruck by her appearance.

'Who's the lucky man, *tonight*?!' he exclaimed.

'Depends on who takes my fancy,' she toyed. He laughed. He liked her flirtatious repartee – it matched his own. He was never happier than when he was engaging in back-and-forth banter with a female ('I like to keep sharp,' he used to joke to his old friends) – one of the few old habits which Marlena hadn't eradicated during their marriage.

'So, what brings you here?' he asked.

'I just wanted to spend some friend time with you, so sue me!' she replied, smiling thinly. 'We could get some Chinese take-out or a pizza, watch some movies – whatever you feel like!' she said.

'Why me? What have I ever done to deserve such generosity?' he quipped. Her face fell a little and, upon seeing it, the regret was instantaneous.

'I'm joking, okay?' he said, softly. 'You look stunning. Is all this really for me?' The question was genuine and she knew it. She could detect a lowering of self-esteem having taken place, perhaps due to the divorce (or the marriage itself!).

'I thought I'd put in a little more effort for you,' she said.

'Well, it's working!' he said, grinning. But behind the grin and twinkling eyes, his sadness shone. At that moment, she knew she had him. It was just a matter of time before…

She shook the image from her mind and was glad to see he it hadn't been registered in him.

Her work could begin.

After tonight, he would belong to her, in heart and mind.

His soul would come later – when she took it.

·········

She lay sleeping, exhausted after their encounter, his seed dry, stuck to the inside of both thighs. He lay on the pillow, gazing adoringly at her. She was a keeper alright, but there was something else there which was proving much harder to nail down into one word. Her passion while astride him had been self-evident, almost ruthless in her absolute command of her own body and his, as they had brought each other to one shattering climax after another. Then they had collapsed into a deep sleep, completely sated. Now awake, he looked upon her curvaceous, ample figure, wondering how she had encouraged such a fire in him. He got up and leaned over, kissing her lightly on the shoulder. He needed a cigarette badly. He descended the stairs slowly, his legs still aching from her brutal, almost-possessed assault on him, and he smiled.

He turned on the kitchen light, opening the drawer, his hands still trembling as he struggled with the sealed pack of Camels in his hand. He chopped and changed brands now and then. He had a little tobacco store on Daly where he could buy various international brands to try out. He found he enjoyed the Amer-Turkish blends on occasion, although he was good with the good ol' Camels for the most part. There was nothing (at least up till this point) he liked more than to be sat in front of his laptop; the purity of a blank page waiting to be desecrated by his demonised mind; a case of MGD; and two packs of Camels.

Now, after one mind-blowing night with Kari Hanley, all he could see in his mind was that dark shadow gyrating steadily back and forth, draining him dry of every drop of fluid he ever had the inspiration to produce. He was smitten beyond the ability to function. He marvelled at the fact that, at this very moment, the very same dark shadow was next door, concealed under dampened black satin bedsheets, dormant and regenerating...ready for the matinee performance which would inevitably follow suit.

His mind shivered at the prospect as he noticed his hands shaking slightly more than he expected. He stared at the screen, waiting for inspiration to strike. It would not come quietly into this dark night. He sat back and thought about death.

Then, he thought, only would the words flow rampant.

∙∙∙∙∙∙∙∙∙∙

The bedside radio alarm clock, like a metronome, was ticking away contentedly as the hour passed into 3am. As the 2.59am flipped to 3.00, Kari's eyes flew open like she had just received a personal message from God. Her pupils were opal black, just as Melissa's had been in that soul-wrenching dream a few nights before. She sat bolt upright, her arms limp and controlled by an unseen, external force, her well-rounded ample breasts, full and swollen, bouncing off her chest as her head turned to the attic office above. Her breathing became erratic and raspy, as her black eyes rolled over white. Her body began to jerk violently, her arms and legs limp, as blood ran from her tear ducts. She felt a physical message being transmitted through her, instructing her of what she had to do; a dull, reverberating humming in her ears, reaching fever pitch as it progressed.

*Kill him! Kill him! KILL HIIIM!*

The room returned as it was as a flitting, transparent blob passed through the air vents, hurtling into her nasal passages like a *Shinkansen* (Japanese high-speed 'bullet' train).

She collapsed in a sideways heap as the evil began its insidious journey to her soul.

The clicking of David's laptop strokes rang through the ceiling like the jingle of a Mr Whippy ice-cream truck.

Completely ignorant of his impending conversion to the depths of depravity, David hit the return button on the last paragraph of the night's writing session, happy in himself and looking forward to returning to the incredible woman waiting for him beneath.

Or, at least, that's what he *believed* her to be. He saved the work, closed the lid on his laptop, and stretched his arms out, groaning. He stood, reaching for the table lamp, descending the small attic office into darkness. As turned the light out, from his peripheral vision, his eyes caught sight of the door for an instant.

There it stood. The outline of a horrifying manifestation in the guise of what once was Kari, now transformed before his eyes into a glaring, cruel creature, her black eyes filled with absolute contempt for him. From her throat came a low guttural moan, rising in pitch until his eardrums felt like they were splintering, his hands clamped over them. It was like a hologram, or so he thought, the door behind her faintly visible as it flickered lightly in places. His eyes opened when the faint reproduction of a very familiar voice was pushing through the cacophony.

A voice he knew only too well...

*'Daaaad-eeeeee! Heeeelp me – pleeaase!'*

He started saying the Lord's Prayer. The moment he started, the monstrosity vanished and a blinding flash filled the room as if in answer.

Disoriented, he looked around the room. Not a hair out of place. Shattered, he turned off the lamp, negotiating the two-foot distance to the door. He needed a drink. As he passed the bedroom door, he paid no attention to the still sleeping Kari. As much as he had fallen for her, he wanted no part of her in his sight. At least for now.

••••••••••

Marlena rushed around her bedroom, rifling through cupboards and drawers, in the end resorting to coats and purses she hadn't worn or used in decades. She knew it was here somewhere – it *had* to be!

*Oh, dear* Christ, *let it be here*, she thought. She waded through boxes upon boxes of paperwork...bills, letters and every other combustible form of hoarded paper she had stashed out of the way over the last few years.

Still nothing.

Dejected and silent, she sat behind her office corner desk, and looked down by chance. The drawer was ajar. Strange, because it was always kept locked. Then the hope surged in her, knowing she might just well be setting herself up for a fall again. She slid it open slowly, biting her bottom lip, and draw a stack of hastily-tossed papers from it. She flicked through them, her heart racing in anticipation, praying it was in there.

*Bin-gooo!*

She had always despised this piece of paper. It represented her only major failure as a woman. They had been trying for a child for a while after they met, but the quacks at the Medical Centre, in their infinite wisdom, had informed her that a case of endometriosis had put paid to any change of her bearing children. The proof was right here in her hands. She would, hopefully, be able to convince David finally, that his 'daughter' existed only in his mind. Maybe then, she hoped, he would seek help. She jumped up, shoving the chair out of the way, as she ran from the room, the sound of her footsteps as they thundered down the stairs.

············

David finished his ninth bourbon in one shot. He sighed, standing up out of the armchair, walking to the stairs. He had calmed down, now, wanting nothing more than to sleep. He didn't even care that that monster might be lying up there. He was so worn out, he thought, she could take him straight to hell for all of him!

He reached the upper landing and swayed, staggering backwards. He lost his footing and grabbed a bannister post to save himself. Regaining his balance, David walked to the bedroom, swinging the door open.

The bed was empty. Where had she gone?

The voice in his head told him to forget her and he lay face down on the bed, the only way to stop the room spinning. The banging coming from the door downstairs made him raise his weary head in the direction of the bedroom door, reluctantly rising as he cursed under his breath. He carefully walked back downstairs, unlocking the still-banging door.

'*Alriiiight, already!*' he yelled, his voice hoarse and cracked. He opened the door, storming out in a belligerent manner to face whoever the fuck it was.

Marlena stood, stunned at the condition he was in.

'You screen all your guests like this, David, or am I especially charmed?' she quipped.

'What do you *want*, Marlena? It's five am, for *Christ's* sake!' he said.

'I've got the proof you need to snap you back to reality. Read it and weep, honey,' she said, sighing. 'I had undiagnosed endometriosis when we were dating. After we got married, the hysterectomy soon followed. There is no *way* we could have had a child. It's all there in black and white.'

He took a cursory look at it, and took it from her, looking it over. It seemed to be in order but he knew as well as anyone that even doctors, with their 'great god objectivity' had been wrong in the past. Motorcycle accidents resulting in a "you'll never walk again" prognosis who, with careful physiotherapy, were up and around within six months, the resultant newspaper claims of how "doctors were baffled at the recovery" taking centre stage. That's why second opinions were available. Hell, nobody was perfect. He handed the paper back to her.

'It could be wrong,' he said.

'Well, it's *right*, David. It's *right*. I oughta know, because I was the one stuck in that operating theatre having my femininity ripped out of me!'

'Go home, Marlena. Get some rest,' he said, sighing. She shook her head in disbelief and stormed out of the house. He closed the door on her, sliding down against it, breaking down into tears. He remained there all night.

· · · · ● ● ● ● · · ·

He had taken the bus into Chicago, desperate to get out of the house. He needed contact with society to make him feel he wasn't losing his mind. It was St. Patrick's Day and the parade would be in full swing, the Lake Michigan dyed green as usual in celebration as thousands of the city's Irish contingent flocked into Michigan Avenue to witness and take part in the Windy City's most famous annual civic events. He was a born Chicagoan, raised in Cicero and, later, Berwyn. It was a great city, filled with great people, the cultural nexus of Midwestern diversity. You had the black markets in Maxwell Street, the enviable selection of soul food and blues music, with live musicians wailing the harp and bending the strings to the adoring crowds, all of them singing, dancing and clapping to the 12-bar blues boogie pumped out of the Marshall amplifier stacks behind them; the tremendously popular and gaily festooned Gay Pride marches, celebrating the LBTQ contingent – fun for all the family!

He walked along the sidewalk taking in the action, his mind trying hard not to focus on the events of the previous week. He was worried about Melissa. Where had she gone? She had crawled into bed with him that night, unable to sleep, only to find her crumpled PJs under the duvet. The cops answering the call had found no trace of forcible entry, and neither of them had thought for one second that he had complicit in her disappearance. They had known the couple too well over years for that to be a viable avenue to pursue. But without forced entry, and her height eliminating any chance of her own exit from the property, they had left satisfied.

*But Marlena…* he thought. *How could she ever deny the existence of her own daughter, her own flesh and blood? It made no sense at all. And that obstetrician report! That was pure, undiluted horse-shit. He had been with her during Melissa's Caesarian, had held Marlena's hand as they removed their only child from the womb! So the hell could she be infertile? He didn't imagine it, did he? Was her horrible version of events the 'according to Hoyle' gospel truth? Was it possible that it could have been that way, and that he had chosen not to accept his wife's tragedy in order to block the torrent of pain he felt?*

This and a thousand other thoughts surged through his mind, a whitewash of harsh, stark light, impervious to penetration from rational analysis. The noise of the parade was deafening, as he gazed out at the marching band approaching the intersection. His eye caught a flash and he followed it. It was dark, curly-haired five-year old girl emerging from between two parked cars. She looked familiar to him. He strained his eyes to focus as her eyes met his directly. She looked at him like he was the only human left alive besides her.

It *was* Melissa!

She wandered into a side street and he ran after her, jostling the crowd as he struggled to keep her in sight. There she was, aimlessly walking across a stop sign as a car roared towards her. He watched helplessly as the car ploughed straight into her, her broken body launched into the air, her head shattering the windshield upon impact, being dislodged from the vehicle as it sped through the stoplights. The asshole had been on his cellphone. He hadn't even stopped.

*Too scared to stop*, he thought. *It was keep goin' or do time in Atlanta for murder one. Not much of a choice for his type.*

He raced to the demolished corpse of his daughter, screaming at the top of his lungs for help. A street derelict with a shopping cart filled with empty beer tins looked on at him, his expression a curious mix of compassion and fear. People came from all over to find out what had happened. Eventually, a small detail of cops turned up. He just wanted to hold her, love her. He felt them prise him from her and he lashed out at them with an anger borne of shame and helplessness. They pinned him down on the ground, cuffing him, and dragged him to the waiting blue'n'white, cramming him in. The last thing that he saw as he craned his head back was a cop covering his daughter's head with a tablecloth donated by a nearby coffee house.

Sirens wailing, the car took off as he looked out of the rear window, dejected and forlorn as the parade raged in the adjacent street.

・・・●●●●●・・・

The room was exactly as he would have expected it to be, had he had the capacity to register his bearings. 'Institutional green' walls, caged windows, chamber music on the turntable mic'd to the PA system – fun for the whole family! He sat in the chair facing the caged pastoral scene outside, completely zoned out, his features numb by the 300mgs of Thorazine they zapped him with on arrival.

Doctor Phillip Leitman strode down the corridor to the Acute Admissions Unit (patients first point of contact when admitted) of Cook County Psychiatric Hospital, looking at his watch. He turned the corner and opened the door to AA. The cops who had signed him in had related their version of events and booked out of there soon after, but Leitman's junior had gotten the details and had them printed off. That had been *something*, at least. Joanie Hartman was a good psychiatrist, and was heading for being a damned good consultant, if she kept it up. Her note taking was beyond what he had experienced in his entire career, and he was proud to have her.

The young orderly handed him the police report and stood waiting.

'Christ!' he said under his breath as he read it. He couldn't believe what he was reading. This poor schlep had been through hell.

Dr. Andrew Gaiman emerged from David's room. Leitman gave him a cursory upward glance.

'Have you read this?' he asked Gaiman. Gaiman nodded before speaking.

'They lost their five-year old daughter due to SDS. His ex-wife's medical history indicates an erroneous report stating endometrial failure, and she's lived with that belief since. After the death of the daughter, Melissa Joanne, friends and relatives claim they withdrew completely from their usual social circles...pretty much became hermetical, which is understandable enough. Bad enough dealing with a miscarriage. But losing a child at five years old is a shattering thing to deal with. From the reports we already have, and the information that we got from neighbours, courtesy of Chicago PD, it appears that he refused to believe she was dead, while his ex-wife blocked everything out - the pregnancy, the birth – every memory of the child she ever had. The wrongful endometrial report had taken hold instead, reinforcing the belief that the child could never have been conceived, much less born. The reports of cops from yesterday, and those of the witnesses, all confirmed what he told us during his initial evaluation session. He claimed he saw his daughter emerging from nowhere, that she looked directly into his eyes, and stepped into the path of a used, cherry red 1965 Dodge Charger. The cops ran a DMV on it. No such car exists on the their books with the license plate Mr. Kent supplied the cops.

He was discovered in the street, lying beside what he believed to be the corpse of his dead child, stroking her head. Witnesses statements indicate hallucinogenic visions, due to him stroking the air with his finger, presumably stroking her face or moving the hair from her face had she actually been there. He mentioned a woman he was involved with at his house the night before. We checked it out. The name was traceable to his High School, this morning having confirmed attendance of both of them the year he stated - but it turned out she was an honour student, barely making it as a cheerleader despite her lack of popularity. She rejected him in their Senior year, according to school incident records. Apparently, this girl was British by birth. Her old man worked for Ford Automotive was transferred by promotion. Her name was Kari Hanley...Kari with a 'k' and an 'i' at the end - got freaked out by his constant attentions and filed a report after three weeks. He went downhill from there. His grades slipped, his entire attitude changed, according to his teachers. The only thing he remained true to was his writing. The rest of his life he dropped like a bad habit. He, uh...*claimed* that she turned up on his doorstep last week and they hit it off big-time, so much so that they slept together just before she was said to have appeared to him as a kinda hologram in his attic doorway. Scared the hell out of him, according to Mr Kent. He said her mouth opened wide and he saw his daughter's terrified face staring out at him. He also maintained that she called out to him for help. Freaky shit, huh? That's about it, besides his vitals. What's your next move, Phillip?' Gaiman asked.

'I'm going to have him committed for six months. We need to study his pathology before we can justifiably release him without fear of legal reprisal. That way we can be sure of his future plans. I don't want *that man* wandering this city in the condition he's in. He's a time bomb with legs. Get him on suicide watch. I realise he's not identified as a suicide, but I want him on constant obs until I dig a little deeper. There's an unspoken evil in that man, Andrew. I can't risk letting him out until he's been tested and verified, but it's *there*! It's just fucking *there*, and I want it rooted out before I watch him ever leave this institution. Document that and I'll sign it later today. The Thorazine will wear off in about an hour. I want someone good on him before that happens. Get on it straight away,' Leitman stressed politely, but Andrew Gaiman knew the urgency in that voice. He nodded, walking off down the corridor, leaving Leitman staring at the man in the room, his eyes leery as hell as his mind traversed the possibilities.

··········

The snow was coming down hard and fast, soon covering the basketball court. David, still under the harsh light from the winter sun, stared ahead. The small figure of a young girl with dark curly hair passed by on the other side of the yard. She stopped dead, then her head spun around to face him.

A malevolent smile crossed his weary features.

# ONE NIGHT ONLY

Ten years is a long time to live with someone. Being monogamous in a rapidly hypergamous society is the biggest slap in the face to every beta male on the planet. He is happy supporting his wife or girlfriend, working hard to make their lives better, taking more than his fair share of the childcare because the bitch can't get off social media long enough to change a diaper, or taking *her* turn making some coffee for a change. Dinner is always late, she's overtired, "time just got away from me" ... just some of the excuses of the so-called 'modern woman' to extricate herself from the traditional role, once accepted by all, of nurturer, caregiver...there are others.

Jim Thompson was feeling abandoned. Even though these last ten years had seen many happy times and memories - and God knew Jim loved Lainey more than any woman he had ever known, over the past two years things had started eating at him. He had been warned by enough people of the dangers of marriage, that the passion would die, but he had been convinced otherwise. He and his wife had enjoyed their passionate nights in, making love for hours, been there and worn the t-shirt...

But life had gotten between them over the past few years, with the kids, career and their future plans creating small fissions in their

# OUT OF THE ASHES

once-solid relationship. Every time he tried to initiate sex, it was one excuse or other not to go there. He was becoming spiteful towards her.

He had needs, even if she had forgotten *hers*. But, he was expected to remain monogamous? It was hardly a fair exchange. The simple fact of human existence is that we are here to procreate, to sustain the balance between nature and humanity. Part of marriage – a *major* part, whether they like it or not – is the sex that comes with it. It is inseparable from the concept of committing your life to another.

Yeah, there will be times when you can't be bothered or are tired, but to completely wipe out any future outlay of lovemaking to your partner is cold and calculated. Jim would reach over at night, and touch her, skipping his finger lightly over her skin, hoping he could invite his *wife* to return his increasingly rebutted attentions. He loved her too much to leave her – in most other ways, she was a keeper – but one way he wanted her was emotionally and romantically.

They had agreed to set aside a date night, in which the kids would go to her parents for the night (usually, by the time she got round to calling them, it was too late – they had already gone out themselves) and he would supply the snacks and wine.

Tonight, it was gonna be different if it killed him, he thought. He started his drive home for the night, looking forward to his 'quality time' – if she didn't fuck him off yet again.

・・・・●●●●・・・

Lainey Thompson sat on the porch swing in front of the house, reading a magazine and nursing a drink. She had been feeling remorseful since Jim had stated his case, and the guilt was creeping up on her. She *had* neglected him and, yes, she knew it was an important – *vital* - part of marriage for a man. Why the hell would you give your life to one person otherwise? It's the dumbest fucking thing on earth for a man to drop his free-wheeling life for the monotony of seeing the ever-changing face of one woman for the rest of his life. The illusion of emotional bonding through the sexual act is enough for most men to be content. But women are different.

They are far too emotional to think logically or laterally. They respond to everything *emotionally*. She knew she had nailed Jim when they married. He had always seemed happy, so she had never thought she was in any way unhappy. But she was gonna have to give him some tonight if she wanted to keep him. He was a refusal away from screwing that little bitch down at the mall. He had never thought of that before, but she knew he was popular with women, able to talk easily to them, and – quite likely – his confidence was a magnetic field to other women.

It would only be a matter of time before he asserted his manhood and started fucking around on her. Yeah, she could give off those 'I-don't-need-a-man-to-live' vibes all she wanted, but – as she well knew – she was done without him. Her sexual marketplace value – SMV, as it was called – was in the shitter and 'the wall' loomed ever larger these days. She had better quit fucking around and let him in – or she was histoire!

She shivered at the prospect of trying to start all over again. She went back to her magazine, and the article about the pregnant man in Louisville.

··········

When Jim's car pulled into the drive, he found the lights off in the house. They never were. He got out of the car quickly, hurrying to the house.

As he opened the door, he was greeted by a trail of rose petals, leading to a small gift-wrapped box on the stairwell. He grinned as he opened the card attached to it.

IF YOU CAN FIND ME...
YOU CAN TAKE ME!

He rushed upstairs, excited as he used to be in the early days. Lainey hadn't pulled this shit in years. He crept upstairs and searched all the rooms but she was nowhere to be found. Panic overtook him, his heartbeat rising fast. He went into the bedroom and he stood at the window, wondering what the hell had happened. He was so lost in the moment that he failed to hear her coming out of the closet, walking seductively towards him, smiling coyly.

Without a word of warning, he was wrenched off his feet, and thrown onto the bed. Grinning, his fears disappeared as he lay there, submissive and yielding to her desires.

The room was filled with headlights as a car drove past the house, inbound. They paid no attention, peeling the clothes from each other.

Outside in the street, the passing car had parked and two men, heavy-set, stood looking up at the shadows of the couple making love and smirked. This was gonna be easier than they thought.

He rolled off her, and they lay there, exhausted. She was beginning to see what she had been missing all these months, and was starting to regret her treatment of him. Maybe she should cut him a break, she thought, biting her bottom lip.

After all this time, and he hadn't lost anything in the bedroom area. Most men would have shot their bolt long before now after waiting such a long time. The simple promise of sex after a time of forced celibacy is enough to bring on too much stimulus in a man, making him get there too prematurely. She had to admit, however, it was the most invigorating he had been since their first time. He lay there, waiting to refill, smoking a cigarette to pass the time.

She was ravenous tonight, not like her at all.

*Christ*, she reflected, *what else do you expect? You've only kept him cold for nine months!*

She hated to admit it, to accede that one little credit to him. He *was* amazing in bed. Even back then. So what was the issue? Was it just her? Had she travelled that old route of marriage where, if the man became too predictable or supplicating, the woman loses all respect and desire for him? That old chestnut? Maybe, she thought.

Maybe she had let herself get too hooked up into the whole Facebook thing, where the dopamine rush is better than that of your man being attentive and providing to you. The incessant rush from constant likes, shares, praise and validation she had never known. The flirtation from strange and, frankly, more appealing men out there sent her dizzy with possibilities. She had turned up her icebox gradually, without realising it, and her resentment towards him grew by the day. She hadn't much of a moral barometer. Never knew, *really*, how to keep interest in anything. Her old man had never really shown her much interest as a kid, and she had watched him suffer the same indifference – the worst thing a loving man can take from an increasingly cold wife – that her mother had shown him. Her father was no breeze, but she had watched too many confrontations about the lack of affection from her to him.

The words of yesteryear reverberated in her head, as she pictured her father (although he failed to see her watching him) sitting there at night, his face sad as he sat in front of the kitchen television, pretending to watch his favourite shows, usually *Airwolf*, *The Persuaders*, or *Sgt Bilko*.

His silence shattered the mirrors of her soul. Although she didn't know it then, she always remembered his face and, when she finally discovered what 'returned love' meant to a man, she swore she would never freeze her own husband out. Yet, here she had been – for almost a year – doing the very same thing. This was gonna be changed – tonight. She was gonna reward him for his efforts, from hereonin. Make certain he felt appreciated...loved...hell, even *cherished*. She looked back at her foolishness. She had been a cunt, to put it bluntly. She had a *real* man the whole time - and had thrown him to the wolves, cast him into the outer-darkness of emotions, and for what? The illusion of attention from assholes who would only give her physical attention instead of what she had craved her entire, miserable life?

*Fuckthat!* she swore to herself.

Time to make amends – before he started looking around himself. Same as with women, there's only so much bullshit a man can take before he loses it and finds someone else. He was – and always had been - a keeper.

She was keeping *him*. *He* belonged to *her*. End of discussion. The die was cast.

That is, she thought, if he hadn't already lost interest and was just taking advantage of what he had been missing for damn near a year. She prayed that wasn't the case. But he could hardly be blamed for that, and she knew it.

She climbed back into bed, cozying up to him, smiling and kissing his body, with her mind in full DEFCON 2 setting. It was a world war of risk, here, and the war was keeping his mind on her.

They began again, and soon became so caught up in the moment that they didn't hear the masked sound of glass breaking downstairs...

·········

The window gave way fairly easily, aided by the thick doormat behind the door, below.

A thick, dark clad arm snaked its way through it, fumbling for the keys, hanging just below reach. The arm extended a little more and grabbed them. Easing them out of the lock, it scooped them up and out of the window.

The door was unlocked, and opened. Two men entered, ski-masks around their heads, as they closed the door. The biggest of the two put his hand in the air, listening.

'We got a live one!' he said, gesturing sex with both hands.

The other one – much younger – clamped a hand across his mouth to stifle a burst of laughter, and composed himself quickly.

They had a job to do, although this presented 'complications' to say the least. Shit like this could escalate into a prison term if the shit hit the fan. *Sieges* were formed from jobs like this.

The woman screams as her husband is knocked unconscious, tending to him; the burglars ransack the place for as much as they can find; a concerned neighbour calls the cops.

The rest?...by the end of the night, a holding cell until their arraignment - two months later if they were lucky. They had came prepared. The taller one pulled out a .38, checked the chambers, and handed it to his partner.

Putting a finger to his mouth, he began the torturous ascension to the landing upstairs. One creak out of sync, and they were done for. They managed to make it, and crept towards the bedroom door. Lainey's passionate moans were louder by the minute as they had negotiated the stairwell, but were deafening now, having gotten closer to the source. They suppressed a laugh, grinning instead as they slipped the masks around their heads.

Fingers signalling a three-count, they barged through the door, causing the table lamp behind it to crash to the floor.

The young thief was at Lainey's side in seconds, being that she was the more risky of the two. He had to deal with her first or the gig was up.

She opened her mouth to scream, but the young man backhanded her hard, knocking her out cold, spread naked across the exposed mattress, blotted by crimson drops from his attack.

Jim leapt out of bed, but received the .38 barrel at his nose.

'You know the score, asshole. Keep your mouth shut, and we're out of here. You don't? Well, lemme put it this way...my boy ovah theah is gonna give her a *real* night to remembah! Got it, Spah-ky?' he drawled, smiling slightly.

'Your call, my friend. What's it gonna be?'

Jim just wanted them out of there. Standing there, naked as a jay bird, he nodded his head.

'Mind if I see to my wife?' Jim asked, his voice shaky.

'You go right ahead, bud! Just remember, though. Any shit, she's done,' he replied, a little too matter-of-factly for Jim's liking. It contained no ambiguity whatsoever. She would be violated furiously if he resisted. His tone had left no doubt of that.

He walked over to the other side of the bed, cradling her head in his arms, the shame coursing through his veins, both at not having heard them enter and at his inaction against them when they made their entrance.

The threat to her was far too great to risk, though, and he cuddled into her. They began to look around the house, one taking a room each. They weren't concerned, which was frightening. But they knew their threat had had its desired effect. He knew that they knew that he wasn't gonna do shit.

And they were right. Watching her being taken was more than he would be able to bear, and far more than she could live with.

They had been all around the house, their sacks full, when they returned to the bedroom to find the happy couple in the same position.

Smiling, the tall thief tossed them a handkerchief.

'Ok, we're outta here. If we see so much as a crossing guard looking at us funny, We'll *both* be back to make her acquaintance.

You got insurance, make the claim. Have a nice life!'

They walked out of the bedroom, and Jim rested his head backwards, angry with himself.

He jolted his head forward. He remembered he had something hidden in the linen cupboard outside the spare bedroom. They were almost downstairs, now. It would be too late. They had to be caught *inside* the house for it to pass as a 'righteous kill'.

He had a minute at most. He walked swiftly and quietly to the cupboard and searched frantically between the linen to locate the small safe he kept their savings in. He expertly flicked the numbers in, yanking the door open.

*There it was!*

*...the salvation of his pride...a shiny, well-oiled .50 calibre Desert Eagle.*

He grabbed it out of there, checking the mag.

*Full.*

He inserted and cocked it, looking in at Lainey, still out of it, and walked onto the landing.

He aimed the Eagle at them. Calling out, the turned around.

'You forgot your stamps, boys!'

He unleashed a hailstorm of rapid fire shots at them, sending them crashing against the solid oak panelling, the impact of the hits carpeting them in their own blood and spilled intestines, as he watched them both slide down the wall, their heads – or what remained of them – flopping over to the side. Dead as Dillinger.

He stared down at them, impassive and coldly, before returning to his wife. He walked to her and picked up her naked, blood-encrusted body, resting it on the bed, laying next to her. He stared at the ceiling, feeling vindicated completely. He found the box she had left on the stairs, and opened it.

Tears welled in his eyes as he extracted an eternity ring with a small card beneath it, saying only *I'm so sorry, baby! I love you.*

He looked over at her, smiling. All would be well in his world from now on.

He *hoped*.

# OUT OF THE ASHES

'OH...MY...*GAWD!*' Marianne Kessler exclaimed, removing her cupped hands from her face. She had been dreaming of this trip for five years since their hastily arranged wedding, itself being crammed in between their hectic schedules. Michael had kept it a secret for six months while he saved for the trip. It couldn't have been easier for him, as they had been passing lanes in life, due to work and social commitments since relocating to Upstate New York two years before. He was an ad executive; she, a marketing manager for a rival competitor. It was an awkward situation, but they made it work despite the natural espionage inherent in it. They didn't bring work home with them for that very reason, and the distance kept the marital bed alive, at least for the first three years until some new start-up clients came along and whipped their billable hours up quite a notch, denying them the evenings they had enjoyed, either alone or with friends. That had, sadly, become a thing of the past for them, and they had sworn to take a late honeymoon at the earliest opportunity, and it was only now - in their third year of marriage - that they had wangled an entire week's vacation. They had no intention of wasting a moment. She walked to the small bare patch of land, breathing in the cool, fresh air, as she surveyed the area. Completely alone. She had plans for this week that weren't entirely on either of their to-do lists, but she was pretty sure he would go for it with a little 'persuasion.' She turned to look at her husband, struggling fifty feet away to get the bicycles they had hired earlier untangled from the roof brace.

The wind picked up a little, and she shivered as she spun around, her eyes betraying a new uncertainty as the area began to assume an aura of suspicion within her, contrasting bluntly with her initial feelings on arriving. She shrugged it off, and returned to her husband who, now at rest, was lighting a cigarette. She didn't mind the occasional one. He had earned it, she supposed. She refrained from mentioning it, and took the bags inside the cottage. She re-emerged, closing the door, and sat behind him, wrapping her arms around his neck, nuzzling it. He smiled, and kissed her on the cheek quickly. He didn't want the smoke in her face too much.

'Thanks, hon! It's stunning - really,' Marianne said.

Mike smiled, patted her hand, then gently stroked it. She smiled. This was one of his little affectionate things - one of the rare few that had survived past the third year, when the tsunami of expectant corporate loyalty had engulfed them both.

They had talked about going somewhere warmer, but his idea of going to England - a distinctly more chilly proposition - appealed to them both, especially when he explained it. He wanted to snuggle up at nights like they used to. That sealed the deal with her, and she had no problem after that.

The sun was going down and Mike locked the car. He walked to the doorway, where Marianne stood, her slim, perfect ten body framing it nicely, wearing the same heart-stopping smile she had given when he had asked her to marry him.

God was good, he thought, as the door closed on the cold, as she wrapped her arms around his neck in a passionate kiss.

Outside in the darkness, the stiff wind which had been building was now whistling through the eaves, as two wispy spectral figures ascended from the bowels of the woods.

··········

THEY AWOKE WITH a start, the cold air piercing the warmth of their skin as they lay naked under the sheets. Raindrops splashed onto their bags which sat on the soiled carpet beside the broken window, and they got out of bed, heading for their joint shower, a tradition they maintained since meeting, which Mike often joked on claiming they were "steamin' out the creases." They got dressed, and headed downstairs for breakfast". Mike found some wooden slats and nails to board up the window while Marianne fixed the food.

'Nice start to the vacation, huh?' Mike said. 'I can't wait to get the bill'.

'Must have been really bad to do that, though,' Marianne replied.

'If this keeps up, we'll be stranded here,' he joked. 'It could be worse, I guess. We could live in Detroit.' Marianne sprayed her coffee out, almost choking. He began laughing as she regained control.

'Yeah, I can just see us living in Sunny Dearborn. Thank you, nooo!' she said. 'Anyway, what are we going to do today? The weather's not exactly 'picnic-friendly,' is it,' she quipped.

'I'm sure we can think of something. We ARE intelligent human beings, after all,' he said.

'Typical man. You're two steps away from being a sex addict, you know that, don't you?' she retorted.

'One. One step,' he said as he winked at her. They put on their parkas, and locked the cottage door, walking arm-in-arm along the driveway towards the nature walk.

They hadn't done this for such a long time and the memories of old came flooding back as they walked, taking in the fresh air. By the time they returned, the grocery van had turned up and the driver helped them in with the bags. Marianne signed and smiled as the driver walked off towards the van. They closed the door and took the bags to the kitchen, unpacking and storing them.

'Jeez, these refrigerators are tiny! We'll be lucky if we can get it all in here!' she said. Mike laughed.

'You're a fridge mamma, what do you expect!? We'll just have to be careful how much we get next time. Come on! Get your skinny butt over here and kiss me!' he said, patting the couch seat.

'Hmm! Something in mind, Mister Kessler?' she asked, offering a coy smile.

'It's in the back of my mind, really,' he countered as she walked towards him, her eyes inviting and alive. This is what they had needed.

They descended into the couch, her arm reaching up to turn off the small table lamp.

Outside, the dampened ground was alive, pulsating as the earth rose and fell, the ethereal light spewing out from the gaps in the dirt.

••••••••••

THE GLASS BLEW inwards, window after window, as Mike grabbed the screaming Marianne to the floor, covering her head with the blanket as the blinding white light dazzled them through the broken window frames. They looked up to see the glow of the spectral figures of two young women gliding through the window, their faces lapped in a storm of fury, their voices howling in anguish. The entire room came alive with the tempest they invoked. Marianne cowered under the blanket, petrified, as Mike found it difficult to keep his eyes on them. Their ocular cavities were black but for a emerald pin prick that blazed at them. In the maelstrom which ensued, household objects flew wildly around the room, smashing into the walls with terrific force.

'MAKE IT STOOOOP!' screamed Marianne, terrified beyond anything she had ever known. Mike was lying unconscious, knocked cold by the impact of a small wooden bookshelf, the volumes included in which being scattered throughout the wrecked living room.

The figures spoke, their voices ear shattering and high-pitched - as if being filtered through crystal, almost. Mike and Marianne held their ears to dampen the racket they made, their eyes screwed up in agony as they prayed silently for it to end.

As they heard the prayer, the spirits screamed and sped out through the window into the cold night air, vanishing as they went.

Mike looked up, seeing they had gone, and wrapped his arms around his wife who was almost convulsing in terror.

They stayed there all night, together in fear, until the rays of daylight crawled over the laminate floor. It was over.

At least for now.

∙∙∙∙••••∙∙∙

MIKE HAD WOKEN earlier than Marianne and had driven into town to find a hardware store. He thanked God for his good credit rating, being able to afford an extending on his AmEx card. He found replicas of the things that had been irreparably damaged, and took them back to the cottage, storing them in the only spare cupboard he found find, although it wasn't nearly as large as the American storage cupboards. There was little point in wasting further resources until they left. If it happened again, he would have to spend even more money to fix up the place, so it was a moot point for them both. He would spend the last day and night re-decorating the cottage to its former state, and get the hell out of there before the shit hit the fan.

··········

THE DOORBELL RANG twice, and they looked at each other, dubious as to who might be on the other side. Marianne chewed her bottom lip, her saucer eyes wide, as Mike walked to the door, and tentatively reached for the door latch, lifting it slowly, ready to close it on wherever monstrosity was out there. The door opened a crack and saw that it was a clergyman.

'What can I do for you, Father?' he asked, tired and irritable, trying to curb his dejected mood.

'You must leave this place, now, my son,' he said, his tone in no way ambiguous. He meant every syllable.

'I can't leave, Father. I have to return the cottage to its natural state as it was when we assumed the occupancy,' Mike replied. 'Then we can leave,' he added.

'May I come in, my son?' he asked

'Actually, Father...the place isn't exactly fit to receive guests at the moment,' he offered.

'We need to talk about your experiences, here,' he insisted, his voice as calm as he could manage.

'YOU have answers for this?' Mike asked, incredulous at the suggestion.

'I have an idea I'd like to elaborate on, shall we say?' the Priest said.

'This oughta be interesting,' he said, his tone ice-y as he opened the door wider, allowing the Priest to enter.  He closed the door behind them.

・・・・●●・●●・・・

FATHER THOMAS HOPE looked around the house, taking each room in turn, starting upstairs.  He said nothing until he entered the living room.  The hairs on his arms stood up as he took the surroundings in.  There was something here, faint traces of electrical charge burning.  He KNEW that smell from the texts in Seminary.  The energy a spirit harnesses in order to cause a coin to traverse up a wall takes a great deal to achieve and expends them quickly.  The damage done to the room was far beyond anything he had heard of, but he nodded his head in self-agreement that this incident was another in a series of spiritual events he had been studying since the events here forty years earlier, and every decade since.

'So! What say, Father?' he asked.

'Oh, It's an epic saga.  Forty years ago, this area was the scene of the brutal murders of two young women...friends...who came here to seek solace from abusive young husbands.  They met with a far worse fate than that.  Attacked and beaten to within an inch of their lives, they were finally burned to death in an inferno that lit up the sky for an hour.  That's the legend.  Now, for the science.  Spirits are metaphysical, not conforming to our laws of life.  If human life is taken, the spirits of those bereft may return to fix what has been left unfinished.  In many cases, it seems, these are less than happy departures, and manifest themselves in this realm - the physical - in various ways.  Poltergeists, spectral hauntings, and so on and so forth.  What you have here is an astounding level of energy being generated by the spirits of those two women. Powerful enough to show themselves to you and inflict the damage you see here. That's the spiritual side. The truth is rather more disturbing, and the single strongest reason I advise you to leave immediately. The rage in these two women was strong enough to survive the grave and they took it with them, unable to receive God's grace until they let this rage die in the power of forgiveness. Such a thing being unforgivable? I'm sure you can appreciate their position. But they are unable to make the transition between this life and the next...caught between the two, until they leave the hate they both bear far behind them. For the last four decades, this cottage has been tormented by them, each time beginning on the anniversary of their deaths.'

Marianne had paled as the realisation finally dawned upon her. She knew the answer before she asked, but went on, anyway.

'Father...you said they were attacked, right?' she started.

'Yes. They were viciously raped and beaten by a group of three passing transients, all of whom were never to be found, despite the best efforts of the Police.'

She continued, hesitant but in need to confirm her nagging suspicion.

'Were they attacked upstairs?' she asked.

'Well, I, uh — I don't think —,' he started.

'Humour me, Father. Where did it happen?' she pressed.

The Priest cleared his throat, and looked her straight in the eye as he gave his matter-of-factly reply.

'Exactly where you sit, now.'

Marianne jumped off the couch like it had a tarantula crawling along the armrest, staring widely at the couch in horror.

'We're short on suggestions, here, Father. If you have one, we'd like to hear it,' Mike said, sighing.

'Normally, people use spirit boards to communicate with the dead. That often makes matters worse, sadly. Many spirits can find their way into your lives that way, and none you want to know about, I dare say. A spiritualist medium might be useful but, again, we tend not to encourage that sort of thing,' the priest said.

'If we could find a way to communicate directly with them, to tell them you're sorry for what happened to them but that it wasn't your doing, perhaps they would vacate the premises. Highly doubtful, of course, but its an option,' he added.

'What about an exorcism? Would that work?' Mike asked.

'It's not easy to get approval for it. And I'm not certain it would be entirely practical in this case. We're not dealing with demons, here. It's just two women who can't break free of their bondage. They will have to forgive those who harmed them, and they can, again, see the light enough to enable the transition. Beyond that, I can't see any way out of this unless you leave the house. But, as you said, you're not prepared to do that, are you?'

Marianne piped up from the corner of the room.

'Could you bless the entire house? At least take a shot at it? she asked.

'It'll have to be done at night because that's when they come to you. I'll be back at seven pm and take care of it. Now, if you'll excuse me, I really must return to the church. I have a novena to prepare and a funeral at 5pm. Then I'll be back,' he said, checking his wristwatch.

He offered his hand, which Mike shook.

Marianne approached, keeping a noticeable distance from the couch. The Priest took both hands in his.

'We'll do what we can, Mrs Kessler. I promise we'll try. These things are never easy. See you at seven o'clock,' he said, walking out of the cottage to his car. The sunlight was starting to fade, and they stood at the door watching him drive off, his tires crunching at the gravel beneath.

Cold and dejected they re-entered the cottage and shut the door.

············

FATHER HOPE HAD returned as promised. He looked around the bedroom, taking in the ambience, judging just how big the Kessler's problem could be - and the resulting complications as far as the Church was concerned. Such matters were touchy subjects and infrequent, intense Papal conferences were conducted when they arose.

The history of the cottage hauntings had been an anomaly for which they had no real answers. Demons, yes; spirits, not so much. Demons tended to be of a more satanic bent. Spirits, on the other hand, were harder to quantify. He reached for his bag, removing his purple stole, a carafe of Holy water and the catechism.

'Bless this house. Release these unfortunate spirits so that they may return to the comfort of Your eternal grace. Forgive them their sins and allow them, in turn, to forgive. In God's name—'

Upon the mention of of the deity, a blinding flash filled the room, accompanied by a gale force wind, leaving him struggling for breath.

As he turned inward, the priest was impacted by an invisible jolt backwards, propelling him with tremendous force against the thinly boarded window cavity, splintering it as he crashed through it, falling the sodden grass mound five feet away - dead upon impact from a broken neck. Hearing the crash, Marianne dashed into the bedroom, surveying the carnage as she walked through the room towards the window - or what there was of it - and looked outside. She screamed as she saw the inverted, blood-soaked body of Father Hope strewn across the front yard. Her hands flew to her face, and she turned her head away, burying it in the shoulder of Mike who had come running in.

There would be few left to help them now, he thought. There was only one thing for it.

Leave now, while they still had their lives intact. If the spirits were bound to this property, they would be safe if they got the hell out of there before they WERE killed.

They wasted little time in packing, and ran to the car, shoving their bags in the trunk. The tires did their duty, and the car was barrel-assing it's way to the main artery road leading to town. They didn't even look behind them, too relieved to be out of that place.

Next time, maybe Key West might not be such a bad idea, after all, she thought.

# PERFECT STRANGER

KARLIE KAYLEN SAT on the window seat of her log farmhouse ranch she had once shared with her late husband, Mike, staring blankly out at the untracked, snow covered fields.

They ran a stud farm together, mostly Arabians, with a couple of Lipizzaner stallions to add to the domestic, American-born horses they maintained. Most were their own stock, but to bring in extra money, they acted as a 'horse kennel', where people would pay Karlie and Mike to board and care for their animals while they went on vacation. It was a pretty good income, too!

She and Mike had spent so many happy times here, in the wilderness of the Tennessee backwaters, rarely visited by outsiders. The heavy rain cascaded down the glass as her eyes, red from tortured tears, pierced the veil of reality she had so desperately fought to deal with these last three months. She had remained aloof until the funeral, and assumed full hermit status after it, ignoring the telephone, disregarding the door when friends came around. She didn't want reminders of what she couldn't have.

Empty, well-meant platitudes held no resonance for her any longer, adamantly refusing to entertain them. The horses were asleep by now, she felt sure of it, having been fed and watered. The trees scattered across her 35 acres were bending with the sheer force of the stiff wind, which was wreaking havoc on the garden furniture. A magazine from the trash appeared from nowhere, thumping against the window, startling her. The creak of the porch swing drew her attention to it. The memories of when they had bought the house came upon her, fast and furious, but only one registered in her. The two of them sitting on it, wrapped together in a thick fleece blanket, staring out at the snow, much as it was now. She had been snuggling tightly into his chest, leaning around with dreamy, sleepy eyes, as she craned her neck to him, kissing him lightly, her contentment evident as the snow began to fall once again. Those were the days - days she wanted back.

She snapped out of her isolation at the sound of the doorbell. Cursing quietly, she stood up, resignedly, walking to the door. It was a courier with a parcel. She opened the door, taking the parcel, placing it on the unit stationed at the door, and signed the delivery note before closing the door on him. She watched him return to his van, and her heart sank for the final time that evening. She was reminded of an old maxim she had heard (but couldn't recall from where) : 'Tomorrow is promise to no-one'

She had been forced to agree.

··········

THE TOWN PARK was quiet, the snow having chased the families off for the season. Christmas was around the bend, her first without Mike. It was going to be a nightmare this year. Sitting alone in that big farmhouse, perched in the porch swing, a blanket wrapped around her – but no husband to wrap his arms around her as they stared out at the setting sun. She wanted to sleep through the entire thing this year. No gifts, no big dinner – just her and a lazy week in bed, with only bathroom visits to get her out of her self-imposed isolation. She finished her sandwiches and tossed the wrappers in the trash as she walked to the exit. Fumbling for her keys, she wasn't watching where she was going. She walked right into the man, knocking him over.

'Oh, my God! Are you alright?' she asked, picking up the gifts he had been carrying. She helped him up.

'I'm so *sorry*! I wasn't looking where I was going,' she said. Looking down, wiping the snow from the front of his overcoat, he looked up, meeting her eyes for the first time.

Her breath clogged in her throat.

*No...no, it wasn't* possible, she thought.

He was the image of her late husband, his doppelgänger. She looked down and away, afraid to look him in the eye.

'Are you okay, Miss,' he asked, his voice soft and filled with care.

'Y-yes, I'm...I'm fine. I'm really sorry about that,' she managed. Her heart was thumping, pulse racing. She sneaked an awkward glance and he smiled, that perfect mouth and closed lips making her quiver internally.

*Dear Christ, it* couldn't *be! He even smiles the same way!*

'Did you find what you were looking for,' he asked.

She was staring at him, unable to digest the stark, unforgiving likeness to her husband.

'Uh, huh,' she droned, quietly. 'I seem to have dropped my car keys around here, someplace,' she replied, absently, as her eyes scoured the vicinity.

He held up his hand, his forefinger raised.

'Hold on one second...,' he said, turning, his finger thoughtfully placed against his lips as he looked around. He walked over to the park seat, delving his hand into a minute body of rain water, fishing something out of it.

'Ta da!' he proclaimed, jangling the keys in front of her.

'I'm not called the miracle worker for nothing, you know!' he joked, winking.

Karlie heaved a sigh of relief.

'Thank you so much! I'm really grateful,' she said.

'Anytime, Mrs-?'

'Kaylen. Karlie Kaylen.'

His face showed a liking for the lyricism of her name.

'Very nice!' he countered. 'Very nice, indeed.'

'Karlie with a K,' she offered, and she instantly regretted it.

*Why the hell did I tell him* that? Karlie thought.

'My name's Matt. Matt Thompson – might as well tell you, since I know yours,' he replied, his face alive with mischievous fun.

'Well, Karlie with a K…would you like a quick refreshment?'

Her face exploded in a blush which would have rivalled a blood moon, and she backed off a little.

He saw this, and held up his hands.

'Please don't misunderstand me, Miss Kaylen. I don't mean you any harm. It's just – well, I always have a drink around this time, and just thought you might like to join me. But if you don't feel comfortable -,' he said. She looked in his eyes, sensing fear that he may have weirded her out.

Sympathy washed over her, feeling bad.

'Okay. Maybe just one, though. I have a lot to do at home,' she said, scarcely believing she was entertaining this. She was *not* in the habit of courting male regard.

'Great. There's a terrific little Irish theme bar around the corner,' he said, flashing his smile, wider this time.

Her heart burst just looking at him, barely managing to conceal it. They walked across the park to the exit.

That was the beginning of it.

··········

SHE LAUGHED HEARTILY as they sat in the corner booth of Paddy O'Hanlon's, a large and boisterous Irish theme bar, always crowded at weekends, but this day it was curiously deserted but for one or two of the senior citizens who called it home – quite literally so. It had been an hour or so since they entered the bar, and several drinks had been partaken of, since. Mr Matthew Thompson was quite the entertainer. Funny, obviously musical – as his astounding rendition of the Jeff Beck/Rod Stewart classic, *I Ain't Superstitious*, clearly proved. He was the only one participating in the afternoon karaoke session, but the bar staff had been suitably impressed. The conversation had been mind-blowing. He was the first to admit that he was a Jack-of-all-subjects - master of none, although he did exhibit a real knowledge of his first love, which was creative writing. "Short stories, mainly, but that's only 'cos a novel takes up too much time at the moment. Besides, it's more fun when you have only so many words to make it as good as you can get it." Her late husband had also been a scribe of sorts, but he had no persistence, and let it slide over time, only indulging in the craft when he *really* had a decent story nagging at him to put it on paper.

Not for the first time, her heart had been softening to this amazing man she had tried to be indifferent to. In truth, and deep inside, she had to admit it, he had had her from hello, and she knew it. Despite her feelings of guilt, being so close to the funeral and all, she found herself actually *wanting* him. It was too much to take. She stood, picking up her purse from the table.

'I'm sorry. I have to go home, Matt. Thank you for a great afternoon. Maybe we'll meet again.'

'Maybe we will,' he replied. She studied that *face* for what seemed like an eternity, before coming to, smiling, awkward as a blushing schoolgirl. She hurried out of the bar.

Matt smiled to himself, sardonically, and walked to the bar, inserting his finger in the air.

The blonde barmaid approached.

'Who's the new woman, Matty?' she asked.

He stared at the door, his eyes distant, as he bit his bottom lip for a second, replying.

'I...don't...know. But it sure would be nice to meet her again. I haven't had so much fun with a woman in years.'

The barmaid smiled, feeling sad for him, and left him deep in thoughts about Miss Karlie Kaylen – the woman he could never have.

・・・・●●●●・・・

IT HAD BEEN a long five weeks since she had first walked into Matt Thompson, and Karlie Kaylen was feeling like the tortured admirer of someone she couldn't have. Problem was – there was nothing stopping her, besides herself and her own inability to accept she could move on. She dried the last dish, and her hands before walking to the kettle. A mug of coffee would go down very nicely with the orange-chocolate profiteroles she had bought earlier. She hated to admit it but she had developed a nasty habit of not exercising, electing instead to consume junk food. Something had to give her pleasure in this life. The thought of Matt flashed across her mind but, once again, she felt the guilt come over her. She still loved her late husband but she had needs which had begun to resurface, triggered by her having met Matt.

Her body was crying out now, aching for that electrical charge of fingers touching the small of the back and working upwards...the scintillating feeling of light kisses on the nape of her exposed neck...the undeniable surge of near climax she received when her body was rattling against the gyrations of the man she loved. It had been a long time, now, and she was feeling like she wanted that intimacy again. But the memory of Mike was still very much omnipresent, and it was beginning to destabilise her. The fear of what he might think of her being around another man, much less after such a short time. At least, a short time to everyone *else* – forever for her. She stood, picking up her coffee, and walked to the rear porch, where the view was magnificent at sunset. The snow added an almost ethereal quality to the scene laid out before her, as she emerged from the house, making her way to the porch swing, and resting back into it. She looked up as a light shower of snow cascaded onto her shoulders, and she felt a stiff, Arctic breeze. She looked up as the dark clouds formed into large clusters. The distant thunder made its presence known, getting closer by the moment. At least the horses had been tended to, she thought. The stable door had been secured, and they would be asleep by now, anyway. She sat alone in the frozen darkness, and waited for the dreams to come.

The shutters were thumping against the window frame when she woke. Flashes of lightning lit her face as she looked around the room. Something wasn't right. Not entirely sure *what*, but there was something amiss, a light odour pervading the room. She lay back down on the bed, letting sleep prevail. She had been out for a bare ten minutes when the bedroom exploded with blinding white light. A figure stepped out of it, walking to the bed, as the light diminished behind him.

It was Michael David Kaylen, not quite 'in the flesh' *but near as, dammit!* she might have thought, had she been awake. He sat on the edge of the bed, looking sadly at his wife, allowing himself the luxury of some fleeting happy moments. He had little time, and he wasted no time. Mike leaned over to her ear, whispering for a few seconds, and kissed her lightly on the lips, barely perceptible but enough to be felt. He smiled. He stood, and returned to the pulsating light field from where he had came and, blowing a kiss, stepped into the light, vanishing forever. The light began to fade, eventually engulfing the room in darkness, punctuated by the fluorescent blue glow of moonlight.

She licked her lips as she slept. Her eyes opened wide and she sat bolt upright, her eyes darting left and right. Mike had been here, she had tasted him. Satisfied that he had gone, her head collapsed in her hands. She remembered his words, his voice, telling her it was "okay to move on. There's a man who loves you as I did. Go to him. I love you, baby," he had said. She looked at the alarm clock, which read FRI 7.15PM. There was still enough time if she left now. She prayed she would find him there – alone. It was a big risk to her psyche to put herself out like this, but she just hoped it would turn out alright. It was early on in the game, still. The pain would be easier than if she were further into life with someone new.. She hopped into a quick shower, straightened her long hair, and got dressed into jeans and a t-shirt before leaving the house. The car started first time out – a rare occasion, indeed – and she grinned from ear to ear. She tore off down the driveway.

'Please, God...let him feel the way I do,' she said, putting the car into third, the streetlights reflecting off the windshield.

············

MATT STOOD AT the bar, talking to a grizzled old man, who had been insistent in sharing his old war stories from 'Nam, but he hadn't minded. He ordered them both a drink, as he sat listening to how 'Charlie' had used whores as spies to pass on troop movements to their High Command in Hanoi, and how they had violated the Tet ceasefire with a brilliant execution of Sun Tzu's classic, *The Art of War*. So engrossed was he, that he failed to see it coming. A quick tap on the left shoulder, causing him to turn. He smiled widely, and stood to greet her. They spent the evening in the usual fun-filled fashion, and her joy was apparent. By the end of the night, she was exhilarated, intoxicated with life, and they danced together for the last time as friends. Matt took her to her car.

'Give me the keys. I'll take you home,' he said.

'What about your car?' she asked.

'It's fine where it is. We'll get you home safe, first, and you can call me a cab back here.'

'Sounds good to me,' she said.

*I hope you've parked your car someplace safe, guy – you won't be seeing it again, tonight.*

She got into the passenger side, and he pulled into the quiet street.

The drive was strangely silent, but they both had had a good deal to drink, and he obviously didn't want to be distracted while driving. He entered the driveway, relaxing somewhat. He had escaped the cops and made it to her place, unmolested by unwanted problems. He turned off the engine, and she got out, walking towards the porch steps. He followed a few seconds later, looking up at the ranch-house.. Two stories of log cabin, massive in dimension, at least in comparison with his apartment, a modest studio apartment on the outskirts of Memphis. This was another world to him. Wide open spaces, horses, the elevated view of the unspoiled countryside...everything he had dreamed of as a boy. It would take him at least ten years to be able to afford this lot. Being a 'horse boarder,' it must surely have paid for itself by now, he thought inwardly. His face betrayed his approval, as he turned to her.

'This is beautiful,' he said.

'*Babies* are beautiful. The Northern *lights* are beautiful. This...this is freakin' *awesome*!' she said, her hands gesticulating like an eccentric mad scientist. They laughed. He handed her the car keys.

'You want the VIP tour?' she asked, more sobered now.

'Might as well. I have to wait for the cab, and I don't care for the idea of waiting in the storm that's about to bless us with its presence.' He climbed the steps and she unlocked the door, turning the lights on as she entered. The moment the light was on, he gasped in disbelief. She had an original 50's Wurlitzer jukebox in the far right corner, an entire wall-length fixed book-shelf unit, crammed with books on every subject imaginable (judging from the sheer volume of books filling it). She closed the door.

'You want a nightcap?' she asked him.

'They don't suit me, thanks anyway,' he said.

'Funny, ain't ya,' she said. 'Heads up!' He caught the beer she tossed him, tapping the top to settle it. Waiting a few moments, he cracked the tab on it and took a gulp from it.

'Canadian Mist. How did you know?' he joked, dead pan.

'I always keep a few on reserve for family and friends dropping by,' she replied. 'That's the kinda gal I am,' she said, winking.

'Ok...where's your phone? The torture chamber in the storm cellar?' he quipped.

'And where do you imagine you're going?' she asked him, walking towards him seductively.

'Well, I... *could* change my plans,' he replied.

She reached out, bringing him closer to her, his face in her soft hands, looking him straight in the eyes.

'I'm in love with you, Matt. I know it sounds crazy, only having known you a short while, but I can't hold it in any more. Stay here with me. Tonight, and every night.'

Matt was stunned into silence. He couldn't believe she was expressing, *herself,* what he had been feeling these past few weeks.

'Ok-aaay,' he said. 'So, what do you suggest we do about it?' he asked. She handed him a drink she had poured for him.

'I know it's a bit soon, but how would you feel about moving in here? Have you got a lot of stuff to bring?' she asked.

'Got a few things, but most of it's in storage. I can bring what I really can't live without and leave the rest where it is. When did you have in mind, exactly?' She leaned in kissing him on the lips, hard.

'Tomorrow morning. Once the horses are fed, I'll drive you home and you grab what you wanna bring. I'll make room in the house for your stuff. There are no man caves, here,' she said. 'Now, get over here and whisper in my ear,' she purred.. He leaned into her as her arms enveloped him. His hands cupped her ample breasts as the kiss became deeper, and passion overcame them.

Tearing at each other's clothes, they were so engrossed that had they seen them, they would scarcely believe it. Two malevolent and ice-cold blue eyes were looking on, unforgiving and vengeful, surveilling the lustful carnage playing out on the sofa, Karlie's ecstatic moans grating his ears. He – this *Matt*, whoever the hell he was - was gonna have to be scared off. He looked on in disgust as their lovemaking became fiercer by the moment, unaware they were being watched.

They were in the throes of their love so intently, when the crash of a vase on the floor made them both disengage and look around. Exhausted, Karlie stood and wrapped her housecoat around her.

'*Fuck!*' she said, under her breath. 'To be continued, honey – don't you *dare* get dressed.' He laughed, his grin stretched wide across his face, as the beads of perspiration ran down his face, his hair all over his face, matted and dripping with sweat.

Karlie grabbed the brush pan and swept up the broken pieces.

'Valuable?' he asked.

'I don't think so, but I couldn't say for real. We got it as a third anniversary gift. Never did like it, but Mike wasn't too keen on it, either, to be honest. Still, was nice of them to give us it. College friends, y'know?' She dumped the pieces into the bin, and entered the kitchen, pouring another two glasses of wine, taking them to the staircase. Winking at him, she asked,

'Well? You're not too tired, are you?'

He grinned, his face reddening, as he rose from the sofa, following her.

It went on all night, both being finally spent as the sun began to rise. It was still fairly dark when they went out on the rear porch, sitting together on the swing set she and Mike had bought two summers ago. It was on the large side, easily accommodating two people, and she sat between his legs, a throw wrapped around her, her arms around him, cuddling in as he craned her head to face him, as he leaned down to meet her bruised, dark lips, lightly kissing them. She was happy again.

She prayed silently to herself that this would last forever, or at least until she was taken first. She couldn't deal with losing another man again. As they watched the sun rise, thoughts of eternity crossed her mind.

••••••••••

MATT WOKE UP in the huge double bed and wondered how he had gotten there. Last thing he remembered was the two of them lying blissfully in the porch swing. Karlie came in with a tray, filled with toast, bacon sandwiches, and coffee. He sat up, and she placed the tray on his lap.

'Breakfast in bed, huh? Wow! You must *really* like me!' he quipped.

She leaned over him, smiling, her eyes sparkling. He didn't have a *clue* just how much she loved him. *Like* didn't enter into it. She kissed him full on the lips, but softly, careful not to spill the coffee.

'Eat your breakfast. I've got to go feed the barn nags,' she joked.

He took a sip of the coffee.

'This is amazing coffee! What is it?' he asked.

'Mike always used to moan about my freeze-dried tasters-choice crap. He'd say, "When I drink it, I wanna *enjoy* it," so I found this stuff and he loved it. Been buyin' it ever since. Glad you like it, though. It'll save me changin' brands. Ok, enjoy. I'll be back in a flash,' she said, putting on her parka. He watched her walk out of the bedroom, hearing her feet thumping as she repelled down the stairs. He looked down at the plate and began eating. It was the best breakfast he'd had in years.

Because real love and care had been invested in its creation.

For *him* alone.

・・・・●●●・・・

MATT'S CAR PULLED into the driveway and made its way to the farm house. It had been two months, already, since he had taken up residence, and things had been amazingly good. He looked around him. The horses were grazing in the slowly melting snow, the grass underneath it more exposed by the elements. He removed the bag from the passenger seat, and locked up the car, walking to the door. Karlie ran out of the door, running to him, embracing him tightly and planted a firm kiss on his lips, linking arms with him as she led him to the warmth of the house.

'How was your day?' she asked. He smiled, and handed her the bag.

'What's this?' she asked.

'Whyn't you open it and see?' he replied.

She opened the bag and pulled out a number of designer tops and outfits. She gasped. They were expensive from what she could see. She walked to him.

'I can't have my woman walking around with nothing to wear, now can I?' he said.

'I *am* your woman. And always will be, as long as you want me,' she said, hugging him tightly, cradling her head in his breastbone. She released him, kissing his cheek.

'Come on. Dinner's already done. It just needs dishin' out.' She took him by the hand, and they walked to the kitchen, where it was low-light with a beautiful red tablecloth, matching serviettes and two candles, lit. She had obviously gone to a lot of trouble. And it made him feel even closer to her. It couldn't get much better, he thought. Except maybe cementing their love with a child at some point. But that would have to wait, he thought. It was too soon after her husband's funeral for him to be bringing that up. That would come in due course, or she might propose such a thing on her own. He was open to it, having never found anyone he wanted to risk raising a child with.

He sat down, removing his coat, hanging it around the back of the chair, as Karlie approached, serving him his plate, and a magnum of Bollinger RD champagne. He loved it when he saw her plate was as stacked as his was.

Usually, the women were salad junkies, and they spoiled their men with enough food to last a month. But not this time. Her plate was crammed with roast chicken, potatoes and vegetables, as his was. He smiled as they enjoyed the meal, eating heartily and chatting about their day apart. He popped the cork, and poured some of the champagne into her flute, then his own. He could barely stand taking his eyes off her. When she had returned from the bathroom after his arrival, she had emerged a transformed woman. Glowing, radiant and delicious to the core. She had changed into a long, Chinese-style dress, barely exposing her neckline, but the opening beneath the top button, showed off her heaving bosom and he was transfixed by its fit. It hugged her form perfectly, not too skinny, but curvaceous enough to please him more than she could imagine. She registered his expression, and it filled her with joy that she had achieved her goal – to stun him into submission. They finished off the meal and she picked up both plates, taking them to the bin, scraping off the remains before putting them into the sink. He watched her as she bent to put them in, and he felt glad to be a man – especially *hers*.

In all the years of dating neurotic losers and psycho bitches, he had been blessed with a woman who made him feel he was worth such extra effort. She brought in dessert – *schwarzwaldenkirschtorte* or, as it was better known, Black Forest cake.

'I've loved this cake since I was a kid,' she said.

'The trifle based on it's a close second, though,' she continued.

'While you're enjoying that, there's one little thing I have to tell you before we move on. I have to know what your feelings are about kids. It has to be discussed, so I figure it's better getting it out of the way, now. How do you feel about having kids?' she ventured, tentative and braced.

His heart exploded in his chest. She had just opened the door for him. He had wanted kids with the right woman, but had never found one who had been 'mommy material.'

'Are you serious?' Matt asked her, his face stunned.

*Ooooh, SHIT!* She thought, her heart deflated. *I've scared the poor bastard off already.* But she wasn't prepared for what came next.

'I wouldn't be asking you if I wasn't,' she replied, watching him intently. This could be the end of a beautiful beginning, and she prayed it would go well. He put his serviette to his lips, wiping the excess cake from his mouth.

Without breaking his stride, he leaned over to her, looked deep in her eyes, his gaze unwavering.

'Exactly *when* would you like to begin?' He kissed her full on the mouth and retracted, sitting back in his chair, smiling. Her heart was out of her body. She couldn't believe his response, thinking she had heard wrongly.

'You're...you're okay with having a kid someday?' she asked him, nervously. It was no mean feat asking a man to commit himself to such a profound responsibility. So many men would be out of there so fast that the woman's head would be blinded by the dust from his departure.

'Ready when you are!' he said, smiling widely.

She handed him an envelope, bracing herself again. It was now or never. He opened it, wondering what was in it, as she watched intently.

He pulled the object out of the envelope. It was a pregnancy test strip.

With two clearly stated blue parallel lines, thick and undeniable.

His heart jolted like a jumper cable.

'Is this for *real*?' he asked, almost unbelieving. She nodded, her eyes filling with tears of joy.

*He's really up for this!* she kept telling herself.

'The doctor confirmed it this afternoon. That's the first one it came out on, the rest are in the basket on the counter. Four of 'em. All blue. You're gonna be a daddy!' He stood up, followed by her, and he held her in his arms, both of them looking into each other's eyes, unable to contain their joy. At that moment, she felt more alive than she ever had.

At the same time as she had that last thought, a high wind appeared from nowhere.

··········

THEY LAY IN bed together, naked and unfettered, sleeping soundly. A loud crash came from downstairs, making them sit bolt upright. Matt stood, grabbing a heavy glass paperweight, as Karlie got up, slipping on her bathrobe, following slowly behind. He crept down the staircase, hand moving down the rail, as he looked around the room. His hand reached for the lights, and clicked the switch. The lounge was normal. He relaxed a little, walking easier, as he moved towards the kitchen. Nothing was out of place. Anywhere.

He made a move towards the staircase when a dark shadow flew across the room. He caught it out of the corner of his eye just before it slammed into his sweat-matted chest, propelling back against the wall, knocking him unconscious. Footsteps creaked on the bedroom above as a gowned and frantic Karlie came running downstairs, stopping halfway down, her hands on the rail. A loud, eerie wail filled the room. It was like numerous voices filtered through a voice processor but it was mistakenly that of her late husband, Mike.

And he did *not* sound happy.

'*YOU CAN'T KEEP HER!! I AM NOT YET DEAD!!*'

Karlie's hand flew to her mouth, a flood of confused emotions traversing every nerve ending in her body.

He had come back before in her dreams, saying it was okay to move on. Why the change of heart?, she asked herself, as a wash of posthumous regret came over her.

The lightbulb in the lounge begin to gradually dim higher until the bulb shattered spraying glass, like shrapnel, across the room. Karlie wanted to tend to Matt, now coming out of his little snooze and rubbing the small if his back, groaning in severe pain, but she was rendered immobile. Without warning, a harsh white light bathed the room and both of them covered their eyes. The farmhouse began to shake violently as if a magnitude 9 quake had just begun. The cupboard doors flew open, the windows imploded in showers of frosted glass particles which rained on the carpet, and the grandfather clock which had been in the family for generations was chiming like the end of time was nigh. Then silence.

The light circulated inwards on itself, swirling in both directions until it was gone. She ran to Matt who was, by this time, covered in glass. She carefully picked the pieces out, and held him close, her petrified eyes darting around, as he comforted the man who had given her so much love barely ten minutes before. It was over, now.

They had a lot of cleaning to do in the morning. She stood, helping Matt to his feet, and guiding him to the staircase. Together, they made it to the upper hallway and into the bedroom, where she tucked him in, lying on top of the duvet besides him, gently tickling his face with her finger until he fell asleep again. She lay there for a further hour, until her exhaustion claimed her.

· · · · · · · · · ·

# OUT OF THE ASHES

SHE AWOKE THE following morning to an empty bed, and got up to take a shower. His coat and wallet had gone from the bedside cabinet. She felt sure he'd booked out of there, and who could blame the guy she thought, as she rinsed her hair. It was one thing to have to deal with an ex-husband or boyfriend, and all the crap that implied for the 'new man' in any relationship. But to expect him to deal with a dead one was a touch much. She grabbed a towel and wrapped it around her as she walked to the bedroom. It was over for sure. It was nice while it lasted. The door closed after her.

··········

MATT SAT ON the wooden porch swing looking out at the dead, winter landscape, hung forward, his hands clasped together as if in prayer. Karlie walked out into the porch and lit a cigarette. She hadn't had one in ages, but felt she needed something to relax her.

'Those things'll kill you, you know,' he said, in reasonably good Southern accent.

Karlie dropped the cigarette, realising then that the porch was wooden, and stubbed it out. She turned to see who it was, thinking it was the mailman. When she saw Matt sitting there, her heart jumped and she ran to him, almost knocking him over.

'You thought I'd booked, didn't you,' he said with a grin.

'I could hardly blame you if you had, after last night. I had no idea Mike would feel so strongly about it. Well, not enough to do all that, anyway. You're gonna I'm nuts but he came to me in a dream, sayin' it was okay for me to find someone. He *told* me that you were the one. Why else would I have come to see you that night at the bar? Maybe he had a change of heart, or somethin.' I'm so sorry, Matt,' said with profuse sadness. 'I thought you'd left when I saw your keys and wallet gone.'

'What kind of guy would I be if I *did*? I told you last night I was in for the duration, and I meant it. So...! What do we do *now*, Mrs Kaylen?'

She knew what she wanted, and his continued presence made it possible. She took his hand, pulling him towards the screen door, and opened it, pulling him inside. Her back, obscured by the warped glass of the door, was pressed up against it, her gown falling to the doormat, while his palms resting firmly on the glass section. They collapsed together as one, and spent the next ten full minutes getting to know each other on a deeper level.

·················

THE HOUSE WAS colder than usual, and it wasn't lost on Karlie. Matt had stepped into the shower, and she was sitting at the kitchen breakfast bar nursing a mug of coffee. The events of the previous night had shaken her, and she had spent the entire day feeling confused as to why Mike was so pissed at her that he would come back to her with such malice. He had always claimed that he would be fine with her finding someone should he depart this world, although she had always sworn it off as not being an option. And she had meant it. But time does things to us, and love rears it's hindquarters just enough to let another in there. She was beginning to truly love Matt at a level almost equal to the love she had shared with Mike; with time, maybe even more. She lay in his arms, both of them gently swinging to and fro as they stared idly out at the snow-covered fields, listening to the rain's rhythm tapping on the porch ledge above, lost in time.

# OUT OF THE ASHES

THEY PULLED UP outside the ranch house, knowing something was out of sorts. The house was dark and foreboding, radiating a surge of something she could only surmise to be malevolent.. The heavy rumbling of thunder in the near distance was of little comfort to her, itself a sign that bad things were on their way. They emptied the trunk, carrying the groceries inside the house. Matt walked back down the steps and closed the trunk, setting the alarm. He walked towards the house and stopped dead, pausing for what felt to be an eternity, and turned to face his suspicion. His breath clogged in his chest as he beheld the monstrosity in the clouds above. They had taken the form of a giant grey face, it's eyes deep, cavernous wells. The mouth which looked not unlike a jack o'lantern, with its short, stumpy teeth, was grinning at him with maniacal defiance. Matt backed up slowly, his eyes never leaving it, petrified inside. This was something *else*, he thought. He had never bought all that spiritualist crap, ghosts and shit, but what he had seen the night before had had radical impact on his belief system.

He *believed* now. There was nothing to challenge your ideals and perception of the universe than witnessing the elemental forces at work. But *this*?

*This* was some other kind of force – a dry charge that hung suspended in the air like a malign storage battery, the faint whiff of sulphur being almost tangible in the atmosphere around him. He turned and strode to the open door, beside which a frightened Karlie stood, her head hugging the wood, her eyes wary. Matt ushered her inside gently, and closed the door.

*Just an atmospheric anomaly, nothing more*, he mused to himself. The key turned in the lock, the sound echoing in the stillness of the night.

Above them, something was stirring...accumulating...as the cloud bank converged over the ranch house, the faint rumbling of thunder increasing with an exponential potency.

It was *time*.

・・・●●●●・・・

KARLIE WOKE WITH a start, her eyes rolling up like window shutters, wide and aware. She was not alone. Matt lay sleeping next to her, spent after their love-making marathon. She regarded him with loving, kind eyes, but there was something more there. A slight trace of reluctance to remain with Matt after the debacle of the previous encounters had began to creep into her mind.. She could have had no idea that Mike – and she truly believed it *was* – would unleash his dissatisfaction like that, and she had borne a sneaking suspicion that there would be more to follow, if not worse.

She put on her robe, tying it, for some unknown reason feeling a reticence to being exposed she hadn't felt since she and Matt had started up. She leaned over and kissed him lightly on the forehead, exiting the room. She needed some brandy to ease her. The kitchen light turned on and Karlie entered, taking a mug off the wooden tree in the corner of the counter, and retrieved the brandy from the fridge.

She walked to the lounge and, as she went, knocked a box of Matt's as-yet-unpacked belongings. Down one side was the dusty spine of a leather bound journal. She dusted it off to see the year 1871 on it.

She hesitated for what seemed an eternity. It was Matt's personal things. She had no right to intrude, but it was just too intriguing to turn down. She opened the cover with tentative care, and started reading. Half an hour had passed and, besides a few risqué entries scattered thus far, she had deemed it to be the errant ramblings of the unhinged. Then it caught her eye – the diamond in the rough. Hitchcock's famed 'MacGuffin.' It horrified her to discover that someone back then, with Matt's surname, had committed a heinous physical attack upon his wife in late 1871, the severity of the attack (caused by "aggravated, mitigating circumstances," resulting in him being committed to Ocean Vale, a revolutionary new (then, at least) Psychiatric Institution, now a festering shadow of its former gothic eminence.

She slowly closed the book, closing her eyes, as a million thoughts raced through her scattered mind.

*He knew*, Karlie thought. *Mike knew. That's why he was so fucking pissed! He thinks that Matt's gonna do the same thing. Holy Mother-a Mary!*

She replaced the book exactly as she had found it, and sat back in the couch, debating whether to tell Matt about Mike. He deserved to know but she knew that, in her telling him, she would reveal that she had invaded his privacy. It was a catch 22. He might not give a shit, but then he *might*. She bit her bottom lip, deciding to come clean. Their relationship had been borne of truth, and there, it must remain. She got up, walked to the staircase, and turned off the light. As he reached the upper landing, she walked to the bedroom where she found Matt sleeping soundly. He looked so cute, like a sleeping lamb. She decided not to awaken him. She had a serious heart-to-heart to attend to. With that, she left the bedroom, closing the door behind her. As she walked back to the staircase, running her hand along the bannister, her eyes never left the darkness beneath her, the staircase vanishing into the void below, wondering what was waiting for her. She placed one cautious step after another until she, herself, was consumed by it.

She felt her way to the lounge, sitting on the floor, and began to speak softly.

'Mike? Mike, honey, can you hear me?'

Silence.

'Mike, come to me...*please*!!'

A shrieking scream came from the other side, imploding the newly-replaced windows, as Karlie held her ears amidst a rain shower of plate glass shards. A harsh, bright, white light filled the lounge as a distorted voice boomed in anger and frustration.

'*LEAVE HIM BE! YOU WILL ONLY LEARN PAIN BY REMAINING HIS. GET...HIM...*OUT!!!'

Karlie had never had been given any reason to distrust Mike in life, why would she have one in the aftermath of his death.

'Mike, *please*, honey...if only you knew him like I do. He's as close to you as a husband as I could ever hope to find. I didn't go looking to find a replacement, because you'll never *be* replaced, baby. I want your blessing, Michael. I'm having his baby and I love him as much as I loved *you*!! Leave us in peace...please. I never stopped loving you, and I never will. But I love Matt the same way I loved you all those years. He deserves the chance to prove he's different. Please say you'll let him try. For *ME!!*'

The silence was deafening as she waited in fear for his response.

The white light began to fade a little, then gradually more. She felt a light brush of lips on her forehead before it vanished completely. The light turned on and Matt ran to her, bringing her to her feet. He looked around at the shattered window frame, and then around the room. He turned back to her.

'I take it you had a visitor. Are you alright?' he asked in his usual tender manner.

'It's over. I think...I think it's over. Mike's gone for good. We can move on, now!'

Matt held her as she sobbed openly in his arms, listening to her wails of heartache. It was time to put it all behind them and look forward.

The sun began to creep over the hills but he couldn't care less. He was there in body and soul with her.

The way it always *should* be.

# A RIDE TO REMEMBER

'*CAN IT NOW!* Carole yelled over her shoulder. Quieter, under her breath, she continued,

'At least till we get there.'

It had been a long drive, and she was shattered. The girls in the back - her daughters - were acting up again.

*Can't blame 'em, really*, she thought. *Maine's a long way off*, and it was way too far in to turn back home to Sidewinder. They had cooled off a bit now and were immersed in their iPad. One twelve, the other six, she hated herself for letting them this close to the outside world. That crap was for adults.

"Too many predators online these days" would be her excuse, and she would be right, too. You had those 'to catch a predator' tv shows on re-run, and it had scared the shit out of them. That was before the divorce she instigated, citing "irreconcilable differences".

"Fuckin' around with the bitch ass blonde next door," she had retorted. Or at least that's what she had began to suspect. The rain was battering on the roof, cascading down the windshield only to be spread over it by the wipers.

A light came into view, and she heaved a sigh of relief. As she took the right exit into the parking lot, the welcome sight of the Golden Arches lit the interior of the car.

She pulled up in front and turned to face the girls.

'Momma's gonna go get some chow. Sit here quiet, and don't move. I'll be a coupla minutes, tops. I'm locking the door so you should be fine.'

The girls nodded, still immersed in their phones. She got out the car and found the rain had stopped. She looked around and made sure no-one saw her, then activated the car alarm. The girls looked up, watching her walk to the entrance. Returning to their own world, they zoned out again.

··········

SOMETHING WAS WRONG out there, she thought as she stood inside watching the car intently. She could see no movement inside it, just two motionless forms.

*They're good girls*, she thought to herself. The server called her, and she walked over to the counter, taking her order.

Smiling, she took it and walked briskly to the door where a young man held the door for her. Shyly, she smiled at him in thanks. His good looks weren't wasted on her.

*Shit! If I were ten years younger, you wouldn't have a prayer!* she mused. She began to laugh inwardly as she walked to the car. Pushing the car alarm, she opened the door, put the bag on the passenger seat, and returned to full height.

She stiffened, her face pale, as a low, guttural voice spoke from her waist.

'They die if you make a sound. Gimme the keys right now!'

Terrified, she handed them over. He stood up quickly and walked around to the other side.

'Get in,' he said, and she complied. He got in and closed the door. He handed her the keys.

'Drive.'

Trying to remain calm for the girl's sake, her high pitched, hoarse voice squeaked.

'Where to?'

He looked in the right-hand side wing mirror, distantly answering her.

'Just get us outta here, lady. Head for I-95, and I'll tell you what from there.' She pulled out into traffic, the journey into her nightmare about to begin…

··········

THE RAIN HAD been hammering against the car for the last half hour, and the silence had been excruciating. She could see he was looking absently out of the side window. He was looking at her via reflection but she wouldn't know that. She reached under her seat, fumbling around, trying not to attract his attention. He turned to face her, opening his jacket. He flashed her own pistol at her, a .38 Smith & Wesson, snub-nosed.

He glared at her, impassive and distant, his eyes vacant rooms. He spoke, his voice calm yet cold, droning.

'This what you're lookin' for?' he asked.

She looked away, biting her lip, waiting for his next move.

Instead, he closed his jacket, returning his steely, frozen eyes toward the passing traffic.

'Take the next exit. There's a 7/11 just after it,' he instructed. She saw the off ramp, taking the lane leading to it.

Carole Hardin was not, by any stretch, a stupid woman. She had graduated in the top 2% of her class and had achieved a lot since then. But that had all changed when her firstborn had come along. She had found herself married to her boyfriend, and it had been good for the first two years, sliding off after that.

*What the hell*, she had conceded ever since. You *weren't the grand prize, either!'*

Now, where was she? Heading east for two thousand-plus miles let her girls see the father she had cut out of the picture out of sheer petulance.

The lights of the 7/11 forecourt appeared, and she pulled in.

'Park it over there,' he instructed. She drove the car into the vacant spot at the far end of the lot and turned off the engine. He turned to her, head on.

'Alright, here's what's happenin'. The munchkin's comin' to the store wit' me. It's major league snack time. My treat. One warning, only. Anything goes down, she dies first,' he said, indicating the youngest daughter, Hallie (her sister, Samantha, had just 12 a few months before).

'You want anything?' he asked. She stared at him, choked and unable to vocalise much of a reply.

'I'll get you somethin' for the trip. Let's go, sweet stuff!'

Hallie looked at her mother, unsure of what she should do. Carole hated it but forced the words out.

'It's ok, Hallie. Be happy when you go in there, okay?'

Hallie nodded and opened the rear door, getting out. The creep opened his door, stepping onto the concrete. He took her hand and walked to the entrance. Hallie looked back at the car. Her mother and Samantha were watching, fearing for her. Half-relieved, Carole heaved a sigh and watched as he entered the gas station with her. At least he hadn't disappeared with her, she thought. Having said that, she thought, he could easily sneak out of there with her daughter without them seeing them.

The following ten minutes were absolute torture for Carole, lifting her cellphone to her eye-line so that she wouldn't miss anything by looking down at it.

Movement caught Samantha's eye and she shook her mother's right shoulder. Carole whipped her eyes up to him. The image would remain with her forever.

He was walking toward the car, smiling (a nice smile, too, she thought despite herself), a large bag of snack food in one hand and Hallie wrapped around his neck, laughing happily. Her heart skipped a beat as she looked on, the sight of her potential rapist bonding with her own daughter. It wasn't as far-fetched as she thought, as they had no inkling of his eventual intentions once she had taken him where he wished to go. She had to accept that it was a contentious possibility. It could well be only a matter of time before he...

She shook the image from her mind as he opened the rear door, letting Hallie get in with Samantha, handing her the bag before closing the door, walking around to the passenger side, resining his seat. He handed her the keys and gestured the exit. The engine turned over, and the car pulled out of the forecourt, headed out to the interstate and I-95, Maine-bound.

・・・・●●●・・・

THEY HAD TAKEN the wrong turning and ended up on a deserted country road. His agitation was rising, but he kept it in check for the kids' sake.

Samantha looked in the rearview mirror and saw a glint of movement. But there was no headlights on if it even *was* a car behind. A thought occurred to her. Biting her lip, she finished her banana, rolling down her window. Feeling the sudden blast of cold, damp air, he turned, staring at her with those lifeless eyes again.

'What? I want some fresh air, alright!'

He turned to face the road, and with a deft move, her eyes on the jerk the whole time, she flicked the banana skin out over her head.

She *prayed* it was what she believed it to be.

Seconds later, the car was lit up by the red, white and blue lights of a Sheriff's Department squad unit, its siren piercing and *loud*.

The creep didn't budge an inch as she had expected, having heard the cops. Carole almost cried with the release of it.

'What do you want me to do, now?' she enquired. He didn't seem to care about getting caught.

'Pull over,' he purred.

She pulled the car over and rolled down the window. He watched the Sheriff get out of his car, followed by his deputy, Norm, and put the gun under the seat, ready for use. The Sheriff arrived at the window and tapped it. Carole rolled it down.

'Was I speeding, Officer?

'No, ma'am,' he said.

'What did I do?' she asked him.

'We were on our way to the all-night deli when all of a sudden, this falls outta the sky,' he said, sternly. He held up Samantha's errant banana skin in the air with two fingers.

'We don't cotton to litterbugs in these heah parts, ma'am! Y'all step out the cah, now, y'heah? You and your kids can talk to my associate heah, and I'll talk to yo' husband for a few ticks. Go on, now.'

The creep didn't move an inch. He had a gut feeling it was the end of the road.

*Let's just see what happens* he mused to himself. *Maybe – just maybe the old timer would just give her a ticket or a warning or whatever.*

As soon as the kids and Carole had been safety deposited in the rear of the squad unit, Norm returned to the Sheriff's side.

'Y'all mind showin' me yo licence and registration fo' second,' he asked, thinly smiling a humouring smile.

'You'll have to ask the lady. She's got the papers in her purse. She's just givin' me a ride to Lewiston.'

Wade Miller had been a lawman for the last thirty years, from as far out as Texas and the Florida swamps, and a few places in between. He knew bullshit when he heard it and looked at Norm. It was a code between them, a silent order. Norm pulled his gun out quickly, as the Sheriff stood back.

'Get yo' ass out of the cah, buttercheeks!'

The creep got out of the car, standing in front of the open door, blocking it. Miller proceeded cautiously. This was a slippery little sum'bitch. He frisked the stranger down, standing back as he spun him around to face him.

'Listen hahd, son...we gonna be takin' y'all down the station house to take a lil' pop quiz. In the meantime, I'm arrestin' you under suspicion of abduction. We'll come up with more after we sort this hoss-shit out.'

He made a grab at Miller's holster, and Norm shot him twice in the chest. He slid down the rear passenger door, holding his wounds, his eyes incredulous. He collapsed in a heap at Norm's feet. The Sheriff motioned for Norm to return to the kids and Carole. He walked away, and Miller took a good, hard stare at the stranger. Almost sneering, he turned and headed for his car.

He was five feet from the squad car when Carole stood up, her face panicked, screamed out.

'*NOOO!*'

The Sheriff saw Norm pulling his gun out. He cursed under his breath, turning on a dime (despite his proud South-Western gut) to see the once-dead stranger bearing down on him, gun pointed.

Without hesitation, the adrenaline rushed through him, as he put five shots, perfectly grouped, into the crazy asshole and the last one hit home, point blank between his eyes. Miller walked over to the corpse, checked the neck pulse. He was gone. There could be no mistaking that. He walked to his car, talking to Norm.

'Get on the wire. Get sum'body get ovah heah to clean this shit up. I'll wait heah while you take care of *them*. Case closed. Get Wally to come ovah, quick. I'm gonna need a ride back to the station house. I gotta block this end of the road – you get them roadblock signs on the junct'yin at the other side. You kin do that on yo' way back. Now, g'on, git! Make them calls, heah me?'

Norm pulled away into the night, the cold, destroyed shell of the creep lying empty on the deserted highway. The meat-wagon would be on its way presently. He popped some chewing tobacco in his mouth, then spat a stream of it at the creep's corpse.

'Aaw, shoot! I missed; you dumb sum'bitch!'

He sat on a wooden log, taking his hat off, rubbing his bald patch. It was over – finally.

# SCREENSHOT

THE LIGHT ABOVE flared down on him as he studied his options carefully. The women in front of him were all beautiful - some in a plain, girl next door type; some with looks to compare with the goddess Aphrodite. He didn't care. He got off on the idea of the fear he was about to spread, just like he had done before a year earlier. He printed off the pictures from his phone and pasted the eight-by-tens into the top of each page, followed by their bios, taken by screenshot and printed. Soon, this book would be filled, a narcissistic scrapbook from whence Hell would follow. He was smart. Too smart, he reasoned, for his own good. The last scrapbook culled from the unsuspecting 'friend suggestions' sections on Facebook had yielded horrendous returns. He had tracked the women to where they lived, watched their daily patterns for a month each, and then once their husbands had left for work, and the women left to go shopping, he would follow them in his car. He was in no way creepy, as women might say these days. He was short, at five-seven, but handsome in a dark way, a way that most women couldn't do anything but imagine themselves being alone with. He set off - unknowingly to him - electrical signals that drove them nuts as they passed him. He possessed a kind of confidence that was undeniable, although he did nothing to project it. As if he was oblivious to it, himself. He printed off the last bio, sticking it to the scrapbook under the screenshot photo of the woman concerned. He closed the book, smiling inwardly, his eyes glazed, and sipped at the steaming coffee made only moments earlier. A million thoughts traversed his mind - all of them being various methods of dispatch for the lead female roles in his so-called 'casting directory.'

It was time to sow the harvest, he thought. His eyes glistened, intent and malice-ridden, and a cold, wide, closed smile stretched from ear to ear.

∙∙∙∙●∙●∙∙∙

MAGGIE THORNTON STOOD silently at the bus stop, waiting for her ride to appear. Her husband, Jay, was going to be a little later than stated, and she was instructed to stand in public to offer her some security, and safety in numbers.

'It's a dangerous world, after all', her husband always told her, 'and you can never tell when some sex trafficker will transport you into a white van, turn you into a drug-addled prostitute, and pimp you out at leisure.' She knew he was right from the news reports she heard on a weekly basis. It doesn't take a second for these animals to sneak up behind someone in a van with fake plates, slide the door open slowly as it's creeping alongside, and two men to launch out of the vehicle and grab you, descending you into a hell where all manner of low-lives take turns to stick it to you on a nightly basis. She stood waiting, this very thought making her shiver, as she looked at her watch. Her phone rang and she yelled into it.

'Where the fuck are you?!'

He told her to "walk around the corner, that he was only five minutes off."

'Just hurry the fuck up, will ya?!' She stormed off and headed around to the rear of the large McDonalds behind them. She had barely turned the corner when a fist crashed into her jaw, knocking her out cold. The man who stood over her picked her up and carried her quickly to a small white van, slamming the door shut. He got into the driver's seat and, gunning the engine, got the hell out of Dodge. Her husband's large white electricians van passed the smaller one, pulling left into the car lot behind the restaurant, and his own impending nightmare. The small van had disappeared from view.

··········

HE HAD STRAPPED her into the chair; so tightly she could barely breathe. It was pitch black, but she could hear the grating sound of knives being sharpened, metal on metal. The sound went through her, as she tried to wriggle her way out, or at least loosen it a little. But it was no good. It was so dark in there that when his face loomed into view, under the light of a flashlight, her heart stopped in terror. That maniacal, wide grin; that foul, tobacco-burnt breath assaulting her; the black, emotionless, dead eyes boring into her like Rasputin. He plunged her into darkness once more. She found her heart thumping in anticipation at her fate. What was his intention...rape? Torture? Some sick S&M crap? Hard to say at that moment, but she tried to compose herself enough to ask him a question.

'Why am I here?'

The voice that emerged was low and polite, even. This terrified her even more. She had hoped that she could reason with a screamer, a 'Jamie Gumb' nut. Maggie swallowed hard. She knew she was fucked - perhaps, quite literally. She took a deep breath, closed her eyes, and awaited whatever he threw her way, resigning herself to her fate. At least till she could find a way out of there.

··········

JAY THORNTON PACED the car lot around the corner where Maggie had arranged to meet him. Fifteen minutes had passed and still no sign of her. He cursed loudly enough that two elderly passers by scowled at him. He didn't care. The only thing he cared about at this moment was the fact that his beloved wife was taking her sweet time getting to him, especially since she was only, apparently, round the corner. He had put his foot down for the last mile to reach her after his last call. She sounded like she was scared, and he had risked a speeding ticket to get there. Thankfully, no cops had been in sight, and he had gotten there in record time - but not time enough to save her from the fate she had now found herself in. A fate he could only surmise.

Had he known his wife of two years was strapped to a table in a basement a bare twenty miles away, he would have freaked out in panic. He was getting to that point but not quite yet. That would come soon enough. He looked around and walked to the garbage skip. His nose was assaulted by a familiar perfume as grew closer to it. His suspicions began to take root as realisation dawned - that was Maggie's favourite scent. The adrenaline rose in him, racing through his veins as, frantically, he scoured the area and found tire tracks ending at the left of the skip. He could make out some heels next to the tire marks. That could mean only one thing. His baby had been hiding from someone until he arrived and that someone had snatched her into the back of car, or a van, maybe. Fear took over and he fumbled for his cellphone.

·········

'WHAT DO YOU want from me?!' Maggie screamed, as he sat calmly on a nearby cracked, black leather couch, staring at her intently, laughing to himself.

He could see she was freaked out and he liked it. A lot. This was the aim. He had no interest in sexual things - he got off on the terror aspects of it, scaring the bejeezus out of them before killing them; sometimes fast, sometimes he enjoyed taking his time. They were out in the sticks in a big house. For this kind of shit, you needed privacy, something you'd never hope to get in an apartment. You needed the space, the fifty metres or more between houses - or more was even better, to do such things without the cops being called by concerned neighbours. He finished his beer, and crushed it in his hand, tossing it into the large basketball net suspended over the trash basket, burping loudly.

He stood, and walked to her, unbuckling his jeans, slowly and intently so. This had always been a large part of his method. It scared the crap out of the women who were fully expecting to be violated. But he only went as far as, ripping their clothes off, pretending to be an insane sex creep fully prepared to go the full way. He never actually handled them anywhere that was of that nature. Only the shoulders.

He didn't want to add to the charges should he be captured, but he has no real desire to go that far, anyway. Instead, he teased them by withdrawing himself at the crucial stage, giving them a little relief but, then turning back to them, saying, 'It ain't quite time, yet. That'll come soon enough, don't you worry about that, baby!'

He would then leave them in darkness and lock the door behind him. That was part of it, too. He had no intention of taking it that far, and never would. That wasn't the object. His plan was simply to scare the fuck out of them, terrorise them to make them change their immoral ways and become the 'good little girls' they had once been.

He looked at it as if he were restoring them to God fully cleansed of mind. Leaving them alive was not an option, and he knew it. They all had to die. Why leave a living witness to finger him? It would be as dumb as maggot-shit to allow one to walk out that door alive.

His motives were simple enough. No ransom, no sexual fulfilment - just the mission to cleanse the women who pursued him or responded to him on Facebook, betraying their partners or husbands by engaging in flirting, sexting (as they called it these days), and meeting up if the location was right. He felt that God had asked him to clean up Facebook and cleanse these women of their adulterous, sinful mindsets. He was only too happy to oblige.

But this one was different. As he had approached her, his belt loose around his waist, the look in her eyes made him feel something he had never encountered. He couldn't place it, although he felt... something. A calming influence of some kind. Her eyes were bright green, lighting up her entire face, bringing it to life. Maggie was by no means the most attractive woman so far, but she possessed a quality he found rare in today's women. An old-fashioned quality that seemed to be lost in the mists of humanity. He began to feel a protective urge towards her, something he had never yet had to contend with.

He didn't want to harm one hair on her head. He wanted her, but he knew she would never want him after all this, not to mention the little fact that she was married. His Facebook profiles showed another man in his photo gallery, so no-one would never identify him easily. Besides, he burnt their cellphones and all evidence of them having been anywhere near him or his house. No prints, no fibres. That was the rules. That was the problem the network planners never took into consideration - the shows like CSI gave people like him (and much worse! he thought) the knowledge of how the system works and how to avoid capture.

He lay back on the couch, staring at the ceiling, wondering what the fuck he was gonna do, now!

············

IT WAS A goddamned circus. The cops were all over the car lot and the lab rats were combing the skip and the area around it for signs of a potential lead. The officer in charge, Sergeant Nate Cook, stood staring absently at the street before him, smoking a cigarette. It was going to be one of those fucking days! The lead lab technician strode up to him.

'Nothing. No prints, no threads. Nada. Zilch. All we got is a pair of dragged heel prints and tire marks belonging to a small van. Michelin tyres according to the treads. But beyond that, just another van out of thousands in this city with the same tires. Like looking for a virgin in a maternity ward.'

Cook laughed at the euphemism. He had a dark sense of humor.

'Shit. Okay, thanks, Terry.'

'What's the plan, now?' Terry asked.

'Christ only knows. Guess I'll get all I can from the husband and check her phone records for unusual calls. Not much else I can do until something better shows it's face.'

Terry slapped Cook on the back, and walked off towards the van he came in. Cook flicked the cigarette butt out beyond the crime scene. He couldn't risk contaminating the area.. He heaved a heavy sigh of resignation, and walked towards the shocked, and very frantic, Jay.

## OUT OF THE ASHES

••••••••••

WITH MAGGIE CONFINED and heavily sedated in the basement at home, he sat in the white van, parked across from the Tavares nightclub, waiting for his next victim to emerge. It took half an hour for Miss Rachael Mulheeny to show her inebriated face, complete with a young man, both of them laughing and staggering along the street.

He started the engine, and followed behind them, far back enough not to be spotted. It was after midnight, and few people would notice the van creeping along the streets at this time of night. All the lights were out in the suburban street where they walked their last stretch.

They walked past a large hedge covering a patch of waste ground, littered with empty refillable gas bottles, broken wooden bed slats and the pre-requisite pile of black bin sacks, food packaging and empty liquor bottles.

They reached the end of the hedge, Rachael laughing hysterically at her new beau. With a violent swipe, the young man's throat was slashed, the blood pouring from the wound, as his stunned, fear-filled eyes stared blankly at the girl. By the time she managed a scream, a fist crashed into her right temple, knocking her out cold. He loaded her into the van, slamming the door, and drenched the young man with gasoline, tossing the empty container into the van along with her. Getting in, he started the engine. Lighting a book of matches, he waited till it burned then tossed it into the dead Lothario on the ground. The body raged in flames as the van careened around the corner out of sight.

••••••••••

NATE COOK LOOKED around the office and wondered, not for the first time, why he did what he did. It sure as hell wasn't the financial benefits, that was for shit sure! He hated the bureaucracy and red tape that held him back from being on the streets; the paperwork that kept him away from the action; and, most of all, he despised the time he spent around the Halls of Justice. He had been married to a lawyer many moons ago, and he detested them after being exposed to the bullshit he was subjected to during the high falutin parties, and the countless conference calls he had borne witness to around the house.

His job wasn't glamorous by any stretch of the imagination, but at least he hadn't brought it home with him too much.

The murders, the rapes, the 8-ball haemorrhages in teenage hookers whose mothers had to be informed that their daughters were dead. Not exactly the dinner conversation he'd had in mind when he marched her down the aisle all those years ago. It hadn't ended too badly as some had, but his savings had been wiped out by the divorce.

Thank Christ his outgoings were minimal, now, and his savings were steadily accumulating again. The office was deserted for a change, usually being frantic with activity. He enjoyed the peace and flicked through the file in front of him. As he progressed, he saw aspects of the case which mirrored the Chicago serial killings from the year before. He had studied those cases out of general interest.

You never could tell if he would come face to face with a case like that. Now, it looked like it had landed in his lap, as if a gift from the Gods. He sat there for hours, going through it, line by line, photograph by photograph, until the janitors came in to clean the office at Ten, and were cleaning around him.

··········

MAGGIE WAS AWARE of someone else in the darkness near her. Another poor woman, she thought. If he was going to kill anyone, it would be her. Why go out and get another? It made no sense. Why hadn't he killed her first? Why risk capture by risking an escape by one of them? The door opened and a shadowy figure entered, untying (she presumed) the woman and carried her out, closing the door behind him, the key turning in the lock. She had seen the shape and form of the woman - or had it been a girl? She had been small in stature, judging by the length of her silhouetted form.

Whoever she was, Maggie prayed for them both. Soon after, the petrified screams emanating from the other room sent shivers up her spine. She couldn't help the thought from penetrating her mind - why am I not in there? She closed her eyes as a piercing scream filled the corridor. Maybe, Maggie thought, it was just as well she wasn't.

··········

THE GIRL HAD barely turned eighteen according to her Facebook profile, but she was a notorious 'man-eater,' despite her going steady with a young plumber who had no idea of her libidinous nature. She lay naked, exposed, gagged and prostrate on a large wooden table, hands and feet clamped in S&M manacles, legs spread apart as he walked leisurely around her.

The girl's eyes were wide with terror, her entire body trembling as he ran the tip of his finger gently along the left of her abdomen towards her lower end and, as he turned around the corner, moved it to the inside of her lower thigh, gently moving it upwards, a cruel smile creasing his serious, cold face. The girl's heart was racing as his toned naked body walked the perimeter of the hard, cold table. The suspense was near fatal. Was he going to take her? Was this some sort of sick ritual sacrifice?

She both wished she knew and, at the same time, hoped she'd never find out. He sensed her fear level, and smiled, walking into the shadows. The sound of a key turning in a lock rang in her ears, and footsteps receding into silence. Her heart was overwrought as it pumped furiously, the adrenaline at its peak. Exhausted, she stared at the bare light bulb above her. The key turned again, and her eyes bulged. The light went off. She screamed under the thick gag, the soul-destroying cry stifled, perhaps for the final time.

············

NATE WAS SHAKEN awake by his partner, Jerry Hamshere.

'You really oughta get more sleep, Y'know!' said Jerry, a wry grin on his face.

'Nag, nag, nag! What's happenin'?' Nate queried.

'It's happened again. This time an eighteen-year-old girl. Parents just called it in.'

Nate cursed under his breath. He reached for a cigarette.

'I thought you'd quit,' Jerry jibed.

'Are you gonna hassle me all day, or do you wanna tell me something I actually need to know?' Nate countered.

'Get your game face on. Our presence is requested at the shrinks. He's gonna lecture us on the finer points of narcissistic personality disorder. C'mon. Let's hit the trail.'

Nate slipped his jacket on, and they walked out towards the exit.

'I think this is gonna be the beginning of a beautiful friendship,' quipped Nate.

'You really should seek professional help,' replied Jerry. They laughed together as they exited the building.

Traffic had been hell due to an accident over between Leyton and Handsworth, and it had taken a good while longer to arrive at the shrink's office. They ambled in and stopped at the desk.

'Dr. Lenkin?' Jerry said, flatly.

'Are you expected?' the receptionist asked.

'Why, does it show?' he replied, rubbing his stomach, taking pleasure in her reddening face. She laughed despite herself. She called up to Lenkin's receptionist and hung up after announcing their arrival.

'You can go right up. Take the right-hand side elevator to the third floor and take a left,' she said, smiling at Jerry. Her eyes watched Cook with great interest. She found him intriguing. She liked the strong, silent type. They walked to the elevators and stood chatting out of earshot as they waited.

And waited. And waited.

·········

'WHAT YOU HAVE to understand, gentlemen, is that these people usually have a history of sexual abuse in childhood. It fosters long-term resentment in them and is usually a sub-conscious shot at getting revenge for the trauma they endured, although it's directed towards another. The fact that the victims in Chicago shared the same modus operandi of non-sexual molestation to the recent victim indicates a far more perturbing subject. If it's a matter of him simply killing his prey, then all he must do is to change the manner in which he dispatches them. He can avoid detection for prolonged periods, due mainly to the lack of a signature killing method, whether it be gun, sharp instrument, blunt force trauma - take your pick. Based purely on what you've told me, I'd say that he'll go on killing. Mostly because he likes it, but the added consideration that no physical evidence has been found on site must also be brought into play. He's highly intelligent, with a deeply creative side - creative enough to investigate forensic matters that allow him to elude capture. You're not dealing with a babbling dummy, so be very mindful of this in your pursuit.

He's probably got no criminal record, so you won't have a sheet on him. It could be anyone out there, from a street bum to a high-society burnout who gets his kicks in seeing women suffer.'

Nate cursed under his breath.

'So, you're telling me we can't catch him? Is that it?' Nate asked.

'I'm telling you that you're dealing with someone who is extremely dangerous and should be treated with a little respect,' the shrink replied matter-or-factly, his logic being defiant to challenge, the tone containing no ambiguity.

'One of the women who have been reported missing, possibly abducted - Mrs Margaret Thornton - hasn't shown up yet. Is there any possible reason for him not killing her?' Jerry inquired.

'If he's not interested in the systematic violation of a victim, it's one of two things - either he's just not ready to take it that far or...'. He paused.

'Or what, Doc?'

'It's entirely possible - and this is just an educated possibility, nothing more - that he's been entranced by her. Somehow sees that she's a human being, someone with a power over him. Someone he doesn't want to kill. If that proves to be the case, then she has a remote chance of escape. But that, as I intimated, is nothing more than my analysing the situation,' Lenkin ventured.

Nate offered his hand.

'Thanks a lot, Doctor. You've been very helpful.

Lenkin extended his hand, shaking theirs, smiling coldly.

'You're welcome. My office is at your disposal should you need counsel. I wish you the best of luck. Good day, gentlemen.' It was a friendly, yet blunt, dismissal. They stood and walked to the door, opening it.

'He won't collect souvenirs, either. He's torturing them mentally and physically. Sexual gratification is not a consideration in this case. It would be pertinent to bear that in mind,' the shrink continued.

'Yeah,' Nate said, drily, nodding his thanks as he closed the door behind him.

They walked to the elevators and Jerry turned to Nate.

'So... whatcha think?'

'I think that if his spine was any straighter, he'd break in two,' Nate quipped. They laughed and entered the elevator. As the doors closed, Jerry looked up at the floor gauge.

'Jesus Christ!'

∙∙∙∙●●●∙∙∙

THE YOUNG GIRL lay strapped to the table, her abdomen and legs slashed lightly, the blood pulsating slowly from her superficial wounds. They weren't deep enough to damage any arteries, instead just 'tastes' of what was to come her way. The creep had stepped out an hour or so ago. Rachael, her perspiration growing, slowly manoeuvred her hands to wiggle her way out of the manacles. She was free - just as soon as she found her way out of there. She prayed that he had gone out again, or was passed out on the couch, drunk as a skunk. She tried the door and found it unlocked. Her heart jumped and, slowly, she opened it wider, edging out into the darkened corridor. All was quiet - too quiet, she thought, but that was a good thing, wasn't it? She wasn't entirely convinced of that. She crept down the corridor, finding a stone stairwell. It was freezing down there, being naked as a jay bird not helping matters much.

She looked around and found an old, empty flour sack and a large bread knife lying around. She made a vest out of it by ripping holes in it for her arms and head to go through. She hunted for something to tie around her waist as a makeshift belt. She had to be quiet. The freak could be back at any moment. She finally found a ball of string in a cupboard drawer and cut a length of it, wrapping it around her bruised, svelte waist. Proceeding to the stairwell, she looked up at the door above. It was slightly ajar, and she thanked God for small mercies. Placing a tentative right foot on the first cold step, she made her way up the flight of stairs towards it. She opened the door, peering out at her pristine surroundings. For a guy, she found it to be odd.

This was the work of a woman, not a grown man. It was too clean and proper for a man's house. She tiptoed across the floor to the front door, trying it. Locked.

SHIT! she thought. She heard the creak of floorboards a little too closely for comfort. Her eyes screwed shut, afraid of what stood behind her. Using her peripheral vision, she edged her head around slowly. There was nothing there. It must have been the house itself.

Houses made strange noises on their own - she had been told that by her mother when she had been frightened as a child. She walked cautiously towards the cellar door, finding it open. She prayed there would be a window down there, something - anything - she could use to get out of there and hitch a ride to the nearest town. Then she would get the cops back here to flush that sick little fuck out of his own torture palace. She had wondered why she hadn't been fooled around with.

Maybe he couldn't. Maybe that was it - sexual dysfunction. Who knew? All she knew was that she would be safe and back home in one piece. She had found it peculiar for a house these days to have both a basement and a cellar. But it was a bigger house than usual. Maybe one of the owners was a wine freak and had had an extension added to include a wine cellar, in order to host those pretentious cheese and wine soirées that most people with serious dough tend to do. She didn't care. All she cared about was getting out of there while she still could, before he realised, she had broken free. She descended the stairwell slowly. There was no light down there - just two steps leading to a veil of darkness. She swallowed hard as she continued.

Her eyes began to adjust to the low light, and she could discern streaks of light coming from the far right. Without warning, she ran out of steps, falling a few feet to the cold cement floor, spraining her left ankle in the process. She bit her lip to suppress any cries of the pain that propelled through her body, struggled to her feet, and limped towards the light source. She could barely make it out, but it looked like a bulkhead door. She hobbled closer, banging her right foot on the short flight of wooden steps leading to it. She clambered up them, wincing with pain at each left step she managed. She tried the doors. They opened outward. She clawed her way to the fresh air which rushed her skin. She looked up to try to find a way out of the area. Her breath clogged in her throat, as she looked up, paralysed by terror.

There he was, towering over her, a stern, evil face regarding her with what she saw as complete contempt. She screamed, the sharp piercing scream filling the countryside air. She picked up a nearby shovel, and swung it against his legs, the metal gouging into his right leg. Screaming in agony, he fell to the dirt, clutching himself. She struggled to get up, and stood over him, shovel raised high, staring down on his furious features. His expression was one of anger and defiant jubilation.  She swung with all her might, hitting him on the right temple, knocking him out cold.  Rachael tore across the front yard to the dirt road and, constantly looking back, kept on walking as best she could.  His body lay there still.  Maybe she had killed him, she thought.  Either way, she was gone.

...........

COOK HATED DRIVING at night.  Especially in the rain.  He was happy enough as the rain had stayed away for the meantime.  Jerry lay in the passenger seat next to him, his head against the window, snoring lightly.  Nate thought about all the good times they had in the 5 years they had been partners.  All the family barbecues he had been invited to by Marianne, Jerry's wife; the departmental baseball games which had turned into laugh riots with all their joking around; and the razor-sharp sarcastic repartee they had enjoyed with their now-retired Captain.

He looked over at Jerry once again, smiling happily.  He was glad to have had him as a friend and a partner.  He'd jump in front of a bullet for Nate, and it was a commonly known thing between them.  He'd do the same for Jerry, naturally.  It was an unspoken pact between them after so many years.

Something flashed across the windshield and Nate jammed his foot on the brake hard, skidding the car to a standstill.  Jerry had been jolted awake and was staring at Nate as if he were nuts.  Before he could say anything, Nate was already out of the car, weapon raised, and storming towards what looked to be a body in the road.  He saw Nate holster his gun, and lean over the object, turning it over.

It was a young woman, naked and soiled.  Jerry got out and walked to his partner.  Rachael lay there, her breath shallow but enough to speak in short bursts.  He managed to get only a few sentences, but one thing she did say struck a familiar, chilling chord in him.  A description of a house he knew only too well.  It had been the location of several brutal, ritualistic murders seven years before.  A house which had evil as its bricks and mortar, in its glass and plaster.  It had stood empty all these years, but from what she had said, it looked like someone had bought the place again.  He lifted the body and placed it across the rear of his back seat.

'Jer, take the car and get her to the hospital fast.  On the way, call for back-up.  The old Sanderson house on Rosemont Drive.  Hurry on, now!'  He took off, disappearing into the bushes where she had emerged.  Jerry got in the car and turned it around, speeding towards town.

Nate surveyed the house from a distance, knowing its dark history.  He was not the type to be spooked, but this place scared the crap out of even HIM.  He worked his way around to the front, making sure his presence wasn't detected.  He crept up to the bulkhead doors, finding a bloodied, weight outline of someone who had recently laid there, and a shovel covered in blood.  He silently bet to himself that this was the blood of the person who had been lying on that spot.  He opened the bulkhead door, and moved quickly down the steps, his flashlight lighting the darkened cellar.

All he could see was half empty wine racks, and a woodwork bench.  Okay, he thought.  So, the guy's a DIY freak.  He swung the light around, looking for a connecting door to the house.  Finding it, he walked across the nail-strewn floor, and saw the first five steps were gone.  That equated with the girl's bruised ankle, he thought.  He climbed up and continued on up to the door, again ajar.  The house was in very good condition, tastefully decorated.  He passed by the basement door, stopping in his tracks.  Was that a cough he had just heard from in there? Gun at the ready, he wrenched the door open, finding another flight of steps.

His arms raised in the Weaver stance, he walked carefully down the stone steps, and found a short corridor with two small doors on either side. Laundry cupboards? Dried goods storage pantry? He tried both doors. One locked, one not. He entered the open door to find a table fitted with S&M manacles, blood (probably the girl's, he thought), and a large, thick, black leather belt. He turned around, laughing to himself, only to be greeted with a closed fist.

Everything went dark.

·········

NATE CAME OUT of it to find the creep sitting nearby. He didn't recognise him, as he thought he might. A complete stranger. Nate felt his bruised jaw, wincing at the pain shooting through it.

'You're a sick bastard, y'know that?'

'Nobody's perfect, Officer. What brings you here?'

'I always wanted a house like this. Thought I'd take a look around,' Nate quipped.

The creep laughed lightly.

'I'm gonna ask you one more time. Why are you sneaking around my house?'

'I'm looking for a missing woman. That means I have to check every building in a 45 mile radius of where she was last thought to be. I came across a young woman who pointed me in your general direction, so I thought I'd check it out.'

The creep stood up, grinning.

'I don't think you'll find her here. Why not try the house two miles further up,' he suggested with a soft, amenable voice.

Nate looked around and faced him.

'Sounds good to me. But one last thing...'

The creep raised a questioning eyebrow.

'Which is?' he asked.

'I'd like you to open that door for me. Then I can leave happy. Think you can do that for me?' Nate asked.

The creep shook his head, laughing.

'That's not gonna be possible without a warrant. Have you got a warrant? You knoooow...a little bitty piece of paper with a judges signatory at the bottom?' he asked Nate.

Nate grabbed him by the collar, thrusting him up against the wall, slamming his badge against the creep's face. Snarling, through clenched teeth, he said,

'This is my warrant, asswipe. It gives me the right to go anywhere I wanna go if I have probable cause to believe a crime has taken place. As it happens, I do. So pretty please - with cherries on top - open the goddamn door before I decorate this basement with your balls!'

'Fuck you, cop!'

Nate pulled him backwards and without warning, rammed the door with him. The creep's weight easily tore the door from its hinges. Maggie screamed at the shock of it, and watched as Nate knocked him out cold. He could hear sirens wailing in the distance and thanked the Lord for Jerry. He untied Maggie and she wrapped her arms around his neck, in hysterics, almost choking him until he broke free.

'What's your name, Miss?' he asked.

'Margaret. Margaret Thornton,' she replied between sobs.

'That's what I thought,' he quipped under his breath. 'Okay, Margaret. Get your clothes on, and we'll get out of here.'

She looked down at her captor.

'What about him?'

'What ABOUT him?' Nate countered.

'You gonna arrest him?' she pressed.

'We're gonna take him to the Boy Scout Jamboree, whaddya think? Of course, we're gonna arrest him! You ready? Okay, let's get the hell outta here before Handsome Dan wakes up, huh?' They left the room, and a scream of rage came from behind them. Nate turned to see the creep charging at them. He pulled Maggie out of the way, and he charged past them. Before they knew it, two shots rang through the basement and he collapsed, dead, onto the cold stone floor. Nate looked up to see Jerry crouched, his gun smoking in his hand.

'You took your time,' Nate growled.

'I was otherwise occupied,' Jerry replied. 'Okay! Let's get this young lady back to her family.' They walked up the steps, sniping comically at each other.

The creep's hand started twitching as a huge rat scurried across the floor.

# STORM OF RAGE

Emily Carson had always been a "very good girl," as her mother, Elizabeth, had always told friends and strangers alike. But that night, in the little Welsh coast cottage, had made her mother begin to question that.

There had been a terrible storm, quite contrary to the last weather report (a joke in themselves which the British *still* take somewhat seriously, enough, at least, to let it affect their daily comings and goings) before leaving the house, which stated a generally "overcast evening, with low-pressure winds and light rain." Nothing whatsoever about the high hurricane winds from which the fixed thatched roof had been swallowed by its relentless attack.

Elizabeth sat in the safety of the coffee shop the following morning, her husband having taken Emily to her granny's house. Her nerves were still jangled from the night before. She couldn't stop her hands from trembling since they had left it following the storm, travelling further south to Barry Island. Her mind returned to that night as she stared out at the bright, sunny morning engulfing the town.

· · · · ● · ● · · ·

The car pulled out of the driveway; little Emily asleep in the rear. They had decided to set out earlier than planned, enabling them to arrive at the cottage as early as possible to spend their whole first day together. They had brought all manner of snacks and toys to keep her occupied after dinner, so they could relax after a day of family 'quality time,' something which had been sorely missed since Emily's arrival home from hospital.

They had all enjoyed a splendid day, and it was time to return to the little cottage they had paid a small fortune to rent for such a fleeting visit. They had finished dinner, cleared up, and went to the living room, where Elizabeth watched happily with her magazine, as her husband, Dave, crawled around Emily, barking like a dog, enjoying her little squeals of delight. The lights had started flickering, and she got up to light the glass-enclosed candles. She opened the front door slowly, looking out at the billowing dark clouds forming in the near distance, as a storm was brewing in its infancy. The wind was growing stiffer, and she felt the cold blast from the coastline surf, as she struggled to close the door, barring it with the plank provided. She would watch this develop from inside, she thought.

It was barely after 9pm, when the baby had finally gone to sleep. They would ride out the storm from the comfort of their bedroom, she thought. Barely had they began to walk up the short flight of steps than the door was wrenched off the wooden frame attached to it. The romantic low rumble of thunder which had warmed her heart earlier, terrified her now. It had become more robust and scarier, punctuated by frequent streaks of forked lightning as the heavy rain battered against the cottage.

'Well...so much for an early night!' Dave joked. 'We can't leave the place like this all night. Get the blankets out – we'll have to sleep down here,' he said. Elizabeth went to the bedroom, re-emerging from the landing, biting her lip.

'I left that bag in the car. Sorry, darling.'

Dave smiled thinly.

*But of course you did, dear!*

He grabbed his coat from the rack, fastening it. The car was parked outside, on the right-hand drive, covered somewhat by the aluminium-sided awning.

'If I'm not back in five minutes...call the Welsh Assembly!' he yelled through the gale. She laughed nervously, as he sped off to the right. This was no time for messing about. If that mess outside got any stronger, they'd be honorary members of the Lollipop Guild before the night was through.

Dave struggled through the furious wind until he reached the car, thankfully still there. He stood in front of it, inspecting it for storm damage for a moment. Without warning, the car lurched towards him, propelled by the sheer force of the gale. He dove out of its path, and watched as it came to a halt – stopped by the large elm tree in the garden.

'Of course. Why not?' he jibed. He walked to the trunk, opened it quickly to retrieve the blanket bag, and struggled back to the cottage.

'Are you alright?' Elizabeth asked him, incredulous at what she had seen through the window, as she cradled Emily back to sleep, having woken up since.

'I think I'll survive, thank you,' he replied with a wink. 'Here.' He handed her the bag, and headed for the kitchen.

'Where are you going?' she asked.

'Going to try to locate a hammer and nails to fix that door. Can't leave it like that all night,' he said, flatly. She returned to the window, watching the lightning crash, lighting up the entire sky through the deafening thunder rolls.

She turned away from the window for a moment and a horrific cracking sound filled the room. She looked up and screamed in terror as the entire thatched roof was being torn off its wooden foundation, spinning through the air. Dave ran through the kitchen, grabbing their coats and whatever else he could manage.

'Enough is enough! We're leaving, *NOW!* Wait here!'

He ran to the car, occasional spears of lightning hitting the ground, barely missing him, as he got into the car, turning the engine over.

Nothing.

'*COME* ONNN!!'

The engine roared to life, and he reversed it as steadily as he could. He didn't want it stuck in the mud. No way, not *now*.

He drove it to the house, opening the car door.

'*GET IN!!*'

She was past persuasion by this time, running to the car, handing him the baby as she got in the rear seat. He handed Emily to her and he slammed his foot on the gas, tearing along the driveway to the main country road and, eventually (if they made it) the nearby town.

············

'Would you like another cup of tea, Miss?' the waitress asked her. She snapped out of her dream-like trance, smiling gently.

'No, thank you. I really ought to be getting back, now.' She paid the waitress and left quickly.

The rain had started again as she walked along the gaily festooned promenade. The thunder rolled in the distance, and she paled under her recently-acquired UV tan as she jumped into a taxi cab, headed back to her mother-in-law.

Enough was as good as a feast, as the age-old British expression went. And once had been *more* than enough of that in one lifetime.

The cab drove off as the elements combined, merging once more.

# THE IVORY SMILE

THE OLD CURIO store on Delfont Avenue had a lot to invite the transient visitor to its gabled entrance. Antiques, bric-a-brac, and other things. But the thing that interested young Harry Lambert - aged 9 - was the black mahogany baby grand piano situated at the back of the store. He would pass by deliberately on his way back from grade school just to peer through the window each day, captivated by the mere sight of it. The raised lid, the silver plaques on each side just above the ivory keys, and the row of yellowing ivory beneath, the black keys between them presenting the appearance of a face leering back at him, tempting him, luring him, even mocking him to take it home. In his fragile fertile mind, it was grinning at him.

His mother, being on welfare, could never afford such an extravagance and, besides anything else, there was little room in their small house for such a large object, anyway. One day, he had bit the bullet and opened the door, walking into that dusty store, making his way through the tables of oddities to the piano in the rear, standing before it, and beholding its opulence, wishing it were his.

Unknown to him, he had been watched by the proprietor, old man McCabe, smiling at the youngster's fascination with the instrument. A former musician himself, he adored the boy's interest in his star item, knowing full well his family's lack of means to buy it outright.

That day was to be a fortunate one for little Harry.  McCabe walked out of his tiny office, running his old, wrinkled, tobacco-stained hand across the wood, sending a light cloud of dust into the air.

'Can you play it, sonny?' he asked.

Harry shook his head, his face saddened at the thought of not being able to.

'I'll tell you what, kiddo.  Come here after school each day, and I'll show you how to play it. Better ask your momma, though. How would that be?'

Harry was incredulous at the prospect.

'Really? You'd show me how to play it?' he asked, marvelling at the old man.

'Sure.  It's rare these days to find someone so young who likes playing music.'  He walked around the area, picking up several small items, dusting them off as he spoke.

'Go 'head, boy.  Have a tinkle if you like,' he invited.  Harry sat on the stool, but became irritated that his feet couldn't reach the foot pedals.

'I can't reach them,' he complained.  McCabe laughed...a huge belly laugh that made him shake a little.

'You'll be reachin' them in no time, sonny.  You don't need them right now, anyways.  You c'n play a tune'r three without them.'

Harry began to hit the keys a little roughly.

'Whoa, there, boy! Pull in the reins a little. You don't have to hammer away like that. Pianos are about finesse. Delicate movements. Watch this.'  He cracked his fingers together, and placed his hands on the keys, both hands working at the same time in a melody that was hauntingly beautiful to someone so young. He caught the kid watching his hands out of the corner of his eye and smiled to himself, making his mind up then and there - he was going to teach the boy to play it. His own wife had died ten years after they married in '68 and, despite trying, it had failed to result in issue.

This would be the only opportunity to feel what it was like to teach a son, pass on his knowledge which, he would openly opine, was precious little. He stopped playing and invited the boy to try. Showing him where to place his fingers around middle C, he watched as Harry began to experiment with his own music, a few slips aside. The kid was pretty good for a beginner, he thought. He picked things up quickly, which is a bonus to any teacher-pupil relationship. The kid would be playing well in no time - as long as he kept that passion aflame. But that was purely up to him in the end. The old man looked at his watch. It was almost 4.30. His mother would be worried about him.

'Better be gettin' on home, son. Your momma's gon' be worried about you.'

'Can I come back and play some more tomorrow?' asked Harry.

'As long as it's ok, by your momma, that's ok by me,' he replied. 'Mind and ask her, now. I can't have you here if she don't know about it. It'd give me a world of trouble if it gave her a mind to!'

'I'll ask my momma,' he assured the old man. He stood up, and walked off towards the door, turning back momentarily.

'Bye, Sir. Thanks for showing me how to play piano,' he called back. McCabe waved back at him, and the boy left the store, the chimes ringing as the door closed. McCabe smiled to himself.

'Good kid,' he muttered before re-entering his office.

Harry walked by the window, headed home, pausing to take one last look at it through the dusty window. There it stood, prominent and steadfast, knowing its place. Harry gasped. Had it just winked at him? No, he thought. It couldn't have. It was a piano made of dead wood and strings. He looked again. The silver plaque on the left above ivory row seemed to disappear for a second and then reappear. Staring at it as he walked, he eventually took off running towards the park, and back to his increasingly frantic mother.

·········

'WHERE HAVE YOU *BEEN*?!' she yelled, both ecstatic and aggravated at him for being late, but grateful he was home unharmed.

'I was at the piano store, momma,' Harry replied.

'What piano store? There ain't one anywhere near here,' she replied.

'It ain't all pianos. But there's one in the back of the store. A big black one. The man let me play with it.'

That wasn't the kind of phrasing that made Miss Arlene Lambert feel warm all over. It sounded downright suspicious to her.

'I don't want you goin' back there, ok,' she said. 'No argument, now. No more, alright?'

'But, mommy!—'

'You don't even know this man. There's bad people all over, Harry. He could be dangerous, for all you know. No more, I mean it. Stay away from that place. He don't sound right to me,' she said, her mind trying to picture him. 'Where is it anyway? Town? What's the name of the place?'

Harry hesitated. He didn't want McCabe to get into trouble just for teaching him how to play a piano. Arlene saw his hesitation by chewing his bottom lip, and it cemented her already suspicious feeling on the whole situation.

'You wanna tell me what the name of the place is so I can go see what all the fuss is about?' she prodded.

'It's just a little store filled with junk. It's next to the bar Daddy used to go to.'

'Oh, yeah. I know it. Some old feller runs it, doesn't he? I'll pop in there and see what's new. Got your Gramma's vase in there 'bout a year back, before she went to the angels,' she said, smiling. It was a fake smile, but she could see that he had been worried about telling her. Once he was in school, she would take a walk into town and pay the old man a visit. Find out EXACTLY what had kept her 9-year old son so late from school.

··········

THE SNOW HAD been falling all night. Arlene Lambert had awoken to the blanket of snow which covered the entire town. The school would have been closed due to the ice on the streets, which meant Harry would be home all day. Shit, she thought. She had made plans for today, and now she was going to have to cancel them - again. It had been the third time, now, that she had kept Mike waiting and she felt sure he was gonna blow her off, pissed off that she kept flaking him.

There was only one option to her. But there was too much risk to that, and she wasn't prepared to take it that far.

But maybe the old fella was okay, after all, she thought. Maybe it was just a mother's instinct working overtime. If the kid enjoyed playing the damn piano, why not let him do it? It might be good to get him doing something with his time besides sitting on his ass all day shooting the heads off zombies on that goddamned console of his.

Maybe then, she could get her day back. Maybe then, she thought, she could ask Mike to come over here and spend the day. He didn't like snow, anyway, and she knew he hated walking in it for fear of slipping and breaking his back. He had come close to that once before and had developed a morbid fear of being paralysed over a fall. Yeah, she was sure he would want to come over. But, selfishly, she didn't want Harry around to screw things up.

The town was only a short-cut through the park, and wasn't like it was a bus run apart. He could walk there, having fun in the snow, and learn a new skill at the same time.

Maybe she WAS being too selfish, she thought, and admonished herself for it. This old guy - what was his name, again? McCabe? - might be just that. An old man who never had any company and had never had kids. Harry might benefit from his life experiences, and would that be a BAD thing? She looked the number up, and called it. It rang for three minutes, and she almost gave up until it clicked and an older voice spilled over the line.

'Magical Mystical. Can I help you?'

'Yes, I think you can. What time do you close up for the day?' she asked, trying to keep the tone of desperation from being too apparent.

'I'm here all day. Was there something in part-ic-uleer you wanted to ask about?' he asked.

'Not really. But I was thinking I might drop in later for a look around. Just wanted to make sure I wasn't wasting a trip, what with the snow'n all,' she said.

'No, that's fine. Come around when you like. Got some new items in just this very morning. Look forward to seein' you, Madam. Bye, now.'

'Bye,' she replied and hung up.

She didn't see the devious smile on the other end of the phone. Probably just as well she hadn't.

It would have chilled her to the bone.

··········

HARRY HAD MADE it into town without incident. He was still only 9, but he was older than his accumulative years. There had only been one major road to cross after the recreation park, an artery road, and he had crossed it as he had been instructed - look left, look right, all way across. He knew cars could come out of nowhere and, himself not relishing the idea of a hospital stay, heeded the sage advice.

He wandered around the half-deserted town, only now filling up gradually with townsfolk who had lives to lead despite the inclement weather, and had began to filter into the streets, albeit most coming in by cab, leaving their cars at home for fear of probable damage. Harry soon got bored lobbing snowballs at the models plastered over the many billboards in town, and headed out to the curio shop, praying it was open, as some of the stores were shuttered. He turned the corner and walked the last twenty yards to the door. It was open. He looked through the window once more.

There it was, unmoved and inimitable in its grandeur. He smiled and entered the store, the sound of the chimes ringing in his ears. He walked to it, struck dumb by its aura of affluent beauty, its white and black toothy grin smiling at him, encouraging him...goading him...to place his fingers on them and make the good times roll. Harry was standing before it, staring at it, as if it were sending out vibes, transmitting a frequency between them only he could hear. The piano was trembling. He could feel the vibrations from the wooden floorboards under it, reverberating up through his legs, and he could almost detect a pale blue glow around it, pulsating ever so slightly. He was so taken by it that he failed to see the old man standing behind him, smiling kindly.

'Wanna learn a new tune, young man?' he asked, making the boy jump. He spun around and heaved a sigh of relief.

'Siddown here and I'll get the paper,' he said, retreating into his office and returning with a small cardboard file box, rifling through it, and finding what he was looking for.

'Bingo! Here it is!' he exclaimed joyously, as he held it up, looking at it. He put the sheet music on the ledge above the keys.

'You know how to read music?' he asked, although he knew the answer would most likely be 'no'.

Harry shook his head.

'Makes no never mind. That's something we'll have to remedy, isn't it!' He pulled out the stool and Harry climbed on to it, putting both hands on the keys where he had been shown. The old man proceeded to explain the stave, measures, the number of notes to each bar, and he encouraged the boy to try playing it. Harry had absorbed the information admirably, and proceeded to play the piece as it was in notation form. It was almost flawless, with a few slips here and there.

The music was hauntingly beautiful, albeit a little strange and discordant. By the time the boy had finished, he was shaking visibly at his own achievement. The old man clapped his hands slowly in approval.

'Now you can play anything that's simple enough, and then some. The same rules apply to most things, but at least you know what to do. The rest is up to you. Practice and perfect. It's the only way.'

He looked at his watch. Quarter after four. Five hours had passed so quickly that he barely believed it. It was almost time to shut up shop.

Harry got off the stool, tears in his eyes, and thanked McCabe for the free lessons.

'My pleasure, sonny. It's a pleasure to teach someone who learns so fast. It's getting late, though. There's a new storm comin' in soon. Better get home quick before it gets here. You don't wanna be caught in this heah storm! See you soon, son,' he said as the boy, jubilant, walked on air towards the door, sending the chimes wild as he danced out into the snow, now up to his knees.

The old man looked down at the piano, his eyes glinting evilly in the darkened parlour area. A red glow washed over the dark mahogany, filtering through the ivory and rosewood keys, a low, grumbling hum throbbing from it.

'It is time,' he whispered, barely able to contain his joy. The boy - a fresh soul - had done what needed doing. He had played the melody that unlocked the void, and opened the seal which barred the exit from Hell.

・・・・●・●・・・

THE DAY HAD been a rejuvenating one for Arlene Lambert. She lay exhausted in bed, her beau lying naked beside her, having fallen asleep. She couldn't have cared less at this moment if she tried. Mike had proven to be an amazing lover, far beyond any of her expectations, and her body still quaked slightly from the repercussions of their secret tryst. She secretly hoped he would wake up soon, before Harry got home. But part of her wanted it to never end. She wanted him to stay forever, giving her the same earth-shattering love he just had barely an hour before. But no, she had to get him home before her baby got back. He was still upset with her for divorcing his daddy, and the presence of another man would only deepen his resentment towards her. Time would heal it, she thought.

*(GOD IN HEAVEN, PLEASE LET IT!)*

But for now, he would have to get out of here. She shook him gently, and he began to stir, his eyes finally opening, groggy and struggling to focus.

'What's up?' he asked.

'You gotta get outta here. My kid'll be back soon, and he's already still sore at me for leaving his daddy. Get ready and I'll call you a cab.' Surprised, but understanding fully her dilemma, he got out of bed, and dressed. She walked him to the rear door, and they kissed passionately once more. At that moment, she wanted to abandon all hope and do it again, but restraint prevailed and she opened the door, ushering him out as the cab pulled into the driveway. She watched the cab from the large bay window in the sitting room, her curvy body aching for a repeat performance. As the cab turned the corner, she saw Harry emerge from the alleyway, struggling through the snow towards the house. She rushed to the door with a large fleece blanket she grabbed from the radiator heater.

He was home.

・・・・・・・・・・

**THE OLD MAN** had been right about the snowstorm. It had hit the entire State with a vengeance. Cars and transit vans had disappeared under the blanket of snow it left behind; houses were snowed in above door level; and the only way to see out was to go upstairs to one of the two bedrooms and look out the windows. There had been a fierce hurricane along with the snow, and the stumps of telephone lines and uprooted trees, now barely visible, poked briefly through the white carpet outside. Harry lay in his bed, hands behind his head and wondered if Mr McCabe had made it out of there okay. He was beginning to look at the old guy as a surrogate dad. After all, who else did he have as an alternative? Some deadbeat joker his mom met in Markey's Bar?

All they could teach him was how to make beer farts and cuss like a sailor. One day, just maybe, his mom would find somebody halfway decent who actually wanted to be a father to him. Someone who wanted to help him with his homework; someone who wanted to take him to ball games; someone who actually gave a crap whether he existed. With his mom's run of luck, her future wasn't looking too bright on that score. He lay back down on the pillow and was soon lost in his snowdrift wonderland.

··········

OLD MAN McCABE sat alone in his office, deep in thought. The piano had to go, and although he knew where he wanted it to go, it was impossible. The boy was only a child and he wasn't eager to put him through what he knew had to be done. He had proven to be a gifted amateur player, but the last tune the boy would have to learn would be the last he would EVER play. This last tune would be final combination of notes to open the portal to the ninth layer of Hell, and release the arch-demons from their fiery incarceration, 'loosed' upon the world to make way for the Antichrist to make his final stand, the final face-off against the Nazarene for the prize - ultimate control of the universe, relegating God to the depths of whence they had come.

This last tune had been carefully, and mathematically, constructed to ensure the portal aperture was fully exposed to the pre-ordained light temperature. If the piano had been normal, he would have gifted it to young Harry, aged 9, but it took an innocent soul to play those notes or it would all be for nothing. The boy had to be sacrificed - and that was that. Tears rolled down his face as a blanket of darkness enveloped him.

··········

# OUT OF THE ASHES

IT HAD BEEN a long four days since the snowstorm had first hit Carson Falls, Ohio. The sun had finally shown its face and the snow was beginning to recede. Soon, he would be able to go back outside. His mother had placed sandbags at the front door to prevent the flood of water from the snow coming into the house and sinking through the cracks in the wooden floor. The dirt under the laminate would rise to the top and the stench would be unbearable. The safest way to guard against it was to employ sandbags. Harry looked outside the window and saw the paving leading to the door was visible. He leapt out of bed, and ran downstairs for a better look. He was greeted by a clear, stark white winter sunlight blasting through the window.

He could see that the path had been completely cleared but that other houses had had no such luck. In fact, his was the only house with its path cleared. Maybe it had been a friend of his mother who had come around to do it. Yes, he thought. That had to be it. He turned on the TV and sat watching Nickelodeon until his mother got up and made him breakfast (whenever that might be, he couldn't restrain himself from thinking). So engrossed was he with Super Wings that he failed to notice the heavy dark cloud forming in the heavens above.

··········

THE OLDMAN sat in his darkened store, conversing with someone.

He was kneeling, almost genuflecting, as he replied to the voice only he could hear. The room had been illuminated by an odd, yet barely perceptible, glow.

*HAS YOUR WORK BEEN DONE?* it asked him, its tone unforgiving.

'Almost, my Lord. The recitation will be performed as ordered. The weather has been less than co-operative.'

*I AM AWARE OF THIS. YOU WILL FULFIL THE TASK, AND MAKE YOUR SACRIFICE.*

'As you wish, my Lord. It shall be done'

The room returned to its normal, cold state and a tear ran down the old man's face. His time was upon him – and he knew it.

But not before the child played the notes which would seal his own fate - and that of Carson Falls, itself.

It was a necessary evil, unavoidable according to the ancient texts.

The child had to die. It was that simple.

·············

THE FOLLOWING MORNING, Harry awoke to the resumption of normality. The snow had gone completely, and he could hear his mother rattling around downstairs, making breakfast before he returned to school, after which he would head out to his piano lessons. He had missed McCabe in his time away, and knew his mother would want some time alone with whatever bonehead she was talking to on Facebook. Might as well give her the space. He had better things to do than listen to her laughing aloud to whatever was being sent to her, listening to the click-clack of her fingers typing her equally tedious response.

He entered the kitchen and ate his breakfast in silence. Harry grabbed his sports bag containing his books, kissed his mother goodbye, and walked out of the door, leaving her to her daydreaming. He knew his mother was trying her best, but her mind had been elsewhere for the past few months since the divorce. He had kept out of her way for the best part of the first few weeks, but he hadn't been able to suppress the flashes of guilt he felt for treating her like he did. His daddy was his hero but, as he was forced to admit, his old man had his 'issues.' But he was a great father, all things considered.

He was always at hand to help him with his homework, watch movies, and play catch with him. No father is perfect although, compared to other kids at his school, Harry's old man was a legend among fathers. Mainly because he was THERE in the first place. Carson Falls was full of young single moms, most of whom had dispensed with their boyfriends to get the financial benefits of child support payments without having their immature, idiot partners hanging around the house, preventing them from experiencing the lives they were desperate to reclaim. The other kids moaned to Harry about the fact their own mothers paraded before them a constant selection of prospective 'daddies,' none of whom had made much effort to bond with them.

It was difficult to see themselves as 'mistakes,' but it was an undeniable fact which could not be easily dismissed, however painful the truth of it was. But Harry's father was one of only two fathers who had shown up at school plays, parent conferences, and other events.

His presence at these tended to elicit dirty looks from the plethora of unattached and deliriously-entitled mothers in attendance, choosing victim hood over accountability. They were the ones who had disposed of their kids' fathers purely because they were convinced that they could do far better, neglecting their own bad choice to break up their reasonably content family (at least in daddy-and-child's eyes) as the reason they were alone.

Harry walked through the broken chain-link fence leading to the street in which his school sat welcoming its pupils once again. All young Harry wanted to do was to sit behind that musty old baby grand, tinkling those yellowed ivory keys, feeling the long-lost encouragement coursing through his tender bones. He smiled at the thought, sighed heavily, and accepted the inevitable as he disappeared into the hallways.

• • • • • • • • • •

ARLENE OPENED THE door to the curio store she had visited only once before. With a sense of trepidation, she ventured inside, unsure of what to expect. Her baby spent hours in here among the old junk, and she wanted to see it for herself; see what the big attraction was. She found herself marvelling at the bill of fare, and discovered that she enjoyed spending time there. She began to slowly

'Get it' and was even more appreciative of the large, old paintings hanging in the rear. She was lost in it all and didn't see McCabe approaching from behind.

'Morning,' he said softly. Arlene jumped out of her skin, turning and almost knocking over a china vase. She caught it just in time and replaced it on the valuable Hepplewhite sideboard where it had been.

'I'm sorry if I startled you. It was unintentional,' he said in the same soft, Southern accent. 'Welcome to Magical Mystical! The place where time stands still,' he recited, his most winning, charming smile used to full effect. It had worked a treat. She was putty in his hands and she began to realise why her son had been here so much. 'Had you something in mind, perchance?' he asked gently, his preferred sales technique being the soft sell, making such an inquiry more of 'casual interest' than feeling out possible sales. He had never liked those people who were overeager to sell their products. Too goddamned pushy, that 'in your space' tactic. Customers buy more when left to browse, and he left them to it.

'My son comes in here a lot. I thought I'd check it out for myself. He seems to think the world of you,' she said.

'You must be young Harry's momma,' he offered.

'Yes. Arlene Lambert,' she replied, offering her hand, which he took, kissing it gently, enveloping it in his own wrinkled old hands.

'I've been teaching yo' son how to play piano. He's a good student. Quick mind, with hands to match. He'll be a fantastic musician if he keeps goin' with it.'

'That's very kind of you, but I can't let you teach him for nuthin'. How much will you take for lessons, Sir?' she asked.

The old man raised his right eyebrow, and his face assumed a pained expression, betraying his anger beneath. He maintained composure and replied.

'I have chosen to teach your son because he showed an interest in it. My own dear wife died a long time ago. She was unable to bear a child. I wanted a child to teach the finer things in life...old movies, music, art...'. He paused, taking a wavering breath, then continued. 'When your son came aroun' here and takin' such an interest in the piano back theah, I had a chance to get acquainted with him. I saw in yo' son all the qualities I dreamed of in my own child, and chose to teach him how to play it on account of him enjoying lookin' at it so much.'

Arlene was both choked up and embarrassed at having made such a slip. The old man had a more than honourable reason for her kid being in his company and she was finally satisfied that he was on the level, and not some senile old preevert as she might, these days, be excused for thinking. It was a dangerous world, and she had to protect her son. But the old man was worth a risk, she thought.

'I have to go, now. Busy day. I just wanted to meet y'all, and see what kind of freak your boy was spending his time with? Don't worry, Mrs Lambert. It's fine. I have no problem with that. You can't be too careful today. So much evil around us, it's kinda hard to tell who's safe and who ain't. Your son is welcome here anytime, as are you,' he replied, grinning warmly.

Her face was bright red. How could he have known what she was thinking? She just wanted to get the hell out of the hole she had dug her thoughts into before she made things worse. Flustered, she said an awkward goodbye, and turned tail, walking quickly out of the store. He watched her with great amusement and smiled thinly.

He looked at his watch.

3.30pm

The boy would be on his way soon.

The last piece would be played and the portal opened. Then Carson Falls would belong to his Master.

Not least the souls of everyone in it.

··········

IT HAD BEEN a long eight hours when the bell rang. Harry collected his things, glad to be out of there at last. School wasn't too bad but he had better things he could be doing, like exterminating zombies and getting pole position on Outrun. He walked the jammed halls to the exit, hurrying down the steps. Next stop - Magical Mystical! It took him a bare ten minutes of walking to the store where he barged through the door, heading straight for the piano. The old man walked out of the office, his face not as happy as it usually was. Harry sat on the stool and tinkled idly on the keys as he waited. McCabe placed the sheet music on the stand.

'What's wrong, Sir?' Harry asked.

'Nothing really. Just one of those days, kiddo. You ready to get started?'

Harry smiled and put his fingers on the keys, and the final notes he would ever play began to fill the deserted store. Before he finished the first section, the old man cracked, slamming the lid down, narrowly missing the boy's fingers.

'What's wrong? What'd I do?' the boy cried. He was confused and becoming a little frightened.

'Get out of here, Harry. QUICKLY! There's something I have to do. *Get out!* Right *now!*'

Harry backed away, the fear rising in him, looking at the old man's saddened, frightened face, confused and hurt. He reached the door, turning one last time to see the old man's tear-stained face, and hearing the cracked, emotion-filled voice call out to him.

'I love you, kid.'

Harry opened the door and left, the chimes ringing in his ears for the last time.

The shop became darker as shadows formed in the alcoves and the corners, screeching with glee, as the thunderous voice of his Master filled the store.

'YOU BETRAYED ME! YOU WILL PAY DEARLY FOR WHAT YOU HAVE DONE!!!' it screamed. The store quaked as dark shadows converged on the old man, their now visible eyes glaring and feral as they attacked. Pain surged through the old man's body and up his left side. It was agonising, a pain he had never known before, as his heart exploded in his chest. Keeling over, his lifeless corpse slammed hard against the wooden floor. The store returned to normal. Seconds later, a gas pipe burst and the store was engulfed in flames, smoke belching out from under the doorway.

··········

*TWO WEEKS LATER...*

CARSON FALLS WAS hit by the worst rainstorm in its entire history. Harry stared blankly out of the window, his fragile mind shattered still by the news of the fire and its resultant death of Mr McCabe. He had grown very fond of the old man, and to lose him like that had a staggering impact on him. He recalled the old man's last words and the tears flowed freely from him as the pain of loss ached every muscle.. He was interrupted from his reverie by the sound of his mom calling him down. Reluctantly, he walked away from the window and trudged his way to the stairs . A delivery courier stood holding an electronic signing device which Arlene signed. The courier handed her a letter, and, in turn, she passed it to her son. He looked at the front and it said, in big letters :

OPEN ME, HARRY!

The boy was too dejected to care, but opened it anyway. Inside was a hundred dollar bill, and a short letter, which he read, his smile returning as he took in what it said :

*Dear Harry,*

*Hey, kiddo! It's your old friend Mister McCabe, here. If you're reading this letter, then I will have left this world. I'm sorry for what happened the last time we met, but it had to be that way to keep you safe. I can't explain it, now, but I ask you only to believe me that I had your best interests at heart.*

*I have sent you a hundred bucks to buy yourself somethin' nice and the man with the van has a little gift for you. The fire didn't destroy everything. The surviving items were sold off cheap, but I made sure this was sent to you. I'm sure you'll find somewhere to put it. Just promise me one thing - that tune you were playing in the store? Don't EVER play it on ANY musical instrument.*

*Enjoy your life, Harry. Look after your momma.*

*In time, we'll meet again.*
*I love you, kid!*
*With my warmest regards,*
*GEORGE McCABE*

Harry handed the letter to his mom, who began reading it. Tears welled up in her eyes and her hand flew to her mouth, trying to stifle herself from crying outright.

The courier rolled up the shutter at the back of the truck and Harry watched him, more interested than before. Piece by piece of the familiar black mahogany became visible until Harry's eyes widened. The shutter, electronically, was raising slowly, revealing the same black, baby grand piano which had caught his eye that cold day he had first laid eyes on it. He closed his eyes, lowering his head, as tears cascaded freely down his reddened face as the courier called his companion from the cab.

The two men moved the piano into the house and found a place where it could be at home, a spare room his mother had cleared out a few days before for a sewing studio.

This, Arlene thought, was more deserving of the space it would take up. The courier left, and Harry went out to play. Arlene closed the door to the room and plunged it into darkness, her eyes still tearful.

In the darkness, a faint, throbbing vibration encompassed the piano as a faint red glow hugged it - possessive and unrelenting in its acquisition.

# THE MAZE

*Sarasota, Florida...1945*

*THE BOY RAN for his life.*

*Whatever was in there was after him, close behind. The hard, heavy freezing rain thrashed off his naked skin, slashing it until blood was soaked into his Mickey Mouse t-shirt. He was weak, and only feeling more anaemic as the pursuit carried on.*

*The thunder was coming in waves of raging anger, punctuated frequently by the sharp streaks of lightning which had begun to strike the structure, causing it to catch aflame. The forks of lightning were getting ever closer, and had almost hit him four times. Almost as if it were teasing him with what it had to offer him; death.*

I'm only a goddamned kid! *he thought as he ran, breathless and frantically praying for the exit.* Gimme a break, whatever the hell you are!

*The feeling of impending doom was getting weaker, now.*

I gotta be closer to the house *he thought.* I've been in here forever!

*He turned the corner, and his heart jumped. The house was barely visible through the storm, due to the rain flooding down his face; his eyes sodden with water, stinging. He ran the last five feet and put one foot towards the joint entry/exit. As he crossed the threshold to safety, he was taken.*

*Dark shadows yanked the boy's exhausted body into the air, flying aimlessly backwards into the tall, imposing walls of razor-sharp greenery. A cacophony of ravenous growls deafened him, drowning out his screams of terror as he passed violently through the hedges, his tiny frame shredded to slivers as it was devoured. The last scream rang in the air, until the storm took the rest. The storm ended as if it had never existed. The air was warm and dry, and the dry fall leaves fell to the ground nearby, waiting to be crunched on by the next feet to tread the area.*

*The maze entrance merged, forbidding its access for the last time. Sarasota, Florida...2015*

· · · • • • • • · · ·

THE CAR CRAWLED along the country road, as it's occupants stared out at the beautiful rural scene unfolding before them. She couldn't believe it. How the hell did he find a place in the sticks? They had dreamed endlessly in bed, staring up at the ceiling, about finding someplace in the middle of nowhere, far from the rat race, where their future kids could have a happier and healthier lifestyle.

*Typical!* She thought. Why do these things always happen after a divorce, instead of coming true when you're happy, when it might actually have saved their marriage?

She cursed under her breath, and swallowed hard as she saw a driveway protruding from behind a tall hedge.

*Here we go*, she mused, a curious combination of hope and envy flushing through her. She felt a wash of guilt envelop her. She should be happy for him if he'd finally achieved the one thing that he'd always wanted. He'd told her on the phone about the book deal, and she had congratulated him, albeit an undertone of indifference had been present. She pulled into the driveway and she hit the brakes, her jaw dropping in disbelief.

A large, brand new, two-tier house with an ornamental garden in front.

The excited voices from behind her compounded her envy, as she recommenced the final approach to the house. As she brought the car to a halt, he appeared from the foyer and stood on the varnished house-length porch. It was immaculate, untouched. She bit her lip with regret at being unsupportive of him near the end of the bad ol' days when his time spent writing had overtaken him. She had *never* understood his passion for writing, and had openly resented it. It was just one more cause to admonish herself as she realised just how petty she had been. He had stuck to his guns, and even when she had asked for the divorce, signed the papers without any animosity. That had *really* pissed her off. She had instigated the whole thing, and she was beginning to regret it now. All too easy to do in retrospect, with hindsight as your vantage point.

He stepped off the porch as the girls opened the door, excitedly, running to him.

'It's *terrific*, Daddy!' they squealed, overjoyed. He indicated with his hand to the rear gate.

'Go see what's out back – and be careful,' he said, his face betraying nothing. They ran around and left them to talk.

'Want the grand tour?' he asked, expecting her to be bitter about it. But she wasn't.

'Why not? It's closest I'm gonna get to living in it.' He ignored the obvious jibe, and held out his hand. She took it, and he helped her up the steps to the hard oak decking. They entered the house, and the door closed behind them. In the skies above, a faint storm was beginning to form.

The girls had finally found their way through the gate and screamed aloud. A twenty foot pool had been installed, and a large hedge with an opening in it stood thirty feet beyond that.

*Looks like one of those maze things*, they told themselves. *Oughta be fun*. They saw two swimming costumes lying on the poolside table, and shrieked in delight. He had two beach changing cubicles installed nearby, and they rushed into them to get changed.

They had been upstairs for a bare ten minutes looking out of the kids bedroom window at the stunning views of the private access stretch of beach beyond the perimeter. She wanted to kill herself for divorcing him now. If only she could have shown more patience and supported him more, they could be lying in bed together, waking up to this every morning.

*Fuck!* she thought inwardly. *You dumb fucking bitch!*

She broached the one subject she feared the most, trying her best to sound as nonchalant as she could.

'So...when do I get to meet her, Jon?' she asked, looking around the beautifully decorated room.

'Meet who?' he asked. He was genuine in his reply. It was obvious in his voice. It possessed no ambiguity. He was out here alone.

Despite herself, she allowed herself a small smile to crease the edges of her mouth.

'You're not the type to live alone, especially in a place like this. They'll probably be taking numbers on the school run to see who gets you in bed.' He detected her inference in seconds, and allowed himself a wry smile. He turned to face her, impassive and normal.

'I'm too busy writing to care, right now, to be honest. If I need company, I'll go to the bar in town.'

Inside, she was both aching to admit she'd made a terrible mistake, although the brutal pride in her wouldn't allow it. She *had* to remain distant. They walked out of the room, and he led her to the staircase.

'Still sleeping on the couch?' she asked, laughing lightly. He pointed with his thumb at a door in the alcove in the far corner.

'In there.' The subject was closed, no invitation being extended to see the room he was sleeping in.

'Well, are you gonna let me take a peek or not?'

He was as blunt as he could be when he shot back, without apparent malice.

'Why? It's not like we're gonna be sharing it, is it? C'mon. Got some champagne in the fridge'

She put her hands in the air.

'Jon...I'm sorry, but I gotta see this room'

'Okay,' he sighed, resigned.

He walked around her, and took his keys out, opening it. He waved her in, avoiding her triumphant glance. She walked into the room and her face collapsed into her hands. It was empirical in stature. Four poster bed, beautiful artwork adorning the walls, punctuated by framed photographs of the kids. She couldn't help but notice there were none featuring her.

Her will was crumbling now, and he could tell. Hell, it was almost tangible! He had to get her out of there – quick. He guided her gently to the door, and she let him, her mind racing with thoughts of 'stupid, selfish, neurotic bitch' reverberating continuously in the chambers of her mind.

*This was the worst mistake of your life. He'll never have you back, now. If he wanted you at all, he'd have thrown you on that four poster, and taken you there and then. Payback's a motherfucker, ain't it?*

*Maybe next time you'll be less of a materialistic bitch, and be there when your husband wants your support. It's your fault and no-one else's.*

They took to the staircase in silence, each fully aware that there was nothing left to be said.

The girls – Claudia, 10, and Sara, 8 – climbed out of the pool, and dried off. Sara's eyes found their way to the maze, and nudged Claudia. They looked at each other, and giggled. They ran to the entrance and slowed to a crawl, as they looked up at the structure; imposing and intimidating. Sara was the first to get over it, and ran head first into the depths of the labyrinth, followed by Claudia who had begun to have serious doubts. She walked in, tentative and cautious, and began her search for her egregious sister. The opening sealed behind her as the thunder rolled in the distance.

*It had awoken.*

・・・・・・・・・・・

THEY SAT AWKWARDLY in the sitting room, sipping on wine, staring out at the thick deluge of rain rolling down the patio doors. A sudden flash of lightning lit up the sky above the maze, illuminating it like a gothic castle out of a 19$^{th}$ century horror novel. Panic gripped his chest.

'Where are the girls?' he asked, he asked with an urgency she had never heard in him.

She stood up, putting her wine glass on the coaster, and hurried to the door.

'What's behind that hedge over there?'

'It's not a hedge, April. It's a *maze*. Been here since 1901, according to the realtor. Been quite a few houses here over the years, but it's outlasted all of 'em. They probably went in for a look around.'

He had a thought, and walked to the glass table, grabbing his winter coat and an umbrella from the nearby stand.

'I'll go in and get them,' he said.

'You can't,' she exclaimed..

'Well, I can't leave them in there in that shit, can I?' he snapped at her.

'I'm sorry. I'll go get them then we'll have dinner.'

'No, I mean you can't. There's no way in.' He looked and sure enough, the opening that had been there was not there as it always had been.

*Strange*, he thought. He opened the door enough to get out without letting the storm in.

'Keep the door closed. Be back soon.' As he opened the umbrella, it was wrenched out of his hands, and sent soaring through the darkness.

'Fuck,' he said, under his breath, as he wrapped the coat around him, heading for the maze.

Without warning, lightning began to fill the sky with streaks, scorching the lawn around him. He hurried back to the house, banging on the door. April wasn't there. She appeared from the foyer and ran to the door, fumbling with the keys, finally finding it.

'Shit! You're drenched.' A pause followed. She looked around.

'Where are the girls?' she demanded.

'Still in there. I almost got hit by lightning four fucking times, so I didn't wanna risk—'

He cut himself off, and realised what he was about to say – and the joy she would get out of it. He grabbed the keys from the couch arm, and went back out, running flat-out this time, reaching the maze wall after the muddied hilltop, almost having slid back down several times. He *knew* there was a way in, somewhere. But it had always been here, dead-centre. How the hell could it have grown in only an hour? He heard faint voices above the deafening thunder rolls. His daughters were in there, and he had to get in, even if it meant scaling the walls or chainsawing a gap in it with the hedge strimmer.

'*DAAAA-DEEEE!!*'

Their joint call pierced through the racket around him, and his heart fell. It seemed all the strength was drained from his body. He yelled back; all he could do for now.

'DADDY'S COMING! HANG ON – I'LL BE RIGHT THERE!'

He took a few steps back, giving him room to get enough leverage, then took off, running towards the wall, and trying to run up it, his arms clamouring for some traction to aid him in his bid to get in. As he hit the wall, he was sent flying backwards, expelled by a blinding blue flash. He looked at his hands; burned and bleeding from the ill-fated assault. He would have to find another way. He *had* to get to his kids who were, no doubt, terrified. He ran back to the house, feeling like a complete failure.

··········

CLAUDIA WALKED QUICKLY, with Sara in tow, lagging behind her. Both of them were exhausted, yet charged just enough by fear to keep going, as the rain cracked like whips against their skin. Claudia immediately wished she'd got dressed after the pool, instead of just jumping straight into this godforsaken hell-hole.

The dark sky, completely devoid of stars, looked ominous as the stratocumulus congregated above like generals, marshalling their troops into an impending battle of which only they were party to. She swallowed hard as, without warning, the thunder crashed and night was almost day with explosions of forked lightning. Turning slowly, she grabbed Sara by the shoulder, backing away, her fear pulsating through her veins. This was *no* maze.

'*RUUUNNN!*' she yelled, as she dragged her younger sister through the labyrinthine passages, each of which were seemingly growing in density with every moment. The rain, at first heavy – now torrential, was so that she could barely make out the heavily weed-forming path beneath. Sara stopped in her tracks, frozen to the spot, took a deep breath and Claudia spun around on her heels, staring at her sister, who was pale with terror, her eyes pleading, and followed her gaze.

A large cloud was morphing into a hideous face like a jack o' lantern, but more seditious. She screwed her eyes up, trying to shed the rain from them, and saw the cloud was pulsating, as if something bad was inside, clawing to get out. She screamed and a bolt of lightning lit up the sky as it struck the hedge above her. She cowered in the corner, holding a petrified Sara close to her. She prayed to God for what was only the third time in her life – but this time she meant it. Dad would be here, soon, enveloping them in his arms and making them feel safe, as he always did. He *had* to come.

··········

JON STOOD IN the doorway of the tool shed, filling the chainsaw with gasoline, all the time the screams of his daughters reverberating around his mind, as his bitch whore ex-wife paced back and forth in the lounge. He cursed her under his breath.

Screwing the cap on the gas chamber, he yanked the cord, bringing the saw to life, its roar filling his ears. He turned it off, covering it with his coat, as he left the shed, walking to his adversary with renewed fervour.

Inside, he was terrified. Whatever was in there, was evil *beyond* evil. Sheer malevolence in the form of topiary, and this was one weed that was about to be whacked.

He strode purposefully up the muddy hill he had created the last time and, reaching the top, pulled the saw from his coat, yanking the cord again. The saw came to life, tearing its way into the structure, punching a hole in its invincibility.

The unearthly scream of anguish filled the air causing his blood to freeze. He had inflicted pain on the unholy spirit that was in those towers. Encouraged, he pressed forward and the hedges parted once more, enabling him free access. He ran into the maze and, with that, the skies gradually turned red. The doorway closed in on him again, it's branches entwining together in an unbreakable fusion that would not be undone.

∙∙∙∙∙∙∙∙∙∙∙

SARA SAT, HUNCHED, beside her sister, her eyes wide open, but her body rigid, immobile due to shock having set in.

Claudia was pissed. She held her sister tight, trying to keep her warm by body heat. The rain was still heavy and the ground had about two inches of rainwater on it. The lightning which had terrorised them the whole time had stopped, although the thunder claps had not relented. They could not move from that spot. Any attempt to escape into one of the inner passages was met with lightning bolts to the ground, barely missing them. Closing her eyes, she prayed to God – for their daddy to come get them.

·········

HE HAD WOUND his way through ten passages, ending up in the same place he entered them. He began to cry, mostly anguish at his inability to find them but also that he had let them down by not being a stronger force in their lives. He thought back to his obsessive desire to get the book finished, and how that obsession had impacted his time with the girls - and *her*.

As he sped through the maze, taking the occasional long path at a run, he could hear faint, yet distorted childlike screams, pleading with him to hurry. This was not his daughters' voices.

He could only presume it was the voices of other children who may have expired in this dark jungle. He tried to blank them out, but they only grew louder. Screams of anguish and pain, folded with abject terror. He held his hands to his ears, screaming in pain himself, as though their pain was being transported through him.

Jon turned right into yet another passage only to find a wall of fire, its light flickering against the hedges. From inside the inferno, the faces of tortured children showed in the flames, their faces, all, contorted in agony as they tried to reach for him. The rain was heavier, now, yet, still, it raged freely, refusing to be extinguished. He backed off and rested up against the wall, wondering what to do next. He closed his eyes, muttering the words of Psalm 23 under his breath.

*The Lord is my shepherd...I shall not want...*

He had everything he had ever dreamed of and now he had to save the one thing he gave a fuck about.

*He maketh me lie down in green pastures......He leadeth me through still waters...*

This must be the green pastures, he thought. Helluva way to see them, he mused to himself. And so much for the still waters! More like a tsunami from the Gods.

*He restoreth my soul. He leadeth me in the paths of righteousness for His namesake. Yay,, tho' I walk through the valley of the shadow of death,, I will fear no evil...for thou art with me...*

Who the hell are they tryin' to kid, here? This goddamned maze was evil personified!

*Thy rod and thy staff they comfort me.*

'I hope to hell You *are* with me,' he said quietly. He braced himself and turned the corner to face the flames once more. Summoning all the bravery he could find in himself, he ran toward the wall of fire and, screaming in defiance, leapt through it. As he did, an ungodly scream of rage, borne of rejection, filled the night's silence, and the fire vanished as if it hadn't existed. He looked around at it, and screwed his eyes up in disbelief. What the fuck was going on around here? He stood and turned another corner, and his heart almost stopped.

There they were!

His daughters, soaking wet – and asleep.

He knelt down, gently rousing them awake. Claudia was the first to respond, her face at first wide-eyed with fear. Her expression soon turned to confused joy, as she threw her arms around him, squeezing the life out of him, then, conversely, letting him go and looking him up and down as if she couldn't believe it was him.

'D-daddy? Is it really...really *yo*u?'

He laughed, grinning wildly at her.

She threw her arms around his neck, breaking down in his arms, her wrenching sobs muffled by his neck. Sara came to, seeing her father and screaming in delight at the sight of him. He let go of Claudia, and gave his baby girl the same attention. Both were breaking down with joy and fear, and he stood up.

'Alright. Let's get out of here, shall we?' he said flippantly, although his voice was cracked with the relief from the ordeal he had been through all night. They took a hand each, and made their way through the jungle of walls, until the last turn to the right revealed the exit, and the house beyond it. They stepped over the threshold, and walked down the hill, towards their waiting mother. He got the girls inside, and took a look back at the maze.

The sky was normal, the clouds at peace, and the structure itself was as mundane a sight as one could expect. The evil was gone.

He smiled, his eyes tired, as he locked the patio door, drawing the curtains. It was all over with.

··········

AS THE CURTAINS were drawn, the maze stood aloof, defiant as ever, as the dark passages began to pulsate with an effervescent kerosene glow, as the doorway closed in on itself for the final time.

*Or was it?*

# BEHIND THE STORIES
## STORY ORIGINS AND CONCEPTS

*I would like to take this opportunity to present to you this short section of notes and concepts integral to the stories which are presented in this book. As some people seem to enjoy such things, I thought it an opportune moment to, perchance, bond ever further with my readers and offer you this insight on how I came to the ideas which (assuming you haven't just skipped right to the appendices as some do!) have, I sincerely hope, terrified and beguiled you from the first.*

*So, without further ado, please join* me, *Martin Eastland, in this, an exclusive notes section on the tales of suspense and terror you have just enjoyed.*

*This section is for all of you... my readers, my loyal Facebook writing friends, and anyone who spent their hard-earned cash on my ramblings, here, and those who love getting more bang for their buck!*

·········

### SUFFER THE LITTLE CHILDREN

The genesis of this story came as a fragment (as all tales in any genre tend to do, and mine are no exception) while in the midst of another activity. My fiancee (at the time) and I had gotten the kids to bed, and I mentioned to her about a story I wanted to write. Being the helpful soul she is, she suggested a few ideas to start with, one of which involved an orphanage.

Being a suspense writer with horror leanings, the idea set my imagination on fire, with her adding many idea fragments, a lot of which I morphed into other ideas, resulting in a story I hoped would be exciting and terrifying. I later identified that one extra key scene was missing, and I inserted it at a key point in the second draft – a scene involving Sammi and Callie, wherein the possession afflicting the orphanage children had to be manifest for the reader to experience as she did. It made all the difference and transformed that which was already an enjoyable story into a far more terrifying prospect.

·・・●・●・・・

**DEADLINE**

I had devised a single tale from two lesser concepts on this one. First, I had a newspaper man being contacted by phone from the grave, which was freaky enough. The other aspect was to have an investigative reporter be the target of the vengeful spirit of a person he helped incarcerate for a particularly brutal crime. The answer came like night from day – composite them together to make a single, terrifying tale of a series of events involving the one character and the resultant devastation of his life over the course of a week.

·・・●・●・・・

**SCREENSHOT**

One of my personal favourites in this book, this story had humble origins. A Facebook killer story. Every idea has been done to death, but what makes an idea original is the writers own voice and style, which may set it apart from others in an ocean beset with similarity. Our job as writers is to mine the ideas which are left in our filters, shape those ideas into a form which may offer the best possible results, and discover the terror that lies dormant within. This was a lot of fun to write, I must admit.

··········

### THE MAZE

My first published piece, released on 15 April 2019 (curiously enough, on my sister's birthday!), was followed by this tale of a topiary maze which fed on the souls of the young who ventured inside its walls. The concept was devised as a follow-up piece for submission to an anthology by the same small-press indie publisher responsible for my debut publication, *'Call Me.'* I wanted to touch on the subjects of divorce and the carnage inherent in them; and also the duality of humanity, exploring the theme of materialism and highlighting someone coming to terms with karma when they realise they have been wrong.

··········

### MIND GAMES

This story was intended to be as disorienting as humanly possible. I wanted, up to a point at least, to mislead the reader as to what was going on, then take them off on a tangent of intrigue where nothing is clear cut as they think it might be. The characters, presented with a heart-wrenching dilemma, and gradually are revealed to be far less in command of their mental faculties as they might wish to believe, as I dragged them (and, hopefully, *you*!) through hell and back.  I try to offer my readers a page-turning experience and with *Mind Games,* I hope I have given it.

·············

**HOME, SWEET HOME**

A wholly unintentional and subconscious retelling of my debut publication caused this little gem to be included in this book.  I had an idea of a 'child in peril' story and having the weather play a major role as a character in itself.  It wasn't till after I had taken some time out and returned to it that I realised – in this instance, quite happily so – that I had essentially re-written my original publishing debut story (*Call Me)*, having changed the age of the child, the gender and made, what I believed – and still believe - to be a superior version, hence its inclusion in this collection.

·············

**CARRY ME OFF!**

One of the more recent pieces, this was a flash fiction piece I wrote for inclusion in a fund-raising anthology publication, geared to attend the medical bills of a extremely-ill and dear mutual friend.  It came to me in an instant and basically wrote itself in a 20-min coffee break. After some tweaking, I submitted it and enjoyed it so much, I decided to include it here for your enjoyment.

·············

**HOMECOMING QUEEN**

Bearing no allusion to the school prom whatsoever, this flash fiction piece has garnered critical praise [see *PRAISE FOR MARTIN EASTLAND* section at front of book] after being published in THE WRITER'S GROUP eZine in 2019, marking my first eZine publication, and is reprinted here for that reason. It was a reimagining of a slightly similar tale I had written while in college in March-April 2000. The challenge being set had been to attempt a story told from a female point of view.

Judging from that terrific review I received, I appear to have produced a crowning piece of work, "reminiscent of classic American flash fiction," remaining to this day one of my most validating endorsements as a writer.

··········

**EVIL IS...**

I was told some years ago, by my youngest sister, a tale about a teenage babysitter who had been confronted by a dangerous man in a baby's nursery, posing as a clown. At the time I was looking for a 'calling card' short film to produce and this seemed ideal with the possibilities endless for my array of modest film-production skills. As usual, I looked for similar videos on YouTube, completely disheartened to discover it was not such an unknown gem I had chanced upon. In my naivete, I had foolishly entertained the notion I had found a potentially unmined tale of terror.

Such was not to be the case, as I found it was an urban legend – the killer clown in the kiddie's bedroom – and YouTube had its fair share of short films exploring the subject. I had no real knowledge of Stephen King's clown opus, *IT*, at that point, however, although subsequently came to find it – and enjoy it immensely. I had the title for my story – *THE OUTSIDER* – and was set to submit it to a magazine. Then, horror or horrors, *again,* the horror maestro came charging in, using the title I came up with for his latest book at that time, killing any chance of using it. I searched for an intriguing title for my own 'take' on the killer clown yarn. I took the title of a previously abandoned story – *EVIL IS...* - and it was apt enough to make an intriguing entrée into the story.

·･････････

**DEATH AWAITS HER**

This story came to me after a discussion of the #MeToo movement. As with all political movements, there is a core idea which is honourable and credible. However, as it regularly transpires, these core concepts are corrupted by its own ranks, twisting the original purpose behind its intended formation. Although the blatantly politically-incorrect material is confined to the motel bedroom scene, it is intrinsic to the character – a sexually aggressive and manipulative businesswoman - and, sadly, a fair representation of a certain 'section' of modern women today, as my research into $2^{nd}$ and $3^{rd}$ Wave Feminist doctrine has tended to confirm.

I write to examine subject matter which arouses my inquiring mind, placing it in a prose setting. Political Correctness has proven to be the sole enemy of free speech and expression, in many cases used to extreme lengths to stem such rights in a rapidly escalating fascist and Orwellian society. As a writer, I assume the additional, and at times uncomfortable, role of social commentator, and I *refuse* to compromise my views over warped ideologies or socially conditioned dialogues which 'Big Brother' imposes upon all. I'm afraid I'm just not as conformist as the herd.

## DARK HARVEST

Started under the title, *SALEM'S INFERNO,* this was a story destined for a future collection, but I thought it strong enough to be fast-tracked to this collection. The reason for the change was due entirely to research, the result of which indicating that Salem Witchcraft suspects were *not* put to the flame, but instead subjected to hanging instead, with the burning of witches having died out, or been brought to an end in Europe years earlier, where the mania was far more hysterical in its intensity. Also, the metaphorical juxtaposition of the inferno of the burning of witches and the inferno of love- between the MC and his love interest.

## PERFECT STRANGER

This story took six months to return to after being derailed after the initial second week of writing – hell, nobody's perfect; I had what I thought to be a better idea – so sue me! (LOL). An old friend, who had been bequeathed a large ranch-type estate after her parent's death, had told be about her lovely home, her stable of horses, and my imagination kicked in like a brush fire in a high wind. The idea of writing my first intentional romance seemed exciting as my usual fare was suspense-thriller, with key horror elements woven in with cinematic atmospheric description. Naturally, I wasn't about to abandon my usual genre and it became a paranormal (or supernatural) romance. All in all, despite the six-month lay-off, the story's second inning stretch yielded far greater results than I could have imagined.

**ONE NIGHT ONLY**

This story was the product of an idea I had about a couple having a night alone together when their home is invaded by burglars. To make it interesting, I changed my specs, making the relationship a bad one, due to the wife's own 'weaknesses.' She decides she has treated him terribly and decides to salvage her dead marriage by making amends in the bedroom. It was an interesting foray into the home invasion topic, sadly a recent American issue from real life events.

**OUT OF THE ASHES**

Originally written as a 'man-in-cabin-in-the-woods' story, I found the development of my story to be too close to comfort, in terms of comparison with another story. It called for a change of direction. Instead, I came up with this story of a busy 'young professional' couple, having rented an isolated cottage in the wilds of England's Lake District. Add in the house possession by the vengeful spirits of two angry young women who had been attacked and brutally murdered there, returning every ten years on the anniversary of that night. I thoroughly enjoyed writing this one.

**'IT SMARTS, DON'T IT?!'**

An extra story written specifically to round off the story count, it was intended to be the most brutal affair-revenge story I could imagine. I had to have it be as concealed as possible from the cheating wife and lover, making certain they weren't wise to the savagely aggrieved husband's plan to teach them both a lesson – not to mention salvage what little pride remained in him.

··········

**STORM OF RAGE**

A flash fiction piece I originally wrote for an anthology submission, I felt there was something special about the writing of it (not necessarily *in* it, though) and was included for certain atmospheric qualities.

··········

**A RIDE TO REMEMBER**

I always heard of 'car-jacking,' but I thought at the time of writing, 'What would happen if the occupants of the car – a woman and her young kids travelling across country to visit their divorced father - were part of the package?' The oldest of the stories in this collection, and a shameless completion addition, I felt it had the resonance and reader-identification qualities to offer a cathartic experience.

··········

**THE IVORY SMILE**

Another slightly older story from the same period as *A RIDE TO REMEMBER*, originally entitled *THE PIANO*. I recalled it from memory as best I could, revamping it considerably, and I think it's a vast improvement on the original, lost to the winds of the ether on a corrupted computer memory stick.

# NOW FOR SOMETHING COMPLETELY SHORTER...

*I first came to learn of the 'Drabble' in 2016. It is the practice of refining a piece of micro fiction until it is stripped of all unnecessary filler words, and learning the discipline of telling a story in a set number of words – usually 50 or 100 in most micro fiction anthologies today. Included here are a small number of the very best alternate 50 and 100-word suspense drabbles I have written over the past 4 years. It teaches one how to encapsulate a story using word economy to tighten one's efforts in fiction writing.*

*I very much hope you enjoy this selection.*

*Martin Eastland*

∙∙∙∙●●●●∙∙∙∙

## WHEN DARKNESS CALLS...

THE DOOR WAS open when Charles Kelsey's car pulled up outside the mansion. The driveway was deserted which was better, he knew, but was grateful. He knew little, only that he had been summoned. The butler led him to the far end of the foyer, stopping at a long, flowing tapestry. He extended his burnt, wrinkled old hand.

Charles reached into his pocket, resurfacing with a small black envelope, adorned by a red ribbon, handing it to him. The butler parted the tapestry, revealing a concealed door, behind it a concrete stairwell leading down, amidst reflected flames, straight to Hell.

..........

**KISS AND TELL**

THEY FACED EACH other, looking into each other's eyes. His deep brown eyes bore into her mind as she felt her willpower draining from her. She was completely lost in him as he leaned into her, feeling her tender lips on his as he drew her soul from her body.

..........

**'HONEY, I'M HOME!'**

THE WIND HOWLED past the cottage as Mary McCann paced the mahogany floor, her infant on her shoulder as she lulled him to sleep.

Her husband had died on the job a year ago, frying himself on a pylon when a power outage had hit the entire West Irish seaboard, plunging it into darkness. She felt Jack snoring on her shoulder and moved towards his pine cot in the corner. The lights began to flicker wildly, and her heart sank. She pivoted on her heels, almost dropping the baby. She gaped. Her husband, Eddie, was walking towards her, grinning maniacally...

..........

**IN THE NAME OF THE FATHER**

THE PRIEST APPROACHED the boy with tentative, calculated steps. He had waited four months to get him alone and wasn't about to waste the opportunity. Backing himself into a corner, the boy, terror trumping confusion, watched helplessly as the young Priest loosened his belt, his eyes glinting.

It became unspeakable.

··········

### NIGHT SHIFT

MIKE JAMISON WAS not enjoying his present position. An Assistant M.E. in the Baton Rouge County Morgue, he had climbed as high as he was to get, and hearkened back to his Medical School days, remorsefully. The 'stiff' lay prostrate before him. Lonnie, the Coroner's assistant, had interred him before he went off duty. The corpse bore no marks, lacerations, bruises or contusions – nothing. Mike donned his apron, gloves and sighed heavily, his enthusiasm dying. Making the first cut, the knife met no resistance. The body was present, but the scalpel touched only steel. The corpse sat upright. Mike screamed...

··········

### BLOOD RIVER

THE GIRL PAID no regard to the water as she waded in to retrieve the Barbie doll, she had been gifted by UNICEF for her fifth birthday and had no wish to lose it.

In seconds, jaws slammed shut around her tiny frame with a sickening crunch, taking her under.

··········

## DATE NIGHT

SAMMI STOOD IN front of the ornamental glass mirror, preening herself for the final time before Scott arrived to pick her up for the Senior Prom. Her make-up was immaculate, her dress devastating – chosen by her dad of all people. She stopped pouting, leaning in closely to the glass. Her eyes glared in terror as her reflection transformed into a mask of bone and dripping blood. Sammi's entire body convulsed involuntarily, the image changing to a white, transparent spectral reflection of an old woman, her eyes two small pin pricks of brilliant white, that *mouth* wide, dripping with yellow ooze...

· · · ● ● ● ● ● · · ·

## DOORWAY TO HELL

THE STREET WAS devoid of life, blanketed in six inches of snow as Carole Martin headed for the railway bridge. He watched her intently, his breath quickening with every unsuspecting step she took. As she reached the doorway, she was wrenched off her feet with a gloved hand, silenced forever.

· · · ● ● ● ● ● · · ·

## THE WOMAN IN WHITE

THE CURTAINS BILLOWED inwards, the rain splashing against the white painted cot nearby. Her mother had left the window open, forgetting to close it as she had intended. The baby – Maryanne – was a bare four months old and staring blankly through the thin, tightly-spaced bars at the curtains...so spritely in colour and engaging...as a thin mist begin to accumulate outside, growing thicker by the moment.

There was something else there.

It looked like...a woman, her eyes a bright, deep yellow, soothing...her teeth rotten and decayed...but pointed, sharp teeth...She came through the mist and floated towards the cot.  She drank.

**NO LOVE LOST**

ENEMIES SINCE TIME immemorial, Caitlin had hated her.  Not content in humiliating Caitlin by filching her bubble-butt boyfriend in High school, *years* of torment had followed that day.  Watching her nemesis, Andi, at the bar, the old wounds still gaping, she fingered the phial of acid in her pocket.

**THE CULLING**

SHE RAN THROUGH the forest, ripping her feet to shreds on the broken branches carpeting the forest floor.  Whatever was in pursuit was intent on tearing her apart, savouring the blood it would soon drain from her bruised and battered carcass.  It was gaining by the second, stalking her...*toying* with her.  It would find her soon if she didn't pick it up a little.

She could see the perimeter fence beckon her, taunting her, to feel it's wires around her fingers, her yearn for it to be behind her.

As she got ten feet from the fence, it took her.

**SKINNY RIPPING**

THE POOL LOOKED inviting as Karen stripped, anticipating the icy water against her skin. The full moon reflected on the surface as she dove in. Exhilarated, she bobbed up and down.

*'Shit!'* she cried out. She wasn't alone in here. Two seconds later, she vanished in a maelstrom of agony.

••••••••••

**DADDY'S HOME!**

THE BOY LAY immobile... He looked at the alarm clock on his bedside table. It was ten after nine. Twenty minutes before the creature walked in the door, tormenting him, berating him, before retiring to his own bedroom, where his poor mother would suffer far worse. Formerly, a loving, attentive father, he had metamorphosed into a cruel, resentful and brutally narcissistic monster. Minor cruelties, such as cutting his TV plugs off at the moulded part so it couldn't be rewired, graduated to full-on verbal abuse, dragging his self-esteem to even lower depths. His little heart leapt – *"DADDY'S HOME!"*

••••••••••

**CAGED AND DEADLY**

MITCH SAT STARING out of the caged window, watching with unease as the clouds cleared above, the effervescent glow of the full moon beginning to encroach on the deserted grounds of the mental institution below. He looked around at his sleeping fellow patients, knowing they would be torn to shreds.

••••••••••

## NOISES IN THE ATTIC

THE THUMPING FROM the attic was intensifying by the moment. Jayne sat, rigid, in her armchair, illuminated by the flickering fire, staring at the ceiling. It was the damn thumping, since augmented by the creaking of floorboards, that was driving her crazy. The lights went out without warning, and she grabbed a candle from the ottoman at her feet, lighting it.

'Shit!' she muttered, walking to the stairwell. She took the stairs one at a time, her heart pounding in her chest as she gripped the handrail, her knuckles rendered white with the pressure.

It lunged towards her, screaming soullessly.

·· • • •• • • ··

## ANGEL OF EVIL

SHE GLIDED ACROSS the grassy plain towards him, her red feral eyes blazing with absolute contempt as she opened her dirty mouth, her gangrenous tongue flashing over those razor-like teeth, as she sank them into his carotid vein, thrashing her head, as the blood drenched her fish-white pallor.

·· • • •• • • ··

## ON A NIGHT LIKE THIS

She looked out of the screen door at him. He was old, at least in his mid-seventies, wearing a Southern Baptist Quaker Oats-type suit. The least threatening type in the world, Kelly thought. Yet, still, he managed to foster a terror in her which she couldn't explain or dispel. He may have been seventy, but his clear, icy blue eyes contained the danger of a much younger man, staring through her, like he was mentally stripping her somehow.

Her eyes felt heavier...

*Was he hypnotising her?* Her heart jumped as he passed through the locked door, into her.

# BEING A WRITER

"**WHY DO YOU WRITE?**" they ask.  And I answer – "I have no choice."  As pretentious as that may sound, it's the truth.  In Grade school (primary school in the UK), I could barely spell, languishing in the second of seven levels, and my reading skills were deplorable.  They used a learning system called I.T.A. (I imagine phonic based), and I had to attend a special school to deal with it.  I was soon out of that reading system after that, but my reading was still at the raw stage, barely able to read much beyond a seriously abridged childrens' version of *Dracula*.   I spent three days there and two at regular school.

Then something miraculous came my way.

It was a Friday morning, around 11am.  I was sitting at my desk and the teacher called a spelling test.  Being on level 2, second lowest of course, I was understandably glum about the prospect.  She set me off from level 1, then 2, and then 3, all the way to seven, the final level.  I aced each level, amazing her and *myself*!

I could, from that point, read any book I picked up.  What was scarier (and lifting) was that I couldn't just understand the words on the page, but the context and subtext of them, too – how they worked together and how to analyse what they said between the lines, as it were.  In one week, I went from *Spot Goes to The Farm* and *Runaway*

*Bunny*, to *Charlotte's Web* and *The House of Sixty Fathers* by Meindert deJong, in the space of about two weeks.

Later that year, I had elevated my ambition to far more advanced material – the *un*abridged, adult Stoker novel, *Dracula*, loving every minute of it, sitting alone behind the bike shed, eating my recess snack and reading this terrific story.

I was soon, a few years later, reading *'Salem's Lot* by Stephen King and my young mind went into overdrive. I read it over two nights – with the curtains shut after a certain stage (partly through having seen the 1979 mini-series adaptation starring David Soul). This book, this *blessing* of suspense, had me reading half a 400+ page novel and planting a desire to write a book one day. That was how it all started, leading me, thirty years later, to achieving my childhood fantasy of writing a book as good as that.

I took a serious apprenticeship by working unpaid at my local library, being taught quickly how to stack the returned books from the cart, in numerical order, into their places on the shelves. My knowledge of books grew at an exponential rate, graduating to Dickens (*A Christmas Carol, Oliver Twist),* to Eric van Lustbader's *The Ninja* and its immediate two sequels, to various other classics, taking in the narrative flow and nuance of each, absorbing them. This set me on path to High School, more interesting discoveries, and the day that changed my life, and my perception on it, forever.

**IN OUR SCHOOL** - and this will be a familiar story for a great many of those who survived to tell the tale, I am sure – you had to be able to handle yourself. It was the fist-fight version of the OK Corral. You were watching your back for the first two years. I had my fair share of 'challengers' (having trained as a boxer, and narrowly missing my medical for what would have been my first amateur effort in the squared circle.)

The club ran out of funds, forcing its foreclosure, but I kept up the training regime up to, and including, my first year in High School. From a skinny, rib-fest to a stocky, six-packed mountain midget, I attracted my fair share of female attention due to my continued regime of training and a chance opportunity to make use of the weightlifting facilities at the local gym (old, rust-encrusted blue machines, but they served their purpose admirably enough.)

When I got tired of defending my non-existent flyweight status, I spent more and more time in the school library to reduce the increasing likelihood of a looming suspension from school due to, by that stage, an increase in playground battles and my propensity to distracting classmates from their schoolwork, via practical jokes and celebrity mimicry. The librarian – a dear lady – had a storeroom at the side of the main counter, with a few shelf units, a long worktop counter and – to my utter joy – a large manual office typewriter from the 70's – the kind you could kill someone with by throwing it in their direction (assuming you could *lift* the fucker, of course!) – with the heavy solid chassis and the long, protruding carriage return bar.

My lips were moist at the sight of it, let alone the idea of being let loose on it. I asked for, and was granted, a turn on it. I sat down in the high stool and slipped the A4 sheet into the roller feed, securing it level. I had no sooner written a random title – *HEART OF THE ORIENT* – and I was taken over, it seemed...a force from without commanding my fingers to race across the keys like a seasoned typist, as I thrashed out a page and a half (perhaps, maybe, two) concerning the son of a Japanese Yakuza *oyabun* attacking the top Hong Kong Triad bosses during a meeting on a heavily-fortified junk (large, wooden chinese boat).

I had never had much knowledge of Hong Kong, or its colonial history (until much more recently, circa 30 years on), but a roving

English teacher (having a sister married and living out there) found it lying, briefly, on the main counter. I had been helping to stack some books for the librarian, and he called me over. I approached with defensive apprehension, not one for receiving much praise to, instead, receive a praise-filled review of the little I had managed to get on paper in the short window of time I had to play around with it.

It was an unexpected boost to my confidence and self-esteem (my home life was less than enjoyable for the most part, and real damage had been sustained and entrenched over the previous years, and beyond). It gave me cause to believe that maybe –just *maybe* – my dream of being a writer had a real chance of bearing fruit one day. So, I continued to write over the years, trying many different genre, trying to find my niche. It turned out, many years later, that my prose assumed a flair for suspenseful, atmospheric, and cinematic tone, with which I had a certain innate skill to create dread and terror, *sans* the gore factor (over-used, mostly, and easily dismissed after a time, anyway). I realised that horror writing had the capacity for cathartic emotional response, and I wanted people to remember my stories for a while after reading them, perhaps them even being discussed by enthusiastic strangers who had been taken by whatever strength my writing possessed.

I have no illusions of my choice of genre. I feel it's connected to my abhorrent childhood and adolescence – most writers and artistes are defined by traumatic childhoods. Some are battered children; some, mentally chastised beyond the pale. Others suffer far more lasting, irreparable damage, the after-effects of which area spread over a lifetime of unspeakable torment in recollection of it. Mine was emotionally and mentally uncompromising (at least for the first ten years between 7-17), slowly reducing but creating an agonising desire to escape it all.

I have forgiven, but I find it impossible to forget the years 7-17, the worst of it (7-12yo) being almost completely blocked out by my own strength of will. There was not a great deal of, shall we say, 'opportunities' to distract me from my troubles, hence, half my life being spent in the local libraries in the immediate and surrounding areas. But my path was clear to me. I was going to be a published writer if it killed me. I had no idea that it would be another 30 years from the day I started out with my freak storytelling frenzy in that warm, balmy school library in 1987.

### *Thirty Years Later...*

**HAVING SPENT TWENTY** years 'karaoke touring' around pubs and sports bars, the singing bug having taken a huge bite on my narrow, trousered and suited ass, I settled into domesticity and travelled around England, having never seen a great deal of it (mostly Blackpool with family, an overnight bus to a South East London park for an open-air concert with an old friend, and a few staggered trips to Nottinghamshire to visit the same friend). My writing had been on the backburner for years, although it was always there if I wanted it. In 2010, the urge returned and living life had fuelled my creativity enough to rattle out enough new stories by the boatload.

Publishing attempts were few as the occasional query email to Simon & Schuster was instigated, receiving a reply inviting me to send three chapters – an outline might follow if they liked what they saw. Fear of rejection reared its head, and those three chapters were never sent. In those days, I still worried about those kinds of things. Rejection can be crippling unless you learn to embrace it.

Mostly, it's nothing personal, with a number of possible reasons behind it, from receiving more than one story with similar theme, to, sadly, the publisher's bias on the subject matter (it shouldn't be a basis for rejection but, sadly, their arrogance outweighs the writer's viewpoint, even more so with the advent of political correctness and the easily-offended, so-called 'snowflake generation' taking a superiority stance on what will be published and what won't be tolerated – mostly out of fear-based image consciousness, with a side of career-destruction paralysis, over what is probably only a few hard truths of how the world and its people have turned out.

It's a fickle industry because of this. Fear-inducing impotence and violation of free speech fuse together to create a toxic industry where the much-expressed "good fiction is the truth behind the lies" is laid out on the literary pathologist's examining table for an extensive 'social conditioning' autopsy, destined for a procedure aimed at removing any offensive foreign bodies which might disrupt their Utopian La La Land.

Your job, as an author (I still prefer to call myself a *writer*, but whatever works!) is to call life as you see it, not stifling your inner voice because some butt-hurt 'snowflake' out there – and there will be plenty of those to go around, rest assured – is waiting to socially crucify you for exposing your thoughts, feelings or humour in your writing, pray God you *have* any!

Say what you feel within the confines of character and story. As long as you report truthfully on life, you can rest easy knowing you did your best to be honest to your work. Let the buyer beware, I guess. It's not your problem. "As a truthful writer," as Stephen King put it, "your days as a member of polite society are numbered, anyway."

My style of writing is much akin to Johnny Cash's guitar playing – I found it by accident or, as one might coin a phrase, 'fortunate serendipity' – "I found my style because I couldn't play no better," Cash would drawl.

The best part about being a writer, for me at least, is when an idea formulates. Sometimes, I get a random title and sit down and just free-write, letting the characters and story take me where it wants to. Other times, I have a very basic 'what if...' premise, and initiate the same process based on that idea. The results are usually fairly good and just need edited here and there. Research is best served by doing it after the initial exploratory draft, returning to insert it insidiously so as not to intrude noticeably in the narrative. A well-developed, albeit 'unthinking,' style is my preference. Using plot works for some but is extremely subjective as to its effect on the finished story.

If I get surprised by some aspect of a character's life or am unaware of the outcome until I get there, then I feel that the reader will be compelled to turn pages in anticipation...a style of working synonymous with music played by ear as opposed to sheet music, fluid versus stiff in its execution. Playing note for note is clunky and mechanical but playing by 'feel' is a lot smoother and the end result is a piece of music which lifts you, filled with life. Writing fiction is, without doubt, no different. You allow the characters, amidst the situations you place them in, to guide you as you go, and you imbue your work with life, heart and soul, imploring, inciting...*compelling*...the end reader to turn those pages with bated breath.

At least, that's how *I* see it.

# ALSO BY

**ALSO AVAILABLE FEATURING
MARTIN EASTLAND...**
FLASH FICTION ADDICTION
(Zombie Pirate Publishing, AUS)
ANGELS Drabble Anthology Vol 2
MONSTERS Drabble Anthology Vol 3
(Black Hare Press, AUS)
BLOOD AND BEETLES
(Nocturnal Sirens Publishing, USA)
HORROR ANTHOLOGY
(Unveiling Nightmares 2023)
FLASH OF THE DEAD: REQUIEM
(Wicked Shadow Press 2024)
**OTHERWISE ENGAGED :**
A LITERATURE & ARTS JOURNAL Vol 6 (WINTER 2020)
THE CASEBOOK
An Anthology of Detective Fiction
(Culture Cult Press)
THE ALIEN BUDDHA's HOUSE OF HORRORS # 6
(Alien Buddha Press)

FLASH OF FANGS
An Anthology of Vampire Fiction
(Culture Cult Press)
A COVEN OF WITCHES
(West Avenue Publishing)
IT'S ALL IN THE MIND!
PSYCHOLOGICAL THRILLERS
Anthology of Short Stories
(Culture Cult Press)